PRAISE FOR 600 HOURS OF EDWARD

"It's a spare, elegantly crafted whizz-bang of a book that, on its surface, is as quiet and orderly as Edward Stanton, but underneath, also like Edward, a cauldron of barely repressed rage and desire seeking escape." —*Missoula Independent*

"Craig Lancaster has created a wonderful character and put him in a memorable story." —*Bookmonger*

"This endearing hero deserves the fine ending the author has bestowed on him. The final pages leave the reader wanting to know what happens next for Edward, in his newly acquired red Cadillac." —*Lively Times (MT)*

"This is a wonderful book. Mr. Lancaster's journey…into the imaginative pages of fiction was one well taken, for himself, for readers and certainly for the lovingly created Edward Stanton." —*Montana Quarterly*

"…A nearly perfect combination of traditional literary elements, mixing crowd-pleasing sappiness with indie-friendly subversion, a masterful blend of character and action…" —Chicago Center for Literature and Photography

600 HOURS OF EDWARD

600 HOURS OF EDWARD

CRAIG LANCASTER

amazon encore

Published by AmazonEncore
P.O. Box 400818
Las Vegas, NV 89140

ISBN-13: 9781612184104
ISBN-10: 1612184103

This book is for Angela Dawn, who believed that I could do it then and believes in me still. Our story goes on and on, sweetheart.

To whom it may concern:

This is a story of how my life changed. That is what one could call a dramatic statement. It's like when people find God; they say, "I found God, and it changed my life." I did not find God. I am dubious that anyone can. When someone says he has found God, he doesn't mean it in the way that one would say he found a penny or something else tangible. He is talking about inner peace or something like that, I suppose. I don't know. I haven't found God, and I don't like supposition. I prefer facts.

Even without God, my life did change, and Dr. Buckley suggested that I write about it. She said that writing about it would be a good project for me and one that might even help me understand how it happened and why. Dr. Buckley is a very logical woman, and I always need a new project.

In looking back, I can fit what happened into twenty-five days, or six hundred hours. I prefer to think of it in terms of hours, as I live my life as much by a clock as a calendar. I will tell it as it happened, from where I viewed it. Others may have seen it another way. They can tell their own stories if they want to.

I'll start with the last day that everything was normal, or what I believed normal to be. That's the problem with belief: if you rely on it too heavily, you have a lot of picking up to do after you find out you were wrong. I prefer facts.

Regards,
Edward Stanton

MONDAY, OCTOBER 13

My eyes flash open. I wait a moment for the dull blur of morning light to come into focus, and then I turn my head ninety degrees to the left and face the clock: It is 7:38 a.m. I have been awake at this time for the past three days, and for eighteen out of the past twenty. Because I go to bed promptly at midnight, I am accustomed to stirring at 7:38, but occasionally, I will wake up a little earlier or a little later. The range isn't large—sometimes it's 7:37, and sometimes it's 7:40, and it has been 7:39 (twenty-two times this year, in fact), but 7:38 is the time I expect. It has happened 221 times so far this year, so if it were you, you would expect it, too. (You're probably wondering how frequently I've been up at other times: fifteen for 7:37 and twenty-nine for 7:40.) Although I do my part by going to bed at midnight sharp, the variances occur because of things I can't control, like the noise made by my neighbors or passing cars or sirens. These things frustrate me, but I cannot do anything about them.

I write down the time I woke up, and my data is complete.

You've probably done the math and know that it's the 287th day of the year. The reason, aside from the sheer scientific fact that Earth has rotated on its axis that many times, is that it's a leap year. I have to take the leap year into account in my

1

calculations, but that's easy for me to do, as it comes up only once every four years.

I can tell when my feet touch the floor that the house is warm, warmer than it usually is for October 13, and this has nothing to do with the leap year. The house has hardwood floors, which are good for reflecting whether it's hot or cold. I have read about newer houses with something called radiant floor heating, where the floors are the source of heat for the home, but this house doesn't have that. While I am intrigued by the notion, I have to remember that this house was built in 1937, and the cost of retrofitting it for radiant floor heating would be prohibitive. My father could afford it, and it is, in fact, his house and not mine, but he never would do it. He's never here, and so it probably doesn't make any difference to him that radiant floor heating would be a lot more economical. It should matter to him, as he pays the heating bill, but my father sometimes is not a logical person. I can't worry about this now, although I have half a mind to write him a letter and tell him that he is being foolish for not thinking of radiant floor heating.

I walk across the hardwood floor of the house, open the front door, and pick the *Billings Herald-Gleaner* off the stoop. According to the front page, the temperature will reach seventy-two degrees today in Billings, and that is as I suspected when my feet touched the floor: It will be warm for October 13. It's far warmer than last October 13 (fifty-six degrees). Of course, I won't know for sure until tomorrow's newspaper comes, the one with the official temperature for today. The number on the front page today is just a forecast, and forecasts are notoriously off base.

I flip over to the back page of the Local & State section and look at the weather data from yesterday, Sunday, October 12, the 286th day of the year (but only because this is a leap year). The weather data is always on the back page of the Local & State section, and while it does bother me that the Local & State section is sometimes Section B and sometimes Section C, I have learned to cope with this inconsistency, as I have no choice. I once wrote to the editor to complain about it, but I did not receive a reply.

The high temperature yesterday was fifty-three and the low temperature was thirty-one, and those are much more in line with the ten-year trends that I have recorded in my notebooks. I write those numbers down, and my data is complete.

— • —

My father bought this house eight years ago. Actually, it was eight years and eighty-six days ago. He bought it for me to live in because I had become "a distraction whose presence was proving divisive in the family home." My father didn't write those words; his lawyer did. I have never heard my father refer to the "family home" before or since.

The reason I know that his lawyer wrote the letter is that it arrived on the lawyer's letterhead. I do sometimes talk to my father face-to-face, but many times, it is followed up with a letter, sometimes on his letterhead and sometimes on the lawyer's. I have not figured out how to predict which letterhead I will receive, although I can always predict the letters. I don't trust predictions anyway. I prefer facts.

I live in this house alone. When my father bought it for me, he made it clear that I was to have no roommates without approval. I don't know why my father worried about it. A roommate would probably mess up my routines and fool with my weather data. I know how roommates are. I have seen the television comedy *Perfect Strangers*, although not in many years, as it was canceled in 1993. I liked Balki Bartokomous. He was very funny. If I had a roommate like Balki, though, I would have to keep watch over my weather data. His rambunctiousness (I love the word "rambunctiousness") would wear on me if he started fooling with my data.

— • —

The two-drawer filing cabinet in my bedroom holds one of the most important collections I have. Inside are my letters of complaint. I have them filed in green office folders under the name of the person I am complaining to, and in those files, the letters are arranged by date.

You are probably thinking that it is odd to keep copies of letters of complaint, and you would be right if not for the fact that these are not copies. These are the actual letters of complaint, and they will never be sent.

The letters are Dr. Buckley's idea. I don't know where she got it, but it's a great one. Eight years ago, after my father and his lawyer persuaded Garth Brooks to drop the restraining order against me, my father bought this house for me. He seemed to suggest that the "Garth Brooks incident," as he still calls it, was what caused him and my mother to decide that I could no longer live in the "family home." I think that my letters of complaint to Garth Brooks were entirely justified. If you look objectively at country music, you cannot come to any conclusion other than he ruined it. He also ruined a lot of pop music, especially when he pretended to be that Chris Gaines person and when he covered that song by Kiss. I merely wrote to him and let him know about the damage he was doing, because I thought that maybe he didn't know and would stop if he did. I had to write to him forty-nine times before he wrote back, but it wasn't really him. It was his lawyer.

After that, I came to live here, and I had to start seeing Dr. Buckley. I have seen her every Tuesday of every month of every year since then. She encouraged me to continue to write my letters of complaint, but she suggested that I not send them so I do not have trouble with other people. I will admit that it didn't make a lot of sense to me at the time, but it really does work. Writing the letters makes me feel better. I find that after I write one and file it away, I soon no longer wish to send it.

Dr. Buckley is a very logical woman.

— • —

Every night at 10:00 sharp, I watch *Dragnet*. I watch only the color episodes of *Dragnet*, the ones that were made between 1967 and 1970. *Dragnet* does not appear on television anymore, so I have to watch the episodes that I recorded on videocassette in 2000, when the TV Land network was still showing it. I have all ninety-eight color episodes on videocassette.

Because today is October 13, the 287th day of the year (because of the leap year), I will be watching the ninety-first episode of the series, "Burglary: The Dognappers." This will be the third time this year that I have seen this episode, which originally aired on February 26, 1970.

Here is my method for watching *Dragnet*: On January 1 of every year, I start with the first episode of *Dragnet*. I then watch the episodes in succession, one each night, until I reach the end, and then I start over.

Because the 365 days in a year—or 366 days in a leap year— are not cleanly divisible by ninety-eight episodes, I will watch each of the episodes at least three times a year, and I will watch the first seventy-two episodes four times. Because this is a leap year, I'll watch the first seventy-three episodes four times. You would think that I would know the first seventy-two (or seventy-three) episodes a little better than the others because of the disparity (I love the word "disparity") in watching them, but I have no proof that's true. Perhaps I should see if I can find the scripts and run some calculations on how many of the words from the first seventy-two (or seventy-three) I know, as opposed to the last twenty-six (or twenty-five). That will be a good project for another time.

"Burglary: The Dognappers," the nineteenth episode of the fourth and final season of the color episodes, is one of my favorites. In this episode, Sergeant Joe Friday and Officer Bill Gannon work a case involving people who steal dogs from cars and then return them to the owners for reward money. You could make a credible case that every *Dragnet* episode has a moral component, but this one does especially. It's not right to steal. Also, people love their pets, if they have them. I do not have pets.

As always, in this episode, Sergeant Joe Friday is a very logical person, and while Officer Bill Gannon isn't as logical, he can be funny. I like them both.

— • —

After *Dragnet*, I get things ready for the next morning. I double-check my wake-up time and weather data and then put my notebook on the end table beside the bedroom door so I can find it first thing after I wake up. I also put three pens beside the notebook, because I don't want to be in a situation where I can't write down the time I wake up and the temperatures from the previous day. One backup pen is just asking for trouble, so I make sure I have two.

The last thing I do before going to sleep is I write my letter of complaint. It's hard sometimes to wait until the very end of the day to do this, but it jumbles my day up too much when I write my letter of complaint at the moment that someone makes me mad. If I'm not careful about the timing, for example, I could miss the 10:00 p.m. start of *Dragnet*, and that would just foul up everything. Also, writing the letter at the end of the day allows me some "separation time" between the incident that made me angry and my response to it. Dr. Buckley says that I can avoid many bad situations by learning to use "separation time." She is a very logical woman.

As you might expect, I'm going to complain to my father. I already have five green office folders that hold letters of complaint to him. Soon, I may need six.

Dear Father:

I think you have erred in not considering radiant floor heating for the house that I am living in. I have read many articles about this type of flooring, and it is my understanding that by utilizing pipes in the concrete floor that carry hot water, you can significantly reduce your energy costs. As you know, in Montana, winter can be very cold. I think that radiant floor heating would bring substantial savings, although I will concede that there is an upfront cost of installation that must be considered.

I also must concede that perhaps you have thought of radiant floor heating and simply have not communicated those thoughts to me. I would ask that you show me the common courtesy of letting me know what you're thinking in regard to this issue, for if you decide to install radiant floor heating, I will have to adjust my life to accommodate the intrusion of a contractor.

Finally, I would urge you to not use the unseasonably warm weather we have been having as an excuse to disregard the heating apparatus of this house. I have ten years' worth of weather data that show conclusively that we will, at some point, come in for some cold weather. That said, I do not like to rely on predictions. I shall wait for the facts to bear this out before contacting you further.

I appreciate your consideration.

With regards, I am your son,
Edward

TUESDAY, OCTOBER 14

The sound of a lawn mower jolts me awake. I turn to face the clock, and it reads 7:28. This is an oddity. Every previous day this year, I have awoken at 7:37, 7:38, 7:39, or 7:40. Now, on the 288th day of this year (because it is a leap year), I am awake at 7:28. Further, I am all but certain that I have never awoken at this particular time. I will have to check my data, as I don't like to trust assumptions. I prefer facts.

I retrieve my notebook from the end table and grab a pen. I record my waking time, and my data is complete.

At the front door, I bend over and retrieve the *Billings Herald-Gleaner* from the front stoop. I can now see the source of my early awakening: The woman across the street, the one who moved in on September 12 (the 256th day of this year, but only because it is a leap year), is mowing her front yard. I have seen her a few times since she moved in, but this is the first time I have seen her mowing her front yard. A boy lives with her, and I assume that he is her son, although I don't like to assume. He looks to be eight or nine years old, but I'm not comfortable with such conjecture. If I could find out the boy's birth date, I would know for sure and would feel more comfortable about the situation. There is a big difference between the ages of eight and nine, and in this case, I just don't know. This frustrates me.

I have not seen a man over there, and so I wonder whether my neighbor has a husband or her boy has a father. I would be sad to think that he doesn't, but having a father isn't necessarily a good thing. I have one, and while he did buy this house for me to live in, he also has his lawyer send me a lot of letters and may not have given any thought to radiant floor heating.

I see now that the woman across the street has stopped pushing the lawn mower and is waving at me. I think it would be better if I looked at the weather information and recorded it inside. I close the door. Soon, my data will be complete.

— • —

After breakfast, I thumb through my voluminous (I love the word "voluminous") data sheets, and I am correct: Before today, I have never awoken at 7:28 a.m. Today is a landmark.

— • —

Because I have many things to do today, including my weekly appointment with Dr. Buckley, I will have to put off my Internet time until later. I meet with Dr. Buckley promptly at 10:00 a.m., just as I have every Tuesday of every month of every year since I started seeing her, save for one.

On Tuesday, June 11, 2002, Dr. Buckley had to move my appointment to 11:00 a.m. It was a disaster. All I could think about was that the shuffling had put my 10:00 p.m. viewing of *Dragnet*—episode number sixty-four, "Frauds: DR-28"—in jeopardy, and so I could not answer questions about how my medication was doing or what projects I was working on or how my letters of complaint were working out. Dr. Buckley cut the session short, which mitigated against the damage done to my schedule, and we both agreed that from then on, we would meet at 10:00 a.m. on Tuesdays.

This is one of the things I like about Dr. Buckley. Although she sometimes makes mistakes, she is a very logical person.

— • —

My first stop is Home Depot, in the paint department. I have decided to paint the garage. I need a new project, and the ten-day weather forecast looks as though it will allow me to do this. I don't like forecasts, though, as they are notoriously off base. I will have to wait for the actual data, and it is my hope that by then the garage will be painted.

There are more paint varieties and colors here than there were the last time I was at Home Depot. There must be an entire arm of the paint industry dedicated to coming up with new colors and combinations, and I instantly wish that I had looked at some possibilities on the Internet before coming here. I'm frustrated with myself for not thinking of this.

The man in the paint department, who is supposed to assist me, isn't helpful at all. He asks many questions, faster than I can answer them, and he is talking about things like ambience, things that I don't care about. I just want to find the right paint.

"Leave me alone," I say.

The paint man trudges away, shaking his head.

Did you know that there are NFL team colors available in paint? I am intrigued by this. I like the Dallas Cowboys, but I don't think that I would want their colors on the garage. I will have to think of a project that would work with Dallas Cowboys team-color paint. This is something I would like to do, sometime after I finish the garage.

After I spend a few more minutes looking at swatches, it's obvious that the paint situation is hopeless. I cannot decide on a color, and I can feel the urge to rip these swatches from the wall welling up inside of me. I close my eyes, as Dr. Buckley has suggested that I do when I feel this way, and I try to breathe. Dr. Buckley says that when I feel overwhelmed by frustration, I should think before I act and find the path that will carry me away from the frustration.

Dr. Buckley is a very logical person. I do as she has counseled me, and my path becomes clear.

I walk over to the unhelpful man and say, "I would like three gallons each of the Behr mochachino the Behr parsley sprig, and the Behr bronze green."

As the unhelpful man walks over to gather the supplies needed to mix my paints, he is shaking his head again.

— • —

I like Dr. Buckley's waiting room. The walls have dark wood paneling, and the lighting sets me at ease. Dr. Buckley also plays soft music in her waiting room. I prefer rock music—my favorites are R.E.M. and Matthew Sweet—but I think that if Dr. Buckley played Matthew Sweet, some of her patients would not like it. Matthew Sweet has a song called "Sick of Myself," and I am pretty sure that is exactly the wrong song name for a therapist's waiting room.

I try to arrive at least ten minutes early for my 10:00 a.m. appointment, although I can never be sure exactly what time I will get here. Things like stoplights and the uncertainty of where in the parking lot I will find a place for my car affect it. I once asked Dr. Buckley if I could have my own parking space, but she assured me that was not possible.

I arrive early for two reasons: First, as I said, the lighting and wood paneling and the soft music help set me at ease. Second, Dr. Buckley's other, less-organized patients are always getting the magazines out of order. I sometimes need the full ten minutes to organize the magazines by title and date. I would do it after our appointment, when I have more time, but Dr. Buckley prefers that her patients not linger.

Today, however, the magazines are not badly out of sorts, and so I have three minutes to just sit and listen to the music.

— • —

When Dr. Buckley emerges from her office to summon me in, I look down at my digital watch, and the time is 9:59:28. I tell Dr. Buckley that it is not quite time for my appointment, and so we stare at each other for thirty-two seconds.

— • —

There is a rhythm to my talks with Dr. Buckley. She asks many of the same questions every week, but it's not by rote. She is interested in my answers. Dr. Buckley has never been less than professional, and she is a very logical person.

"How has your week been, Edward?"

"Very good, I think. My data is complete, and before I came here today, I bought some paint for the garage."

"It's a little late in the year for that, isn't it?"

"The ten-day forecast looks good."

"You're trusting forecasts now?"

"No, but you've told me that I should have a little faith, right?"

"Very good. Have you been taking your medication?"

"Every day. Eighty milligrams every day."

"Any problems with the Prozac?"

"I prefer the term fluoxetine."

"Any problems?"

"No."

"Excellent. Are you still writing letters?"

"I wrote one to my father last night."

"But you didn't send it, right?"

"No."

"What was your complaint to your father?"

"I don't think he's even considered radiant floor heating. Do you realize how much money he could save?"

"Radiant floors are nice. Do you know why this is so important to you?"

"It's not that it's important. I'm frustrated that he hasn't thought of it. It doesn't speak well of him."

"Do you think, perhaps, that it might be too much to expect that your father has thought of radiant floors just because you have?"

"I don't know. Maybe. He makes me mad."

"We can talk about that some more."

— • —

Tuesday is also the day that I go to the grocery store. It just makes good sense. Dr. Buckley's office is at Lewis Avenue and Sixteenth Street W., which means that I can go north on Sixteenth to Grand Avenue, take a right turn, and be at the Albertsons store three blocks later. After shopping, I can take a right turn on Grand, then another right turn on Sixth Street W., then another right turn on Clark Avenue, where I live. I like right turns much better than I like left turns.

At Albertsons, I buy the same things every week: three packages of spaghetti, three pounds of ground beef (the kind with only 4 percent fat), three bottles of Newman's Own roasted garlic spaghetti sauce, a twelve-pack of Diet Dr Pepper, a big box of corn flakes, a half gallon of milk, a quart of Dreyer's vanilla ice cream, five assorted frozen Banquet dinners, and one DiGiorno pizza (usually spicy chicken).

I can get three meals out of each box of spaghetti; spaghetti is my favorite food. I mix the spaghetti with a package of ground beef and one of the bottles of spaghetti sauce. That's nine meals total. The five Banquet dinners bring the total to fourteen meals. I can get seven bowls of cereal from the corn flakes, so that's twenty-one meals, or three a day for the seven days of the week. The ice cream and the DiGiorno pizza are treats.

Ever since the Albertsons on Grand put in self-checkout stands, I have been a happier shopper. Before, I sometimes had to wait behind several people in line, and that threatened to affect the projects I had at home and, conceivably, although it never happened, could have caused me to miss the 10:00 p.m. start of my *Dragnet* episode. I'm no longer permitted to go to the Albertsons on Sixth Street W. and Central Avenue, which is actually closer to the house that my father bought for me.

It was a dumb situation: I was in the checkout line behind an old woman, and she and the checker were talking a lot, and the line was moving slowly. I asked if they could quit talking so I could leave faster, and the checker shot me a mean glance and then kept talking. So then I said, "Please, hurry up because I have to leave soon." The man behind me didn't like this and pushed me, and I ran into the old lady and knocked her down.

The store manager called the police, and my father had to come to the store and tell the police that he would make sure it never happened again, even though I told them that it was not my fault and that I wouldn't have run into the woman if I had not been pushed. Nobody believed me.

You can probably guess that the whole thing ended up involving a letter from my father's lawyer, who ordered me not to go back to that Albertsons ever again.

But now that the Albertsons on Grand Avenue and Thirteenth Street W. has self-checkout stands, I think it's a moot point. I don't have to talk to anyone to pay for my groceries now.

— • —

After I get home and unload and put away the groceries, I notice that the mailman has already been to the house. Ideally, I would like to add to my data sheets the time that the mail is delivered each day, but my projects and appointments sometimes take me away from the house, and so I don't always see the mailman when he comes by. I might be able to rig up a video camera that would record his visit even when I'm not home, but Dr. Buckley says that is the sort of impulse that I need to work on controlling.

I don't receive much mail. My bills go directly to my father, and he pays them. My name is not on this house or on my car, and so even junk mail is scarce. That's how the junk mail people find out who you are and where you live. They go snooping around in public records, like home and car titles, and then they write to you. Also, if you apply for credit cards, you are sure to get all sorts of junk mail. The only credit card I have is for my expenses, and the bill goes to my father. If this card has resulted in junk mail, I can only assume that my father is receiving it. I don't like to assume. I prefer facts.

Today, there is one letter in the mailbox. It is from my father, in an envelope from his office. I am relieved that I am not hearing from my father's lawyer, but hearing from my father isn't necessarily better. I will have to open the letter to find out.

Edward:

I have received your credit card bill from last month. Everything looks to be in order, but I am confused by one charge: $49.95 for eHarmony.
Call me so we can address this.

Ted Stanton

I had a suspicion that this was going to happen. Now it is a fact.

I go inside the house, pick up the phone, and dial the number at my father's office.

"Yellowstone County Commissioners."

"It's Edward Stanton. Let me talk to my father."

"One moment, please."

I listen to the orchestral version of a pop song—Muzak, it is called. Paul McCartney's "My Love."

"Ted Stanton."

"Father."

"Edward, thank you for calling. How are you?"

"I am fine, Father."

"Can you tell me about this forty-nine dollars and ninety-five cents?"

"I signed up for eHarmony."

"What is that?"

"It's an online dating service."

"You're dating?"

"I am looking at online personal advertisements."

"Does Dr. Buckley know about this?"

"My treatment with Dr. Buckley is between me and Dr. Buckley."

"Online dating, eh?"

"Yes."

My father's voice softens. "Well. This could be interesting, Edward. This could be something good for you."

"You're going to pay the bill?"

"Sure. Yes. Why not?"

"It's the only one you will get. I canceled the membership."

"Oh."

"Good-bye, Father."

— • —

I guess I should tell you about eHarmony. I spend a lot of time on the computer looking at websites on the Internet. I used to keep track of how many hours and minutes I spent on the Internet, but I don't do that anymore. It was easy when you had to pay for the time on the Internet, because you could just write down the time when you got the bill. Now the Internet is hooked up through my cable television, and I can spend as much time as I want on it for one price, which my father pays. It bothers me sometimes that I don't keep track of the time I spend on the Internet, but I've learned to "let that go," as Dr. Buckley says. Dr. Buckley was very happy for me when I stopped tracking my Internet time. I'm not sure why she cared.

Lately, I have been spending most of my online time at Internet dating sites. On the television commercials, everyone who is finding dates online seems so happy, and all of them have found a "soul mate," whatever that is. I doubt that they have any scientific proof that they have found their soul mate—for all they know, someone even more special is out there dating someone else—but I cannot argue with how happy they all are. I am envious.

I have not gone on an Internet date. I think I would like to go on an Internet date, but so far I haven't met anyone who keeps track of weather data, and I think it is important that whomever I date on the Internet have something in common with me.

I have not told Dr. Buckley about the Internet dating yet, as there is nothing to tell. I wouldn't have told my father, either, but he got the bill and asked me about it, so I had no choice.

I now use Montana Personal Connect. I tried eHarmony, because I liked the white hair and glasses of that guy on the commercials, and his manner was gentle, but eHarmony told me that its system and its twenty-nine levels of compatibility couldn't find anyone for me.

That hurt my feelings.

— • —

At 10:00 p.m. sharp, I watch episode number ninety-two of *Dragnet*, which originally aired on March 5, 1970.

The episode, the twentieth of the fourth and final season, is called "Missing Persons: The Body," and it is one of my favorites.

In this episode, Sergeant Joe Friday and Officer Bill Gannon have only two clues to identify a woman who was found dead under the Venice Pier in Los Angeles: a wadded piece of paper and a ring. But because of their doggedness, they eventually find out who she was and crack the case. Sergeant Joe Friday and Officer Bill Gannon are good cops.

When I started to learn my way around the Internet, I found that the actors who appeared on *Dragnet* were, in many cases, not difficult to track down. Most of them were not big stars, and some even have listed phone numbers and addresses. That's not the case with the main actors in this episode, Anthony Eisley, Virginia Gregg, and Luana Patten; they are all dead. A lot of other people who were in the ensemble are dead, too, but some are alive. I exchanged some mail with an actor named Clark Howat, who appeared in twenty-one episodes of *Dragnet*. He was very nice. He told me how the star and creator of the show, Jack Webb, who plays Sergeant Joe Friday, didn't want his actors to act because the series had such a small budget and could not afford more than one take on each scene. Instead, Jack Webb had them read their lines off teleprompters. Mr. Howat said it was hard to get used to, as actors' training is to be more natural. But, he said, Jack Webb's methods worked. I wrote back to Mr. Howat five or six times, and even invited him to have a cup of coffee with me if he ever came through Billings, but he never wrote back. It's just as well. I don't like coffee, and I think it would be difficult to sit at a table with a stranger and talk, even if he was in *Dragnet* twenty-one times.

— • —

I am flummoxed by my letter of complaint tonight. (I love the word "flummoxed." I heard a man use it once, and I immediately incorporated it into my lexicon. I also love the word "lexicon." I had to look it up first, though. I used to write down the words and definitions I looked up, but I stopped doing that because the words are right there in the dictionary, and I can look at the dictionary anytime I want. It's harder to keep a record of daily temperatures, because you would have to store a lot of old newspapers in the house, and so I decided it's best that I focus on that and not the words. That way, I ensure that my data is complete.)

I would like to complain to my father for his rudeness about my credit card bill, but I don't like to complain to the same person two times in a row. It's bothersome enough that the complaints themselves don't follow any particular pattern; I don't need the added aggravation of bunching up my complaints about one person, not even my father.

I think I will complain to Matthew Sweet. This will require that I start a new green office folder.

Mr. Sweet:

It pains me to have to write this letter to you, as I am very much a fan of your music. However, two things are bothering me.

First, I can't listen to your music when I am waiting to see my therapist, Dr. Buckley. She prefers quiet, more reflective music, and while it would be unfair to say that you're not reflective, I don't think "Sick of Myself" is emblematic of the sort of healing and self-respect that Dr. Buckley strives for in her practice. Perhaps you could consider something more upbeat, should you, yourself, someday feel a little more optimistic about things.

*Second, as I'm sure you're aware, the middle songs on
your album* Blue Sky on Mars *are substandard. From "Hol-
low," the fourth song, to "Heaven and Earth," the eighth,
you appear to have accepted half-baked songs. You cheap-
ened your talent and swindled your fans by not insisting on
a higher level of performance.*

*I will say, however, that you acquitted yourself nicely
on your next album,* In Reverse.

As ever, I remain your fan,
Edward Stanton

WEDNESDAY, OCTOBER 15

When my eyes open, I'm lying on my back. The clock says 7:38 a.m. This is a relief to me, after the waking-time debacle from yesterday. That's 222 days out of 289 this year (because it's a leap year) that I've stirred at 7:38. There is something in my physiology that favors this time. I do not know what it is. I am not a physiologist.

I reach for my notebook and my pen, flip over to today's page, and record my wake-up time, and my data is complete.

— • —

Today, I am going to paint the garage. I have been in this house that my father bought for eight years (eight years and eighty-eight days). I paint the house and the garage in alternating years. I would prefer to paint them on the same date each year, but weather is too much of a variable.

Technically speaking, I do not need to paint this often. A good paint job, the only kind that is acceptable, can last ten years or more, even in a climate as erratic as Montana's. Dr. Buckley tells me that I will feel better if I remain as busy as possible, and I have found that physical busywork is more beneficial than mental busywork. For example, I like putting together plastic models of trains and automobiles and such, but often, I will start thinking not of the glue or the paint involved in the model but about something someone has done to irritate me—that someone often being my father—and I end up writing letters of complaint that I am tempted to mail, and this interferes with my project. Dr. Buckley does not want me to mail my letters of complaint. I also like painting the house and the garage, and my mind does not go to other things when I'm doing so because the work is more physically demanding. That's why, today, I'm going to paint the garage.

But I can't paint every day. For one thing, paint needs time to dry. For another, Montana's weather is such that there is precipitation—that's rain or snow—every single month of the year. Even if paint somehow magically dried (and there is no such thing as magic) two seconds after you applied it, you would still have to deal with rain and snow. Someday, scientists might make super fast–drying paint. Controlling the weather would be much harder, even for scientists.

There is also a third reason, which I don't want to talk about for very long, as it will make me angry. The third reason is my father. There is no way that my father would buy enough paint for me to paint the house and garage every single day, even if I could. I have to fight with him just to paint every year, and I know he will be mad when he sees that I've bought nine gallons of paint for a tiny one-car garage. It wasn't my fault, though. Home Depot had too many choices, and the paint man was not helpful. I need to write him a letter.

— • —

After eating a bowl of corn flakes and taking my eighty milligrams of fluoxetine—and after changing into my painting T-shirt and jeans, which are very ratty and thus are kept deep down in my bottom drawer so I don't have to see them except when they're needed—I log on to Montana Personal Connect. eHarmony and its twenty-nine levels of compatibility found no one for me, but there are no levels of compatibility on Montana Personal Connect. You just write a profile and post it and wait to see what happens.

My profile looks like this:

Edward, age 39
Status: Single
Seeking: Dating
Lives: Yes
Location: Billings
Region: US-Mountain
Looks: Average
Hair/eyes: Brown/brown
Body: Average (although I don't know what average really is)
Height: Tall (although I don't know what tall really is)
Smoking: No
Drinking: No
Drugs: No
Religion: No. I prefer facts.
Sun sign: Capricorn
Education: High school graduate
Children: No
Career field: Not answered
Politics: Not answered
More about me…

I keep track of the weather and I like to watch Dragnet, *but only the 1967–1970 color episodes.*

There are no messages waiting for me. Montana Personal Connect seems a lot less scientific than eHarmony, but at least it let me post a profile.

— • —

Because I paint the garage so frequently, I need only wash it before painting. When my father bought this house eight years and eighty-eight days ago, the painting on both the house and the garage was in very sorry shape and probably hadn't been tended to in twenty years. It was so bad that I wanted to write a letter of complaint to the man who sold the house to my father, but my father would not give me his address. That frustrated me.

The first year I painted the house, I had to use a wire brush and a putty knife to dig out defective paint, and then I sanded down most of the house by hand. The next year, when I painted the garage, I knew better and bought a power sander. My father was not happy about that expenditure.

Now I need only wash the garage. It should dry quickly. The *Billings Herald-Gleaner* said the temperature was going to reach seventy-two today, which is very warm for this time of year. By contrast, the high temperature a year ago was forty-six, which I know because my data is complete. I won't know for sure whether the temperature reaches seventy-two today until I see tomorrow's newspaper. Today's has only a forecast, and forecasts are notoriously off base. I prefer facts.

— • —

My garage, which is detached from the house, is very small. In 1937, when the house was built, people didn't build the huge houses that are built today, unless they were very rich or very ostentatious. (I love the word "ostentatious.") The house is 1,360 square feet—680 upstairs and 680 in the basement. The garage is twelve feet wide by fifteen feet deep, or just big enough for my car, a 1997 Toyota Camry, and some tools and other things.

Still, it takes me a while to wash the garage, mix the paint (I'm going to try Behr's parsley sprig first), and get my various brushes lined up in the order that I'm going to use them. I also have a ladder for those hard-to-reach areas.

By 11:00 a.m., I am painting, working in the same direction that the sun is moving.

I am happy.

— • —

"I like that color."

I'm on the ladder when I hear the voice, and I'm so startled that I nearly hit my head on the eave. I set my brush on the shelf on the ladder. My heart is beating fast. I steady myself and back down the ladder, and then I turn around.

It's the boy I have seen across the street.

"What?"

"I said, I like that color."

"It's Behr parsley sprig."

"What does that mean?"

"Behr is the company that made the paint. Parsley sprig is the color."

"What's parsley sprig?"

"Do you know that green stuff they put on your plate at a restaurant?"

"Yeah. You're not supposed to eat it."

"That's a parsley sprig."

"Oh."

The boy has his hands in his pocket and he fidgets. This makes me fidgety, too. I don't like it.

"What do you want?"

"Nothing."

"Go away, then."

"Well, maybe…"

"What?"

"Can I help you paint?"

— • —

I am agog. (I love the word "agog.")

There is an eight- or nine-year-old boy painting the garage. Holy shit!

I do not curse often, but I am partial to the phrase "Holy shit!" Many years ago, I saw the movie *Animal House*, which is very funny. In one scene, Bluto and D-Day and Flounder from Delta House take a horse into the dean's office—I am not sure why; the scene flummoxed me—and Flounder shoots a gun in the air, and the horse has a heart attack and dies. The other two guys come in and say "Holy shit!" a lot. It is a very funny movie.

I am giggling now, thinking of this.

"There's an eight- or nine-year-old boy painting the garage."

"Holy shit!"

"He's eight or nine, and he is painting the garage."

"Holy shit!"

"The garage is being painted by an eight- or nine-year-old boy."

"Holy shit!"

I am pretty funny sometimes.

— • —

The boy does not paint the garage exactly as I would prefer, and I would say something to him if not for the fact that he never stops talking as he paints.

"What's your name?" he asks me.

"Edward. What's yours?"

"Kyle. Did you know that your house will be brown, but your garage will be green?"

"Yes. I will paint the house next year."

"Why next year?"

"That's the way I do things."

"Are you married?"

"No."

"Have you ever been married?"

"No."

"How old are you?"

"I'm thirty-nine. How old are you?"

"I'm nine. I was born in 1999."

"That's the year Kevin Spacey won the best actor Oscar for *American Beauty*."

"What's that?"

"A movie."

"I like movies."

"So do I."

"Are you going to pay me for painting your garage?"

I am taken aback. It's not quite the same thing as being agog. "Did we have a deal?"

"No."

"Then I'm not going to pay you."

"I am saving up my money for a bicycle. That's why I was wondering. I have fifty-three dollars, but that's not enough for the bike I want. My mom said that I might get one for my birthday, but she's not sure."

"If you expected money, you should have negotiated a deal with me before you started painting. That's the fair thing to do."

"It's OK. I like painting."

"When is your birthday?" I ask him.

"February ninth."

"That's when you'll be ten?"

"Yes."

"You're nine years and two hundred and forty-nine days old."

"Cool! How did you do that?"

"I'm good with data."

His painting is haphazard. Sometimes his strokes are up and down, and sometimes they are side to side. Little dots of paint are missing the garage and landing in the driveway. And I am surprised that I don't seem to care.

I will have to talk to Dr. Buckley about this.

— • —

The garage painting is finished by 4:30 p.m. It looks pretty good, especially considering that a nine-year-old boy did some of it. I offer to shake hands with Kyle, but he insists on a high five, something I've never done. I've seen the Dallas Cowboys do it, and it looks like great fun. I hold up my right hand, and Kyle slaps it hard. It sort of hurts. It's not that much fun.

"See ya, Edward," Kyle says, and he's dashing across the street to his house, his blond hair flying behind him, his arms flailing.

— • —

At 8:07 p.m., after I've had my spaghetti, I hear a knock on the door. I am flummoxed. Visitors are rare at this house. I have not had a visitor since July 21.

I open the door, and standing on the stoop is the woman I saw mowing her yard yesterday morning, the woman I presume to be Kyle's mother.

"Hello? Mister...I'm sorry, I don't know your last name. You're Edward, right?"

"Edward Stanton. Yes."

"I'm Donna, Kyle's mom. I don't think we've met."

"Not until now, no."

"Kyle told me he helped you paint your garage. I hope he wasn't any trouble."

"No."

"I just thought, if he's going to be hanging around over here, I should know who you are. I hope you're not offended."

"No. But he just helped paint the garage."

"Of course. I don't want to be rude. You just can't be too careful, you know? I'm sure you understand."

"I didn't let him go up on the ladder."

"OK."

She's now just looking at me. I stare back at her.

"Is there anything else?" I ask her.

"No, I guess not. Thanks for letting Kyle help you out, Edward."

"All right, then."

I close the door. I can tell from the sound outside that Donna stands there for a few seconds before walking across the street to her house.

I'm as flummoxed as I've ever been, I think, although I don't keep data on that. I may need a new word.

— • —

Tonight's *Dragnet* is the twenty-first episode of the fourth and final season, "Forgery: The Ranger," and it is one of my favorites. It originally aired on March 12, 1970.

A character named Barney Regal, played by Stacy Harris, who died many years before I started writing to *Dragnet* actors, tries to pass himself off as a forest ranger. In talking to various groups about forestry, he ends up stealing credit cards and other valuables. Sergeant Joe Friday and Officer Bill Gannon slowly work him over at the office downtown, methodically poking holes in his story until he confesses that he's not Ranger Barney Regal at all but a common criminal named Clifford Ray Owens.

I would not want to be a criminal being worked over by Friday and Gannon. They would surely make me admit my crimes. They are very logical men.

— • —

I have a couple of candidates for tonight's letter of complaint. The unhelpful paint man at Home Depot has avoided my wrath so far, and he is deserving of complaint. But I have to concede that the Behr parsley sprig looks pretty good on that garage. He will get a complaint—he deserves one—but it can wait.

Donna:

I did not appreciate your uninvited knock on my door this evening. Had you granted me the courtesy of some warning of your visit, I would have been better prepared to answer your questions and more comfortable in talking with you.

Also, I am uncomfortable addressing you in a familiar way by using your first name. You have left me no choice, however, as you introduced yourself that way. However, I gave you the courtesy of letting you know my last name, and yet you insisted on addressing me as Edward. This, too, is entirely too familiar given our limited interaction.

Your son, Kyle, is a very courteous young man, if a little exuberant. I can only assume that he learned his manners from someone other than you. That said, I do not like assumptions. I prefer facts. Perhaps we can discuss this issue at a more appropriate time, while referring to each other in an acceptable way.

I thank you for your consideration.

Regards,
Edward Stanton

THURSDAY, OCTOBER 16

My eyes open at 7:37 a.m. I am on my side, facing the clock. This does not happen often. I usually wake up on my back. On the 290th day of the year (because it's a leap year), I have awakened at 7:37 for the sixteenth time. There is no correlation between those numbers that I can see, but as I have recorded both in my notebook, my data is complete.

— • —

Through the big bay window in the dining room, I can see both the garage (now the color of Behr parsley sprig, although not for long) and, in the other direction, signs of life on Clark Avenue. People are heading to work and school and who knows where else. Today, I will be joining them. I have volunteered to make calls for the Muscular Dystrophy Association. I do not like to talk on the telephone, as I do not do spontaneous conversation well, but I have been assured that I will have a "script" to use, and that I can do. I can read very well. Dr. Buckley encourages me to stay as busy as possible, and volunteering to help the Muscular Dystrophy Association seems like a good way to spend a day.

I found out that the Muscular Dystrophy Association needed a volunteer through reading the *Billings Herald-Gleaner* a week ago. I am now reading today's *Billings Herald-Gleaner*, and the front page says the high temperature will be sixty degrees today. Of course, that's just a forecast, and forecasts are notoriously off base. I prefer facts. I will know for sure tomorrow what the temperature reaches today.

Today, however, I know that it reached sixty-six degrees yesterday, with a low of forty-four, and I record those numbers in my notebook, and my data is complete.

In any case, I can deduce from the advisory and from what I can see with my own two eyes that the garage should be dry today, while I am off volunteering for the Muscular Dystrophy Association.

— • —

As I'm dressing—brown corduroy pants and a blue button-down, long-sleeved shirt, as today I will be working in an office—I think that it makes me feel good to have a job to go to today. It's not really a job, of course, but it seems like one, in that I will be in my car when everybody else is going to work, and when I get to the Muscular Dystrophy office, I will be making phone calls and writing things down, just like a person who has a job. I wonder if I will get my own desk. That would be neat.

If everything works out all right, I might even take a coffee break. I don't like coffee, but if that's what they do at the Muscular Dystrophy Association, I think it would only be polite to do the same.

I used to have a job, many years ago. In 1993, my father helped me get a clerical job with Yellowstone County. I liked the work very much. I maintained files in the clerk and recorder's office, and it was very orderly work. Paperwork would come in, and I would find the file where it belonged and put it away. I was very good at keeping everything in order, and when I was asked to retrieve a file, I could do so quickly. My boss was very complimentary of my work, and I was left alone to do it. I liked that job very much.

But I stopped working for Yellowstone County in 1997. A new clerk and recorder was elected the previous November, and she wanted things done completely differently from the way I was doing them. She did not like my work at all, and she told me that I had to do it a different way, her way. I did not like her way, and I told her so. She told me I had to do it anyway. I told her that I wouldn't. She told me that I would or I would have to find somewhere else to work.

My father had to come down to the office after I removed every file and shook its contents onto the floor. The new clerk and recorder told my father that she was going to call the deputies if he did not remove me immediately.

After that, I did not have to work anymore.

— • —

The Muscular Dystrophy Association office is in the West End of Billings, a few miles from the house on Clark Avenue, which is in a part of Billings that I suppose you would call central. But I have read histories of Billings suggesting that where I live, at Sixth Street W. and Clark Avenue, used to be the western edge of town. I suppose that the idea of what is north, south, east, or west of something else depends a lot on what point of history you're looking at. These are facts that change. This flummoxes me.

600 HOURS OF EDWARD

At Nineteenth Street W. and Central Avenue, I see the Exchange City Par 3 Golf Course. My father loves golf, so much so that he wears golf shirts no matter what time of year it is. He looks like a tool. (I love the word "tool" in the pejorative sense. I also love the word "pejorative.") He and my mother go on vacation in places like Pebble Beach, California, and Hilton Head, South Carolina. I'm not sure what my mother does in those places, but my father plays golf.

When I was a boy, my father took me to the Exchange City Par 3 Golf Course and tried to teach me how to play. We went once, and I have never been back. Golf is a stupid game. You cannot hit the ball the same way every time and get the same result— not even Tiger Woods, the best golfer in the world, can do this. I do not like such unpredictability. Our golf outing ended when I threw three of my father's golf clubs into the water. He didn't talk to me for two days after that.

I take a right turn on Monad Street (I like right turns), then a left on Twentieth Street W. (I don't like left turns so much), cross over King Avenue W., and see the Muscular Dystrophy Association office. I pull into the parking lot.

I am a little bit nervous. As I reach for the keys, I hear through the car speakers the opening bars of R.E.M.'s "Try Not to Breathe," and it seems to me that this is just about the worst possible advice right now.

— • —

Inside the Muscular Dystrophy Association office, I am met by a woman named Sonya Starr, who smiles a lot and wears too much makeup. She firmly shakes my hand, and I think she notices that I recoil a bit at that, but her smile stays firmly attached to her face.

"Thank you so much for coming in and helping us, Mr. Stanton."

Sonya Starr has more teeth than anyone I've ever seen, although I know this is just an illusion. The normal adult human mouth has thirty-two teeth, and it defies all statistical probability that Sonya Starr has thirty-three teeth and everyone else has thirty-two.

"You're welcome."

She smiles again. "We had expected to have two of you making calls today, but unfortunately, our other volunteer had to cancel, so it looks like it'll just be you."

"Do I have to do the work of two people? Because I don't think I can do that, since I've never done this before, and if that's the requirement, I should have been told of this when I called last week."

Sonya Starr is not smiling anymore.

"It's no problem, Mr. Stanton. You do what you can do in the time that you feel you can give us. You are a volunteer, and we appreciate you for offering your time."

"Yes."

Sonya Starr is definitely not smiling anymore.

— • —

Sonya Starr explains to me what I will be doing today. I am to call businesses on a master list and ask if they would like to participate in the Muscular Dystrophy Association's Turkey Time fundraiser.

I have a script for this:

"Hello, Mr./Mrs. _____. This is (your name) from the Muscular Dystrophy Association of

Montana. I am calling to see if your business is interested in helping with our Turkey Time fund-raiser. Are you familiar with Turkey Time?"

(If the answer is no, read the next paragraph. If yes, skip to the next paragraph.)

"Turkey Time is a fund-raiser in which customers are asked if they would like to buy a turkey for one dollar to assist the Muscular Dystrophy Association. Customers who choose to buy a turkey get a paper turkey on which they can print their name, and the turkey is displayed at your place of business. The money generated goes to the Muscular Dystrophy Association in support of our range of programs for children afflicted with this terrible disease.

"Are you interested in taking part in this fund-raiser?"

(If the answer is yes, proceed to the bottom and explain to the business how the program is administered. If the answer is no, read the next paragraph.)

"I'm sorry to hear that. The program is very easy to administer, requires no up-front cost to you, and helps many, many children and their families deal with the effects of this terrible disease. Are you certain that you're not willing to take part?"

(If the answer is yes, politely thank the business for its time. If the business now expresses interest, read the last paragraph.)

"We thank you so much for your participation. I will now ensure that I have the correct address for your business, and then we will send you a packet with the turkeys and an explanation of how to get the money back to us."

(Now verify mailing address and contact information before hanging up.)

"Again, thanks so much for your time and your generosity to the Muscular Dystrophy Association of Montana. Good-bye."

This is going to be exhausting.

— • —

After showing me to a cubicle and teaching me how to use the hands-free headset, Sonya Starr asks me if I have ever seen the Turkey Time fund-raiser. She says she wants to hear from the "front lines" how recognizable the program is.

"No," I say.

"It's in all the grocery stores this time of year, as Thanksgiving approaches. Are you sure you haven't seen the little paper turkeys at the checkout stands?"

"I use the self-checkout stands. It's easier not to talk to anyone."

Again, Sonya Starr isn't smiling.

— • —

The calls are a disaster.

First of all, I'm supposed to ask for the manager or owner. I rarely get that person. I get a lot of answers like, "He goes home at ten," or "He won't be in this week." I get so many of these, in fact, that I soon regret that I'm not counting and classifying the answers I'm getting.

Second of all, I get a lot of hang-ups. I'll be halfway through my opening—"Hello, Mr. Business Owner, this is Edward Stanton with the Muscular..."—and I'll hear, "We already gave," and a click. This is frustrating.

Third of all, I get a lot of dodges. People tell me that only the corporate office can approve things like the Turkey Time fundraiser, and so I ask for those numbers and fill up another sheet of paper with more numbers to call.

Fourth of all, Sonya Starr's preferred method of keeping track of the calls is terrible. She wants me to mark successful calls—as of noon, I have two of those—with a yellow highlighter. The calls that don't connect with an owner or manager—as of noon, I have fourteen of those—take an asterisk so they can be called back. The ones that turn me down—as of noon, I have eighteen of those—are to be marked with a strike-through.

If you ask me, which Sonya Starr did not, it would be better to mark the callbacks with a yellow highlighter and the successful calls with a green highlighter. (The strike-through, of course, makes perfect sense.) The reason is simple: Green means go (as in, these Turkey Time turkeys are ready to go), and yellow means wait (as in, you will have to wait and try these numbers again). Anybody who drives a car knows the value of these particular colors.

At 12:30, Sonya Starr tells me I can go to lunch. There has been no coffee break.

— • —

At 1:29, I return from lunch and stop in at Sonya Starr's office.

"Yes, Mr. Stanton?"

"I was wondering if I could change the way I mark the calls."

"Why?"

"This way is dumb."

"What do you mean?"

"You have a yellow highlighter for a successful call and an asterisk for a callback. It should be green highlighter for a successful call and a yellow highlighter for a callback."

"Does it really matter?"

"Yes. Colors have meanings. Yours don't make any sense."

"But everybody in the office knows this color scheme."

"It flummoxes me. It's probably why the calls have gone so poorly."

"I doubt that."

"I'm sure of it. Well, I'm not entirely sure. I would have to do a detailed analysis to be sure and talk to all of the business owners and ask them what is causing them to say no, and I doubt that I could do that, since I have had so much trouble reaching them thus far. So it's not right for me to say I'm sure. I prefer facts. But the fact is that I'm flummoxed by this."

Sonya Starr smiles at me.

"Mr. Stanton, I think we won't be needing any more of your help. Thanks ever so much for coming by."

— • —

On my drive home, I'm stopped at every traffic light by yellow. I do not keep data on traffic lights, but I cannot remember this ever happening to me.

— • —

As I near the house, I see that Kyle is standing on the sidewalk where it crosses the driveway. His back is to the street. His hands are jammed in his back pockets, and he is staring at the garage.

I toot the horn, and he jumps aside and waves at me. I pull the car forward, set the brake, shut off the ignition, and get out.

"The garage looks good," Kyle says.

"Yes."

"We did a good job. Do you like the color?"

"Yes. But I'm painting it again tomorrow."

"What? Really?"

"Yes."

"Why?"

"Because I want to."

"Can I help?"

"If you want to."

"Will I get paid?"

"No."

He smiles. "I had to ask."

And then he's gone, running again. I can't remember the last time I ran. I don't keep data on that.

— • —

Dinner is leftover spaghetti with meat sauce, warmed up in the microwave. I eat spaghetti nine times a week, every week, and it is my favorite food. And yet, tonight, I wonder if I am in a rut.

— • —

Tonight's episode of *Dragnet*—the twenty-second of the fourth and final season—is called "DHQ: Night School," and it is one of my favorites.

In this episode, which originally aired on March 19, 1970, we see two *Dragnet* rarities: First, Sergeant Joe Friday spends most of the episode not wearing his customary gray suit, as he is attending night school. Instead, he wears a red cardigan sweater that I can only assume was a popular item in 1970, although I don't like to assume. I prefer facts. Second, Sergeant Joe Friday has a female interest in this episode, a young nurse who is also attending night school. I guess night school was the sort of place where you met someone in 1970, before the Internet and online dating.

Sergeant Joe Friday is doing very well in night school, but he spots a classmate carrying marijuana, and because he is a cop and cops are never off duty, he arrests his classmate after school. This greatly angers the teacher, played by an actor named Leonard Stone, who also played Sam Beauregard in the movie *Willy Wonka & the Chocolate Factory*, which is one of my favorites. He's the one who says, "Violet! You're turning violet, Violet!" Sam Beauregard is also supposed to be from Miles City, Montana, which isn't all that far from where I live.

Sergeant Joe Friday ends up getting kicked out of class on a vote of the classmates for breaking their trust. Sergeant Joe Friday stews about this, then comes back and asks the teacher for one more chance to talk to the class, with the agreement that if he doesn't sway two-thirds of the class, he's still out. The vote is in favor of Sergeant Joe Friday, but not by two-thirds, and he is prepared to leave until a lawyer wearing an eye patch tells the teacher that he has no right to deny Sergeant Joe Friday an education and that he will file charges to keep Sergeant Joe Friday in the class if the professor persists.

This episode, I think, is about standing up for what you believe in, no matter how unpopular. I need to be a lot more like Sergeant Joe Friday.

Sonya Starr:

I wish to express my extreme displeasure with your intractability on the issue of how to label the calls made on behalf of the Muscular Dystrophy Association. Your refusal to listen to my concerns and then your abrupt dismissal of me were not professional representations of your organization.

I think that people who stand up for what they believe in, no matter how unpopular, should be celebrated, not cast aside. I believe that my ideas about green highlighters and yellow highlighters could have served the Muscular Dystrophy Association well, if only they were given a proper and considerate airing.

It is my hope that should we have occasion to work together in the future, you will exhibit a higher standard of professionalism.

Respectfully submitted,
Edward Stanton

FRIDAY, OCTOBER 17

It's hazy in here. The edges of my vision have a gauzy feel. An R.E.M. song I like, "Daysleeper," calls it "headache gray." Michael Stipe, R.E.M.'s lead singer, puts words together in odd yet pleasing ways.

Suddenly, she comes into view. I think I have seen her before, and yet I cannot put a name to her. She is looking at me in a way that sends a tingle through me. She licks her lips and moves closer to me.

She is naked.

I am naked.

She reaches down. Oh my goodness. This can't possibly...

— • —

My eyes fly open. My breath is shallow and rapid. It's 7:39 a.m. It is the twenty-third time this year that I have awoken at this time, although never before like this. I breathe deeply and purse my lips and expel the air in a single blast. I reach for my notebook and pen, flip to today's page, and write down "7:39 a.m.," and my data is complete.

Also, my balls ache.

— • —

When I log on to Montana Personal Connect, I see something I haven't seen before:

Inbox (1).

I had not anticipated this. I try not to anticipate things at all, as that is just supposition about what will happen, and supposition is not fact. I prefer facts. And yet I know that anticipation is also human, and so am I, no matter how much I try to resist it.

I had not anticipated this. It seems silly to say, but I am not sure what to do.

I had not anticipated this. I guess I should click the inbox link. Yes, that's the thing to do.

I had not anticipated this.

Click.

Edward:

I really liked your profile. So many people on here try to "sell" themselves. Its all so fake. But your profile is simple and to the point. I like that in a man.

And your funny too. Anyway I hope you will check out my profile and maybe write back.

Have a great day!

Joy

I am flabbergasted. (I like the word "flabbergasted." It's not quite an onomatopoeia, another word I like, but it's close.)

It's not a perfect letter. Joy does not seem to know the difference between "you're" and "your," or how to use an apostrophe or a comma, and she didn't mention anything about tracking the weather.

It's also the first response my profile has received. Beggars can't be choosers, as the saying goes. My father says that a lot, but I don't think it's a philosophy to him. He just doesn't like poor people. It's not a philosophy to me, either. I prefer facts.

Joy's profile picture is very pretty. It would be a stretch to say she's beautiful. Beautiful is Angelina Jolie or Merry Anders, one of my favorite ensemble actors on *Dragnet*. Joy is not that. But she is very pretty.

She has short blonde hair and blue eyes that are very bright. She smiles very well, and she has dimples. She looks very sturdy, too, which isn't always considered a beautiful trait, but I like it.

This is what her profile says:

> *The guy I am looking for is secure and wants a woman who is secure too. Ive been there done that with guys who are controlling or insecure and never again. I am a simple girl with simple tastes. Take me out to a movie and dinner once in a while and its all good. I prefer H/W proportionate but its the spark that counts. If you can make me laugh its all good. If your in a relationship or living in your parents house don't bother. If your rich that's even better. Ha ha. I have 2 kids who live with there dad. I would like to have more kids.*

Joy is forty-one. If she wants to have more kids, she needs to hurry.

Her grammar is atrocious. I am worried about this desire for more kids. It is a lot to think about right now, since I haven't even met Joy. I can't think about kids yet. It's too much pressure. Also, she lives in Broadview, a small town that is thirty-one miles away. A lot of reasons not to respond are piling up. I am thinking about hitting delete on her note and waiting for another response. It could be a long wait, though.

Dr. Buckley has encouraged me to challenge my tendency to not want to talk to or meet people. I wonder what she would think of this.

She might tell me that Joy was very nice to have responded to my profile and that I ought to be equally nice in return.

She would probably tell me to be more forgiving about the atrocious grammar.

Maybe I should write back.

Maybe I should paint the garage first and figure out what I want to say.

— • —

After eating a bowl of corn flakes and recording yesterday's weather data—high of fifty-seven, low of thirty-four on the 291st day of the year (because it's a leap year), and now my data is complete—I drag the Behr mochachino paint, the mixing pans, and the paintbrushes into the driveway. I have extra brushes for Kyle, in case he decides to show up after school.

I am feeling apprehensive about the painting. The ten-day forecast looked good, so I am reasonably confident that I can get the mocha chino applied and even the bronze green before Billings gets a blast of snow or rain. I don't know this for a fact, of course. That's the problem with forecasts. They are notoriously off base.

So it's not the painting, per se, that makes me hesitant. I don't quite know what it is. I'm beginning to wonder if it wasn't dumb of me to buy three kinds of paint, all of which I will have to see on the garage before I am satisfied. I know this about myself, and I'm now regretful that I couldn't have chosen just one color and been done with it. Even though I want to blame the unhelpful paint man, I cannot. It's my fault for being so compulsive.

But what's done is done. I cannot reverse it now.

I wonder if Joy will think I'm weird for painting the garage three times. Maybe I can wait before telling her. Maybe I'll put it off to sometime between our first meeting and our discussion about the kids.

— • —

I am in nearly the same spot on the garage and at nearly the same time as before when Kyle shows up. I prefer to be more precise than "nearly," but I did not write down the time of Kyle's last visit, as I did not expect that it would be the sort of regular occurrence that would require data keeping on my part. Here, again, is the problem with assumptions. They are sometimes wrong. I prefer facts.

This time, I don't almost hit my head on the eave when he speaks, because I hear him coming. I also expected that he might show up, and I am right. Sometimes, expectations aren't so problematic.

"Can I help?" he asks.

Again, I back down the ladder and face him.

"Yes. I have paintbrushes for you."

Kyle goes over to the lined-up brushes, chooses one, dips it into the mixing pan, and starts sloshing the Behr mochachino on the garage door.

"You should use a steady stroke in the same direction."

"Like this?" He is holding the paintbrush rigidly and moving it up and down quickly.

"Relax your wrist and slow down a little bit, and paint in one direction."

"Like this?" He has done as I asked.

"That's better."

"Why are you painting the garage again?" he asks.

"It's part of my plan."

"Like a secret plan?"

"Something like that, yes."

"And I'm like your partner."

"Yes. On this garage plan, you are my partner."

Kyle giggles.

I let him paint.

"Hey, Edward."

"Yes?"

"I'm nine years old and two hundred and fifty-one days today."

"Yes."

— • —

Boys who are nine years old and 251 days talk…a lot. I am leaning against the hood of my 1997 Toyota Camry, drinking a can of Diet Dr Pepper while I watch Kyle paint. His Diet Dr Pepper is sitting in the driveway, unopened.

Kyle talks about his school. He doesn't like his teacher. He likes math. And he likes a girl. I ask him if she knows that he likes her. He says no. I ask if he's going to tell her, and he giggles again.

Kyle talks about his house, the one he and his mother moved into on September 12. He has a PlayStation 2 but wishes he had a Wii, because those "totally rule." He asks if I want to come over sometime and play PlayStation 2, and I pretend that I didn't hear him, and he goes back to painting.

He talks about his mother. She is a nurse at Billings Clinic, and she works Fridays, Saturdays, and Sundays in the emergency room. She is thirty-four years old, he offers. She has lived with many men—I count a Donald and a Troy and a Mike in his anecdotes. He tells me that the reason they moved into this house is that Mike hit her, and she filed a restraining order against him. I ask him if he saw Mike hit his mother, and Kyle says softly, "Yeah."

"Where do you go on Fridays, Saturdays, and Sundays when your mother is working?"

"I stay with my grandma in Laurel."

"Your mother's mother or your father's mother?"

"My mom's mom. I don't know my dad."

"I know my father."

"What's he like?"

"He is a Yellowstone County commissioner."

"What's that?"

"He runs stuff around here."

"Oh."

"He's not very nice sometimes," I offer. "Maybe it's better that you don't know your father."

"I don't think so."

— • —

A little before 5:00 p.m., while Kyle and I are washing out the paintbrushes, his mother walks across the street.

"Kyle, it's about time to go."

"I know."

"OK, run home and grab your overnight bag for Grandma's house."

"See ya, Edward," Kyle says, and he lights out.

She smiles at me.

"Hi, Edward."

"Hello."

"Kyle wasn't any trouble, was he?"

"No. He's a very good painter now."

"Really?"

"Yes. I taught him how to do it."

"That's great."

I nod.

"Listen," she says, "I want to thank you for being nice to him. He doesn't get much of a chance to do these kinds of things."

"OK."

"I'm sorry if I was accusatory the other day."

"OK."

"You don't have a lot to say, do you?"

I stare at her.

"I'm sorry," she says. "That didn't come out very nice."

"OK. I have to go now."

"OK, Edward."

I gather up the brushes and head to the front door, then stop and turn around.

"Donna?"

She's halfway across the street.

"Yes?"

"What's your last name?"

"Middleton. What's yours?"

"Stanton. I told you that the other day."

"Right. Sorry. I forgot."

We're looking at each other.

"Good-bye, Ms. Middleton."

"Good-bye, Mr. Stanton."

— • —

First, dinner. I will have the DiGiorno pizza.

It's good, but it doesn't taste like delivery, no matter what the TV commercial says. I don't think delivery has a taste. It's nonsensical. Delivered pizza has a taste, but that's not what the commercial says. Imprecision frustrates me.

— • —

Second, I will write back to Joy. I haven't given my reply as much thought as I'd hoped, what with spending the day with Kyle and, for a few minutes, his mother. But I can't put it off much longer, for I fear that Joy will think I am rude.

I decide to wing it. I don't like winging it. I like plans.

Joy:

I hope this note finds you well.

Thank you for responding to my profile. I enjoyed reading yours. It has given me much to think about. It's hard to know what to think of this online dating. I wish a kind face (yours) were a reliable barometer. But it seems that one has to be willing to take a chance. I don't like chance. I prefer reliability and facts.

Here are some things about me:

I am thirty-nine. I was born on January 9, 1969, and so I am really thirty-nine years and 282 days old, if you're counting. I always count.
I like to track the weather and keep track of other things.
I am six foot four and a bit heavy. You said height-weight proportional but also that a spark was most important. I will take you at your word.
I am a nonsmoker.
I have never married.
I have no children. You spoke a lot about children in your profile. I would like to wait to have those discussions.
I live in Billings. You live in Broadview. That's thirty-one miles. I would be willing to travel for the right person. How do you feel about this?
I hope to hear from you.

With regards,
Edward

I hit send. Holy shit!

— • —

Third, at 10:00 p.m. sharp, I will watch tonight's episode of *Dragnet*.

This one, the twenty-third episode of the fourth and final season, is called "I.A.D.: The Receipt," and it is one of my favorites. It originally aired on March 26, 1970. In this episode, a woman accuses two detectives of stealing $800 from a dead man, and Sergeant Joe Friday and Officer Bill Gannon are called in to investigate. They eventually prove that the detectives did not steal the money, because they follow clues relentlessly until the truth emerges.

You may be wondering why, in 2008, my favorite television show is one that was made largely before I was born. I will tell you.

Sergeant Joe Friday, played by Jack Webb, is no-nonsense. He wants only the facts, which he repeatedly tells anyone with whom he is talking. The facts lead Sergeant Joe Friday to the truth, and that allows him to put the bad guys away and make Los Angeles a little bit safer. There are not many TV shows like that anymore. The ones today are full of moral equivalencies, and there seems to be little celebration of the truth. I do like shows like *Law and Order*, which is made by Dick Wolf, who is a big fan of Jack Webb. But even shows like that end up mired in the ambiguity that Sergeant Joe Friday disdained.

Also, some of today's shows have a totally unrealistic view of the world. On that show everybody seems to love, *24*, Jack Bauer can get from one side of Los Angeles to the other in five minutes. This is simply not possible. I went to Los Angeles on a vacation two years ago—my father was apoplectic when he saw the cost. (I love the word "apoplectic.") I can tell you from experience that you cannot get from Hollywood and Vine to the Sunset Strip in five minutes, and those places are very close together, in Los Angeles terms. Jack Bauer is fooling his audience, but he doesn't fool me.

— • —

My letter of complaint tonight requires yet another new green office folder. This letter is overdue.

Unhelpful paint man at Home Depot:

As I have had other things attracting my attention, I have been slow to register my complaint about your poor performance on October 14, when I purchased paint in your store. I would be remiss, however, if I did not cover this ground with you.

I have now applied two colors to the garage, and because of your inability to help me zero in on a single color, I will still have to apply another. This wastes my valuable time and could conceivably cause me to run up against the erratic October weather for which Billings is known.

Still, I also must acknowledge my own role in this failure. I could not control my impulse to buy three colors of paint, and that is not your fault. I had merely hoped that you could help me negotiate the many choices at your store. I will continue to work on my problem. Perhaps you could work on yours.

Respectfully,
Edward Stanton

SATURDAY, OCTOBER 18

I am standing at the edge of a cliff, looking down. I don't know if I've been here before. There is a rimrock that surrounds Billings; it is the signature geographic formation of the area. I know it well. I see it every day. I don't know if this is it, as I can't see the whole rock or a town below. I see my feet and the brown, dusty, weather-beaten sandstone below them, and below that only the murky darkness.

Then I feel myself fall down. Only, it's not me.

It's him. Kyle. I can see his face as he falls away, and I know his little body is going to crash to the rocks that I assume are below, although I don't like to assume. I can feel the black terror inside of me.

And suddenly, a hand reaches out and catches Kyle's wrist. It's my hand, and I feel the snap of my shoulder as his fall is arrested.

"Help me, Edward!" he says.

"I have you," I say through my teeth, straining to keep my grip on his wrist. I'm lying flat on my stomach, my chin hanging over the edge of the cliff, my feet scratching at the rock behind me as I try to find purchase.

"I'm slipping!"

"I have you!"

And then I don't have him. Gravity pulls him from my grip and hurtles him to certain death, and...

— • —

I am awake.
　And I am up.
　And I am out of here.
　I don't know what time it is.
　My data is not complete.

— • —

Once I am sitting in the driver's seat of my 1997 Toyota Camry, I notice three things. First, it's 7:40 a.m. Second, the Behr mochachino looks horrid on the garage in front of me. Third, I am wearing my 1999 R.E.M. *Up* tour T-shirt and blue-and-red pajama bottoms. I sleep in these. I am wearing no shoes.
　I don't care.

— • —

From the house that my father bought, the route to Billings Clinic is easy: right turn on Clark Avenue to Sixth Avenue W., left turn on Sixth to Lewis Avenue, right turn on Lewis to Broadway, left turn on Broadway to Billings Clinic. I can be there in five minutes. My stomach is churning, and not from the left turns.

— • —

At Billings Clinic, I find a parking spot in the lot behind the emergency department. Before I step out of the car, I catch a glimpse of myself in the rearview mirror and lick my right palm, then paw at my head. My hair is puffed up and bent every which way from sleep. I look crazy. I feel crazy. I guess I am crazy.

I'm running for the door.

— • —

"I have to see Donna Middleton."

"And you are?" The security guard at the emergency department's front desk is looking at me with suspicion, and I cannot blame him, but I also cannot care.

"Edward Stanton. You have to get her."

"Does she know you're coming?"

"No. Get her."

"Sir, you need to calm down."

"Please get her."

"Sir."

"Please."

"Sir, why are you here?"

"Please. Just tell her it's Edward Stanton. Please."

He looks me over slowly. I try to stand up a little straighter, as if it would make me look any less ridiculous.

He picks up the phone.

— • —

In two minutes that seem to take forever—it's funny how time can be both fact and illusion—Donna Middleton emerges from the double doors separating the lobby from the emergency department.

"Edward, what's going on?"

"I have to talk to you."

"OK. Edward, I'm at work."

"I know. I have to talk to you."

"OK."

"I need you to call Kyle."

"Why?"

"I need you to make sure he's OK."

Her face, until now perplexed, changes in an instant. It flushes with color, her eyes bore in on me, and there is a snap in her tone.

"What happened? Did something happen to my son? Why are you here?"

"Please, just call him."

"What do you know about my son?" She is yelling at me.

The security guard, having watched us warily from behind the desk, is advancing on me now. Donna Middleton's hands are fists.

"I...I..."

"What about my son?" She is quaking.

I start talking fast. "I don't know. I had a dream. I've dreamed the past two nights. I dreamed that something happened. I couldn't save him. I tried. I really, really tried. You have to call him. Just make sure he's OK. Please. Call him."

Donna Middleton wheels away from me and sprints back through the double doors. The security guard, a very strong young man, grabs my arms and pulls them behind my back. I slump to the floor.

— • —

I am not surprised when my father comes through the automatic doors and into the emergency department lobby. The security guard called the police, and the police called my father. It has happened before, although never here at Billings Clinic.

My father is wearing a tan golf shirt under a windbreaker. Given the unseasonably warm weather—I haven't compiled my data yet, but I would guess that it will get into the sixties today, although I don't like guessing—I have probably interrupted my father's golf game. He looks at me and shakes his head slightly, and then he walks over to the front desk. He talks with the security guard, but quietly. I'm sitting in a chair along the wall, my hands shackled behind the back of it. I can hear my father identify himself, and I see the guard nod, but I'm having trouble hearing more.

After a few minutes of discussion with my father, the security guard nods again, and now they're both walking over to me. The security guard reaches behind me and unlocks the handcuffs, puts them back on his belt, and goes back to the front desk.

My father sits down next to me.

"What happened, Edward?"

"I had a bad dream. I was scared."

"About this woman's son?"

"Yes."

"Edward, what's your relationship with this boy?"

"Relationship?"

"Yes. Why are you so interested in this woman's son?"

"I am not interested in him, Father."

"Considering the circumstance you're in here, Edward, that's difficult to believe."

"He has helped me with painting the garage. He came over one day. That's it."

"That's it?"

"Yes. He has helped me paint. His mother knows about it. She hasn't complained."

"She's complaining now."

"Yes."

My father sighs. He leans forward in the chair, rubbing his eyes with his thumb and forefinger. "Do you understand how this looks? You're in your pajamas, you don't have any shoes, and you're in a hospital emergency room talking about a woman's son being hurt. Do you understand how that might be viewed as unacceptable?"

"Yes. I was scared."

"OK, Edward. But now you've scared someone else."

— • —

After talking with me, my father talks with Donna Middleton, who has come out to meet him. They talk a few feet away from me, and it's as if I'm not here.

"Mr. Stanton, I've never been so scared."

"I know."

"I called Kyle. He's fine."

"That's good. Edward says he had a bad dream. I'm sure your son was never in danger."

"Can I ask you a question?"

"Sure."

"What's wrong with him?"

My father smiles, as if to reassure her. "Edward has a severe case of obsessive-compulsive disorder. He has had it for a long time. What he did today is something new, I'll admit, but he generally does what he has to do to control his condition. He's on medication. He sees a therapist."

This shows what my father knows. The full story is that I'm obsessive-compulsive and that I have Asperger's syndrome. Some people call that "high-functioning autism." Dr. Buckley says it's not my fault.

"Is he dangerous?"

"No. At least, he never has been. Edward's compulsions generally lie in solitary things—the TV shows he watches, the projects he gets involved in, the things that stimulate his mind."

"I see. But you say that he's never done this."

"No."

"Can you assure me that he never will again?"

"I'm sorry. I don't think he will, but I can't promise that."

"OK. Would you please tell him to leave us alone? Will he do that?"

"I will see to it."

"Thank you."

"I'm glad your son is OK."

"Thank you."

Donna Middleton leaves.

— • —

My father lays out the situation for me, which I already know. I am to stay away from Donna Middleton and Kyle. I have scared them, and I am not to bother them ever again.

"Go home, Edward," my father says.

— • —

There is so much to do back at the house. None of my data has been recorded. I start with the time I woke up. The fact is, I just don't know. I was sitting in the 1997 Toyota Camry at 7:40, and so I estimate that my eyes opened at 7:39 and that I took a minute to dash out the door and get into the car. But I just don't know for sure. I write down 7:39—the twenty-fourth time out of 292 days this year (because it's a leap year), but the first time that I've put an asterisk next to the time. This signifies that the time is an estimate. I don't like estimates. I prefer facts.

I also grab the *Billings Herald-Gleaner* and record yesterday's high and low temperatures—fifty-four and twenty-eight. The forecast today is as I expected; it's warm, with a projected high of sixty-three. I will know for sure tomorrow.

And my data is complete.

— • —

In the shower, I think about what a mess today already is. I'm relieved that Kyle is OK. I am scared of these dreams that I'm having. I wonder where they are coming from and why they are coming. It will be a long wait until Tuesday, when I can talk to Dr. Buckley about them. She is a very logical person. I hope she can explain what's happening.

I think about how it's too late now for a bowl of corn flakes, which is going to throw off my system of food consumption completely. I think about my data. I think about how ugly the garage is and how I'm going to have to do something about that soon.

Mostly, I think about Donna Middleton and how scared she was this morning. I was scared, but my fear was nothing like hers. I think about how if it hadn't been for me, she would have been just fine, going about her work as an emergency department nurse at Billings Clinic. I think about my father and how disappointed he seemed. I think about how many times he has had to show up somewhere and get me out of some trouble. This is probably worse than the "Garth Brooks incident."

I slump down into the tub, pull my knees up to chin, and rest my head.

— • —

At Montana Personal Connect, I see it again:

Inbox (1).

I click the link.

Hi Edward!

Your SO funny. I liked your note very much. I would like to keep talking to you. You have a kind face too. I like youre eyes.

Let's do this OK? I will ask you five questions about yourself and then you write back with the answers and five questions about me.

Here are some questions.

1. Where were you born?

2. Do you have any nicknames?

3. What do you like to do on a date?

4. Do you have any brothers or sisters?

5. Would you help the roadrunner escape from the coyote or help the coyote catch the roadrunner?

Write back!

Joy

This is a confounding woman. She has gotten no better at grammar, and I may have to prepare myself for the possibility that she never will. But she also asks really good, although random, questions. I will have to think about this for a while.

— • —

After dinner—a Banquet roast-beef-and-potatoes frozen meal—I write back.

> *Joy:*
>
> *You ask really good questions.*
> *1. I was born here in Billings on January 9, 1969.*
> *2. My mother used to call me Teddy when I was a little boy, but I prefer Edward.*
> *3. I think I would like to see a movie on a date. I like movies. Also, if you eat dinner after the movie, you have something to talk about.*
> *4. I am my parents' only child.*
> *5. I'm not sure why this matters, but it seems to me that the roadrunner needs no help in escaping the coyote—that's the whole point of the cartoon, that the coyote never wins. I suppose I would help the coyote, although what I would really like to do is be the guy who invents things for Acme.*
> *Here are five questions for you:*
> *1. How many online dates have you been on?*
> *2. What is your favorite season?*
> *3. Do you watch* Dragnet? *If so, what is your favorite episode?*

4. *What music do you like?*

5. *Where do you go on vacation?*

Regards,
Edward

At 10:00 p.m. sharp, I sit down for my nightly *Dragnet* episode. Tonight, I am watching the twenty-fourth episode of the fourth and final season, "Robbery: The Harassing Wife." It originally aired on April 2, 1970, and it is one of my favorites.

In this one, an ex-convict named John Sawyer—played by Herbert Ellis, who appeared in three of the color episodes—is repeatedly accused by his bitter, estranged wife of committing robberies. Sergeant Joe Friday and Officer Bill Gannon, having to take seriously allegations against an ex-convict, repeatedly investigate John Sawyer and conclude that he did not commit the crimes he has been accused of doing.

Finally, John Sawyer does commit a robbery, thinking that Sergeant Joe Friday and Officer Bill Gannon won't believe that he did it, since his wife's stories are not panning out. This is a grave miscalculation on his part, because Sergeant Joe Friday always gets his man.

Once John Sawyer is in custody, his wife gets very angry with Sergeant Joe Friday and Officer Bill Gannon for throwing him in jail. She turned him in for all the crimes he didn't commit only because she wanted him to come back to her.

Some women have funny ways of saying what they want.

— • —

I shut off the TV and videocassette recorder, and then I go to the front window to close the curtain. Another day is almost over. It's one of the most exhausting I can remember, although I do not keep data on my level of exhaustion each day. In any case, I am happy that it is through.

Across the street, under the streetlight, I can see Donna Middleton standing behind her car. She is talking to a man. Her arms are moving rapidly. He is leaning in toward her. It looks like he is yelling.

I step over to the front door and crack it open. I can hear them.

"You're supposed to stay away from me, Mike."

Mike. Holy shit!

"I just want to talk," he yells at her.

"No!"

"Yes, goddamn it!"

This is bad. Up and down my block, lights are coming on.

"I never want to talk to you again."

"Why not?"

"You know why not."

"Because you're a fucking cunt, that's why."

This is really bad. I go over to the telephone and dial.

"Nine-one-one emergency."

"A man and a woman are arguing on my street. I think she has a restraining order against him."

"What's the address?"

"Six Twenty-Eight Clark Avenue."

"Do you know the woman's name?"

"Donna Middleton."

"Do you know the man's name?"

"Mike. That's all I know."

"Can you see what's happening now?"

I go back to the front window. "They're yelling."

"What's your name, sir?"

"Edward Stanton."

"And where do you live, sir?"

"Six Thirty-Nine Clark Avenue."

"Can you still see them, sir?"

"Yes."

"What are they doing?"

"Still yelling."

It happens so fast that I gasp in shock. Mike strikes Donna Middleton across the cheek with the back of his right hand. Her body jumps at the blow and lands against her car, and then she falls to the ground.

"He just hit her!"

"OK, sir. Stay calm. Officers are on the way."

Donna Middleton is on her hands and knees, and she's trying to scramble away. Mike grabs her and flings her backward to the concrete of the driveway, where she lands on her back, and then he pounces down upon her and wraps his hands around her neck.

"He's choking her."

"Sir, officers are almost there. Stay with me."

"I have to help her."

"Sir, stay right here on the phone."

As if out of nowhere, three police cars converge on Donna Middleton's house. The officers emerge from the cars, guns drawn. I can hear them yelling at Mike.

"Hands off her. Stand up. Hands behind your head."

After Mike lets go and climbs to his feet, two of the police officers take him hard to the ground and cuff him, while the other attends to Donna Middleton. An ambulance rolls up. My neighborhood is lit up with red-and-blue strobes. I can see my neighbors standing on their front porches, talking and gawking.

After Mike is wrestled into a police car and taken away, one of the officers who tackled him crosses the street and walks up to my house. I meet him at the door. I have seen this police officer before.

"Is she OK?" I ask.

"She's shaken. She'll have some bruises. But she'll be OK."

"She has a restraining order against that man, doesn't she?"

"Yes."

"Why was he here, then?"

"Well, it's a court order. It's not a jail cell. He'll be in one of those soon enough."

"It's terrible."

"Yes, it is. It could have been a lot worse, Mr. Stanton. Thanks for calling it in."

"You're not going to call my father, are you?"

The officer chuckles. "No. You did the right thing."

Mike:

You are scum. You are subhuman. You are a horrible, horrible man.

You have no right to go where you are not wanted, to defy a legal restraining order against you. You have no right to be at Donna Middleton's house. You have no right to yell at her, to hit her, to choke her.

I can only hope that the full weight of the law puts you somewhere you can't hurt her again.

Edward Stanton

I put the letter in a new green office folder, labeled "Mike," and file it away. I want to throw up.

— • —

As appointed, I go to bed at midnight. I can't fall asleep, and I think I have to prepare myself for an unusual waking time in the morning, if I go to sleep at all. My data will be complete, but it will be erratic.

At 1:47 a.m.—I know because I am not asleep and I check the clock—I hear a rap on the front door. I crawl out of bed and go to the door, where I look through the peephole.

It's Donna Middleton through the fish-eye lens. She has a purplish welt under her right eye. Her face is streaked and stained with makeup. She has been crying.

I open the door.

"Hello, Mr. Stanton."

"Hello, Ms. Middleton. Are you OK?"

"Physically, I'll be fine in a few days, they say. But I'm not OK."

"I understand."

She looks down. "I want to thank you for calling the cops."

"Yes."

"And I want to apologize to you for my reaction this morning—God, this morning. It seems like a long time ago." She is weeping.

"Yes."

"I'm having a hard time figuring you out, Mr. Stanton."

"Edward."

"Edward," she repeats.

"I know." I am not sure what to say to her.

"Are you a friend to us, Edward?"

"Yes."

"OK, then. Thank you again. I was…" She is crying again. "I was sure I was going to die."

"That was not going to happen."

She tries to smile but just cries some more. She rubs her face and sniffles. "OK, then. It's late. I probably woke you up. Good night, Edward."

"Good night."

I watch as she turns around and cuts diagonally across the street, from my front yard to hers. She walks up the steps of her porch, opens the front door, and disappears inside.

It's 2:00 a.m. I always go to sleep at midnight sharp, but today has been extraordinary, and here I am, awake. I've never seen my neighborhood at this time. It's quiet and beautiful. I can't hear anything except the beating of my heart.

SUNDAY, OCTOBER 19

I am not surprised to see the man in front of me. It is Mike. Though he is at least seven inches shorter than me, no more than five foot nine, he weighs at least as much as I do, and unlike me, Mike is all muscle. His angular face seethes. He is holding a baseball bat, and he waggles it menacingly. That bat, I am sure, is intended for me.

I am surprised that Mike is not in jail. The cops in this town are terrible.

I am not surprised that he is advancing on me.

I am surprised that I am not running—indeed, that I am standing still.

I am not surprised that Mike has pulled the bat back for a mighty swing and that it is aimed directly at my head...

— • —

I am surprised that I'm awake. I am even more surprised that it's 4:12 a.m.

It seems that there is little I can rely on anymore.

I try closing my eyes, now that I know I am safe.

But it is useless. I grab my pen and notebook and scribble down the time, and my data is complete.

— • —

As I pad through the living room toward the earliest bowl of corn flakes of my life, I stop at the front window and pull back the curtain. Life outside on Clark Avenue looks much as it did just a few hours ago. Only the streetlights pierce the dark. No one appears to be out and about, not at this hour. I tilt my head to the right and find Donna Middleton's house. I wonder if she's having trouble sleeping. I wonder if she is scared. I wouldn't say she was scared when I talked to her earlier—shaken, yes, but there was firmness in her voice and what I would call resolve in her eyes. There is no empirical way to prove these things, of course, but that was the sense I got. I prefer facts, but sometimes sense is all you have to go on.

I've occasionally heard people say something like "I know his heart," and I wonder how someone could possibly know such a thing. A heart is a mysterious thing to know. Doctors know how they work, of course, and can sometimes fix them when they're not working correctly. But the mechanics of the heart are not what people are talking about when they say such things. They are talking about a person's intentions or nature or good-ness—or perhaps, in the case of someone like Mike, the opposite of goodness.

I do not understand how one can know such things, the way people know that the Declaration of Independence was signed on July 4, 1776, or that the cheetah is the fastest land mammal. Those things can be measured and verified. Hearts cannot. Still, I cannot fight the notion that Donna has a strong heart, no matter how imprecise I know that feeling to be.

I feel bad for Donna Middleton. It must be difficult for her. Boys, even good boys like Kyle, must be difficult to raise. She is doing it alone, though she must be doing something right. I guess Kyle will be coming home today from his grandparents' house in Laurel. I hope he is a good boy to his mother for a while.

I don't think Donna Middleton wants to be alone like she is. How could she, having been with the Mikes and Troys and Donalds that she has been with? I think it must be very difficult and sad to want something and to not get it, no matter how hard you try. She lived with Mike, and he tried to choke her.

I feel bad for Donna Middleton. But I do not feel sorry for her. This is a fine distinction, I think, but it feels right to me. I do not think Donna Middleton would appreciate my feeling sorry for her. I don't know her heart, but I feel confident about that. That confidence will have to do until the facts come in.

— • —

At 4:38 a.m. on the 293rd day of the year (because it's a leap year), I'm munching on corn flakes and sitting in front of the computer, logging on to Montana Personal Connect.

Inbox (1).

I click the link.

Hi Edward!

Thanks SOOOOO much for answering my questions. Yours' are great. Here are my answers:

1. *I'm not sure of the number. A bunch. Online dating is hard. But what are you going to do. Its not like Im going to meet someone in Broadview. Ha ha.*
2. *I like summer. Go to the lake, ride in a boat, get a tan. LOL. Do you like the lake?*

3. What is Dragnet?
*4. Any kind pretty much. I like classic rock and coun-
try. I LOVE Garth Brooks.*
*5. I don't go on many vacations. The last one I took was
to Colorado for mountain biking. What about you?
Edward do you think maybe you would like to meet?
Let me know.
Bye!*

Joy

There is so much wrong with this note I almost do not know
where to begin. But then there is that question. Do I want to meet?
I am shocked to realize that, until this very moment, 4:44 a.m. on
October 19, the 293rd day of the year (because it's a leap year),
I never suspected that participating in an online dating website
might actually result in an online date.

Also, I have an idea.

— • —

I'm in the basement, and I'm taking inventory.

The front wheel and the pedals on my eighteen-speed bicycle
will work. It's not like the bike is getting much use from me. My
parents gave it to me for Christmas in 2002. I took it out once and
nearly got run over by a car on Lewis Avenue. It has been down
in the basement since.

I know the big back wheels on my mulching mower, which
is out in the garage, will work. Taking them will render the
mower useless, but I won't need to worry about that until next
spring.

I'm going to need some lumber and some hardware—bolts and nuts and such—and some paint and some lacquer and some other things, too. I need to write my inventory down and take some measurements. Home Depot will be open in two hours and forty-three minutes.

— • —

My idea—for now, I am going to call it "The Big Project"—is one of the best that I have had in a while. I used to have a lot of big ideas, and I have never made any secret of the fact that I enjoy new projects, but many of them never came to fruition. (I love the word "fruition.") It's not that I couldn't do them; it's that they often collided with my other, more established projects, like watching *Dragnet* every night.

I am confident, however, that The Big Project can get finished. It will require close attention not only to the fundamentals of the project itself but also to the clock.

My idea has come on the day that the Dallas Cowboys play football.

— • —

Today's trip to the Home Depot store in the West End of Billings goes so much better than the one Tuesday I can hardly believe it. But it's a fact, and I trust facts.

This has happened for a couple of reasons. First, I know exactly what I need and exactly where to get it, so there is no need to seek out potentially unhelpful store employees. Second, there are no choices involved—even with the spray paint. I can see in my mind exactly what color The Big Project will be, and so I simply grab the appropriate cans and put them in the cart.

As I wheel the heavily laden cart to the front of the store, I see that Home Depot even has self-checkout stands. If I kept data on such things, this might be the best day ever. Until today, however, it never occurred to me that the days were worth rating.

— • —

The total bill at Home Depot comes to $221.95. This sounds like the sort of cost you might hear on a late-night TV commercial, but in Montana, it's common. Montana has no sales tax, which is something that most of its residents seem to appreciate. My father, as a Yellowstone County commissioner, is not so ebullient about it. (I love the word "ebullient.") My father often bemoans the fact that the county doesn't extract more money out of tourists by imposing a sales tax on them. He even led an unsuccessful charge against the state legislature to get it to empower individual counties to impose sales taxes as they please. An editorial in the *Billings Herald-Gleaner* criticized my father over this and said, "In his zeal to tax visitors to Montana, Commissioner Ted Stanton apparently fails to realize that he would also be soaking the many thousands of people who live here and pay his salary." My father did not talk to anybody from the *Billings Herald-Gleaner* for several months after that.

Here's something else that my father will not be happy about: a bill for $221.95. He will get it next month. I will surely hear about it thereafter—perhaps even from his lawyer.

— • —

I arrive home at 9:23 a.m. The Dallas Cowboys will play in an hour and thirty-seven minutes against the St. Louis Rams. I am nervous about this game. The Cowboys' best player, quarterback Tony Romo, is not going to play because he has a broken finger. The Cowboys ought to be able to win without Tony Romo because the St. Louis Rams are terrible, but I am still nervous.

You are probably wondering why I am a Dallas Cowboys fan. I will tell you. First, the Dallas Cowboys are "America's Team." People call them this all the time. I don't think America took a vote on it—and there are probably a lot of people in America who don't even like professional football, although I can't know for sure without taking a scientific poll, and I already have The Big Project.

Also, my father grew up in Dallas, and his parents—my Grandpa Sid and Grandma Mabel, who are both dead now—were very good friends with Tom Landry, who used to be the Dallas Cowboys' coach. Tom Landry is dead, too. The only time I saw my father cry was the day Tom Landry died. He didn't cry when Grandma Mabel and Grandpa Sid died, at least not that I saw.

Tom Landry must have been a very good man.

In 1978, when I was nine years old, my father took me with him to Dallas on a business trip. I mostly stayed with Grandpa Sid and Grandma Mabel while Father did his business. He worked for an oil exploration company then, and he was in charge of its Montana and North Dakota operations, which is why we lived in Billings. He didn't become a politician until a few years later, after the oil business "went in the crapper," as my father likes to say. By then, he had made a lot of money and didn't need to be in the oil business anymore. He was a Billings city councilman for a while and then mayor of Billings and then Yellowstone County commissioner.

But back in 1978, when he took me to Dallas with him, he was still in the oil business. One day, when he didn't have meetings, we went to Irving, where the Dallas Cowboys work out. I got to meet Tom Landry and Dan Reeves, who was an assistant coach with the Cowboys at the time and later went on to be a head coach in places like Denver and New York and Atlanta. I also got to meet Roger Staubach, who was the Cowboys' quarterback and my favorite player. I also met lots of other players, and they all signed my autograph book. I still have it.

It was a great day. I felt very close to my father then.

— • —

Before the Cowboys start playing, I haul the stuff from Home Depot downstairs to the basement and organize it in the order that I will need it later. I can't start The Big Project just yet. There's not enough time before the game, and I have to prepare. For one thing, I have to grab the newspaper off the stoop and record my weather data so it is complete.

— • —

At 2:16 p.m., I am sitting on my couch, facing the TV, agape. (I would say I like the word "agape," but I don't like anything right now.) My authentic white Tony Romo jersey—I also have a blue one for when the Cowboys wear those—has been stripped from my torso and is in a wadded ball in the middle of the living room.

It was horrible.

First, not having Tony Romo is going to be tougher than I thought. His replacement, Brad Johnson, did not do well today. He threw three interceptions. Tony Romo also throws many interceptions, but he throws a lot of touchdown passes, too. Brad Johnson threw for one touchdown. That is not enough.

Second, the Cowboys' defense was terrible, and Tony Romo doesn't play defense, so I don't see how anyone can use his absence as an excuse.

The St. Louis Rams' running back, Steven Jackson, ran for 160 yards and three touchdowns against the Cowboys. That was not Tony Romo's fault.

Third, I think the Cowboys are not as good as they think they are. They have lost three of their past four games and now have a record of 4–3. Even when Tony Romo was not hurt, they were not playing so well.

Fourth, the Cowboys lost 34–14.

If I kept data on the quality of a day, and I'm thankful now that I do not, this would no longer be the best day ever.

— • —

Ordinarily, I do not write my letters of complaint until just before I go to bed, but I think that I need to do it earlier today so I can clear my mind and concentrate on The Big Project.

I have a thick green office folder of letters to Dallas Cowboys owner Jerry Jones.

Mr. Jones:

I am sure you know why I am writing to you today. Your Dallas Cowboys played pitifully against the St. Louis Rams, and I have begun to fear that they will not make the playoffs. After all, Tony Romo will miss at least two more weeks.

I cannot hold Tony Romo's injury against you. Injuries are part of the game, and no one can predict when they might occur. This would be difficult for me to accept if I were in your position, as I prefer facts and things that I can rely on. However, you do not seem to be bothered by the capriciousness of injuries.

I can hold against you, however, the fact that, as a backup quarterback, Brad Johnson appears to be far short of acceptable. This is something you should have known and accounted for in building a roster, as it is at least a reasonable possibility that the backup quarterback will have to play occasionally. With Tony Romo injured, it's not possibility—it's reality.

Finally, I must lay some of the blame at the feet of your defense. I have seen grandmothers who hit harder than some of your players. (This is not actually true. I have never seen a grandmother hit, and I could not, without some physical experimentation, say for certain that any grandmother could hit harder than your players could. This is a literary device called hyperbole.)

I thank you in advance for your kind attention to these pressing matters.

Regards,
Edward Stanton

After filing away the letter to Jerry Jones—the thirty-eighth one I have written to him—I remember that I have more writing yet to do. I am corresponding with more people than I ever have before, and it exhausts me.

I log on to Montana Personal Connect and write a note to Joy.

Joy:

Yes, I agree that we should talk about meeting. You should know, however, that I do not like Garth Brooks. I hope this doesn't make you reconsider meeting me.

Regards,
Edward

I think it is better that I wait a while before telling Joy about the forty-nine letters of complaint that I sent to Garth Brooks.

— • —

My mind cleared of the unpleasantness of the Dallas Cowboys and the anxiety of having to respond to Joy, I am free to turn my full attention to The Big Project. I work away at drilling and sawing and connecting and screwdrivering (which isn't really a word), and I think only a little about how the anxiety of responding to Joy is gone but that the anxiety of actually perhaps meeting her is very much here.

The work goes quickly; I did well for myself by sketching out some plans beforehand. It helps that I am very good with tools. I do not say that to be boastful. It is a fact, and I prefer facts. When I was at Billings West High School twenty-one years ago, the only class I liked was wood shop. There was no high school social strata there. The only question anyone had was whether you could do the work, and I could. Mr. Withers even made me the shop assistant my senior year. He told my parents when I graduated that I was the best student he had ever had. My father was so proud he was beaming. I still get notes from Mr. Withers on occasion. I think he might be the only person who ever noticed that I was at Billings West High School at all, although I would have to take a poll of everyone who was there at the time to know for sure, and I just don't have time for that right now.

I might have liked to have been a shop teacher, but I do not think I could have put up with the rowdy kids and the parents and the paperwork and the demands of the principals. I am sure I could not. I don't think there is enough fluoxetine in the world or enough wisdom in Dr. Buckley to get me through that.

The tool work done, I roll The Big Project up the stairs, out the back door, and into the garage. It's time to paint—The Big Project, not the garage. The garage will come tomorrow.

— • —

Tonight's episode of *Dragnet*, the twenty-fifth and penultimate (I love the word "penultimate") of the fourth and final season, is called "Burglary: Baseball," and it is one of my favorites.

G. D. Spradlin, an actor who appeared in three episodes of *Dragnet*, plays a man named Arthur Leo Tyson, and he cracks safes for sport. He's an ex-convict who is on parole, and it turns out that he misses being in prison. This is a condition called "institutionalization," and it sounds awful to me. And yet, Arthur Leo Tyson has much to look forward to when he gets back in "the pen." The inmate baseball team at San Quentin expects to have a good season, and he wants to be a part of it. This amuses Sergeant Joe Friday and Officer Bill Gannon, who take a liking to Arthur Leo Tyson even though he is an unrepentant criminal. It's nice to think that police officers can be a little human.

G. D. Spradlin is one of the more recognizable actors on *Dragnet*, and he went on to be a character actor in many shows and movies over the years. He has a very distinctive face: It's kind of round, and he has crinkled eyes and a perpetually pursed mouth—the kind of mouth that "looks like a chicken's asshole," as my Grandpa Sid used to say. He has a raspy Southern accent, the kind that Grandpa Sid had, too. If you ever saw the movie *One on One*, starring Robby Benson as a basketball star, then you know who G. D. Spradlin is. He played the coach, and his mouth looked like a chicken's asshole for most of that film.

I would have liked to write to G. D. Spradlin about his experiences on *Dragnet*, but he was well known enough that I never found out his address. I looked him up on the Internet a couple of years ago, and he seemed to still be alive, although he hasn't worked in a long time. He would be old now—eighty-eight, according to the Internet.

That's how old Grandpa Sid would be, too, if he were still alive.

Time flummoxes me.

MONDAY, OCTOBER 20

I'm awake at 7:38 a.m., the 223rd time out of 294 days this year (because it's a leap year). While I seem to be tacking back to normal, if in fact normal can be defined, I don't feel normal at all. I don't want to leave my bed. Michael Stipe's headache gray is settling over me, the residue of my late-to-bed-early-to-rise act yesterday.

I drift away.

— • —

I'm not a part of the scene I'm witnessing. Joy, my online paramour (I love the word "paramour") from Broadview, is standing in a parking lot that is filled not with cars and pickups and SUVs but with a throng of people who stand around her.

Joy is holding a huge controller in her hands, something that looks like a TV remote, only much larger. It has buttons and a joystick. She holds it over her head, and the crowd behind her cheers. The gathered people then start chanting: "Show it! Show it! Show it! Show it!"

Joy turns away from the crowd, lowers the giant remote control, and starts punching buttons. Above her and the crowd, pressed flat against the side of a building, a giant plasma TV screen flickers awake. And there I am, ten times as big as life, sitting at my computer desk. I am naked. Worse than that, if anything could be worse than that, I am cooing as I type on my computer: "Oh, Joy. You are my little chickadee. You are my sweetie."

In unison, the crowd belts out a thunderous laugh, and Joy turns around, a smile drawn across her face, her dimples carving holes in her cheeks, her eyes alight.

The crowd turns around, too, and they're all pointing and laughing.

I look down and I am no longer on the plasma screen but in the parking lot, naked.

I look up in horror, and Donna Middleton is in the middle of the front row of hecklers, laughing at me.

— • —

I'm awake again at 10:26. My data is all fouled up, of course. I'm entering uncharted territory here, and so I improvise. I reach over, grab my notebook and a pen, and record two times:

First awakening: 7:38.

Second awakening: 10:26.

I don't feel rested or happy.

— • —

After recording my weather data—a high of fifty-five yesterday, a low of thirty-four, a forecasted high of fifty-seven today (I'll know for sure tomorrow)—and consuming a bowl of corn flakes and eighty milligrams of fluoxetine, I am ready for the day.

I must give the ten-day forecast its proper due: It has been on the money, allowing me to take another run at painting the garage, which is long overdue. That horrid mocha chino has been on it for three days now, and I will not countenance (I love the word "countenance") another day of the garage's being a neighborhood eyesore. If I hustle, I can overcome the time I have lost to extra sleep and bad dreams.

To do so, I resolve to not check Montana Personal Connect until this evening, after I'm done. I'm anxious about Joy's reply—and, I have to admit, freaked out (I love the phrase "freaked out") now that she has invaded my dreams, although I know logically that there are no giant TV remotes, no plasma screens on buildings in Billings, and that I never, under any circumstances, type on my computer when I am naked. There is some explanation for these dreams, and I will look to Dr. Buckley to provide it.

I have read that everyone dreams, and that even animals dream. There is a whole field of study, called oneirology, that is dedicated to examining dreams. The statistical probability that, before the past few days, I did not dream is beyond remote. But I do not remember dreams before the past few days; the ones lately I cannot seem to forget.

One of my favorite R.E.M. songs is called "I Don't Sleep, I Dream." It contains words about dreams that an oneirologist would probably find fascinating. I'm not sure what it's all about. Michael Stipe uses words in fascinating and strange combinations. I don't know, for instance, why he says "hip hip hooray" in that song or what a cup of coffee has to do with anything. I think not knowing is probably part of the point for someone like Michael Stipe. I do know that Michael Stipe sang a lot more about sex on that album *Monster* than he did before or since. It wasn't until today, the 294th day of 2008 (because it's a leap year), four-teen years after that album came out, that I realized the title of this song could now be about me.

— • —

By 2:00 p.m., I have made good progress on the garage. The bronze green is covering up the mocha chino, and I like this color a lot better. It's the best of the three. I think I will be able to stick with this, at least until the year after next, when it will be time to paint the garage again.

I take a break from painting before I get to the garage door. I open the garage and look at The Big Project, gleaming in freshly painted glory. I dab at the body of it with my left forefinger, testing the paint and lacquer. It seems to be dry. I think it's ready.

I roll it into the front yard.

— • —

Kyle is a predictable boy, at least in terms of coming and going. I'm working the same corner of the garage eave, at the same time, when I hear his voice. This reliability is comforting to me.

"Whoa! What's that?"

I climb down off the ladder, grinning. "You don't know?"

"No. It looks awesome! What is it?"

"It's for you."

"Really? But what is it?"

I start telling Kyle a story. When I was a little younger than him, for Christmas 1977, my parents got me something called a "Green Machine." They tried to tell me that it had come from Santa Claus, but the idea of Santa Claus never seemed logical to me, and by then I knew the truth. By then, I was tolerating their pretending that a fat man in a red suit could live in a place as inhospitable as the North Pole and deliver toys to kids all over the world in one night. The whole notion is preposterous.

I leave out the fallacy of Santa Claus in telling my story to Kyle, though. It's not my place to tell him such a thing. He's a smart boy. He probably already knows that it's not true.

I tell him about the Green Machine. I say it was the greatest Christmas gift I ever received.

It was like a Big Wheel in that it had a big wheel up front, but it was unlike a Big Wheel in every other way. You didn't steer the big wheel. You had two levers that controlled the rear axle, which would swivel the smaller back wheels. You would sit recumbent style, pedaling the big front wheel, swiveling the back wheels and tearing around all over the place.

"This," I tell Kyle, "is your own Green Machine. Except that it's not green, it's blue. And it's built out of way better stuff than the Green Machine. The sad truth of the Green Machine is that eventually the plastic would wear out and holes would develop in the wheels.

"This one has an adjustable seat, so you can ride it even as you get bigger. It has shocks, so it doesn't hurt when you hit holes on the street—"

"It's even got a cup holder!" Kyle says.

"That's for your Diet Dr Pepper. Do you want to try it out?"

"Heck yeah!" He's jumping up and down.

I show him how the levers work—how if he pulls the left one back and pushes the right one forward, the axle will swivel in a way that causes his vehicle to turn left. If he reverses that and pulls the right lever back and pushes the left forward, the machine will make a right turn.

"If you lean into the turn a little bit, it will help, but you're not going to flip it. It's very well balanced. Just ride carefully and watch out for cars, OK?"

"OK."

And then Kyle hesitates. "Do you need me to help paint the garage first?"

"No. I have it. You just give me a little shout when you pass by, OK?"

"You got it."

"Hey, Kyle?"

"Yeah?"

"What are you going to call it?"

Kyle crinkles his nose as he thinks for a second, then he lights up again. "The Blue Blaster!"

And he's off.

For the next hour and a half, as I'm putting the finishing touches on the garage, Kyle is riding laps around the block, sticking to the sidewalk. Every few minutes, I hear "Hi, Edward" as he goes shooting by, a happy boy on his Blue Blaster.

— • —

At 4:36, Donna crosses the street and intercepts Kyle as he's making his thirty-seventh pass around the block. (I have been counting.)

"Whoa, mister. What's this thing you have here?"

"It's the Blue Blaster, Mom."

Donna looks up from the three-wheeled vehicle at me. "Is this yours, Edward? It's really cool."

"No, it's mine," Kyle says. "Edward made it for me."

"Really?" Donna does not look as happy as Kyle.

"Look at this," Kyle says, and he goes through the explanation of how the levers work and how the seat is adjustable and the cup holder and the rest. As he chatters away, Donna keeps glancing up at me on the ladder.

"OK, Kyle, it's really cool. Take it home now."

Kyle starts to complain, but Donna cuts him off with a stare.

"See you later, Edward. Thanks again," he says, and then he plops back into the Blue Blaster's seat and pilots it to his house.

"I need to talk to you, Edward," Donna says.

"OK." I dread what's coming.

"What you did for Kyle is a very nice thing."

I nod.

"And it's too much. How much did you spend on all of that?"

"It wasn't so much." This is a lie, and I think she knows it.

"I would like to pay you for it."

"I don't want you to."

"I would feel better about this if I did."

"I would feel worse. I did it because I wanted to do it."

"Kyle does not need to see you as the guy across the street who gives him things."

"I don't give him things. I gave him this thing."

"I would feel better if I paid you."

"Maybe you can just do something nice for me sometime."

She bristles. "What do you mean by that?"

"I don't mean anything."

"You're not going to use Kyle to get at me." She seems really mad now.

"Get at you?"

"You heard me."

"I don't know what you're talking about. You're flummoxing me."

"I'm just saying."

"It's not even a gift. Your son has helped me paint the garage twice. He told me he wants a bicycle. I made him something better than a bicycle. That's it. I don't want to get at you, whatever that means." I'm shaking.

A bit of softness returns to Donna's face, and I find myself noticing that the eye that seemed so puffy and purple early Sunday morning looks a little better today. Not so puffy anyway.

"I'm sorry. I'm on edge. I'm just trying to figure things out."

Now I'm the one who is bristling. "You asked me if I was a friend to you."

"I did."

"I said I was."

"You did."

"OK, then. I have to go now."

As I walk away from Donna Middleton, I hear her start to say something else, but then she cuts it off, deciding not to. I don't turn around. I open the door, go into the house, and slam the door behind me.

— • —

Dinner—spaghetti—tastes artificial. I'm sure of it now: I'm in a rut.

I fling my half-finished plate into the sink, where it shatters.

— • —

At Montana Personal Connect, I'm greeted with this:

Inbox (0).

The world is stupid.

— • —

Tonight's episode of *Dragnet* is the final one of the color series, which ran from 1967 to 1970. It originally aired on April 16, 1970, and it's called "DHQ: The Victims." It's one of my favorites.

I have always thought it fitting that the series finished on this note, as "DHQ: The Victims" runs the gamut of duties for Sergeant Joe Friday and Officer Bill Gannon. They investigate all sorts of crimes, including two homicides, an armed robbery, and a purse snatching. Days like that must be very difficult when you're a police officer, not only because people are dead or hurting, but also because there is all sorts of paperwork to do. Sergeant Joe Friday always seems to get his man, but some days, he must feel like the criminals are winning.

So far this year, I have been through all ninety-eight color episodes of *Dragnet* three times. Tomorrow, I will start again at the beginning.

I never grow tired of Sergeant Joe Friday and Officer Bill Gannon and the rest of the *Dragnet* ensemble. I can rely on them in a way that I cannot rely on anyone or anything else.

Donna:

> *I hesitated to refer to you familiarly with your first name, as after today's interaction, I have no idea if we know each other or not. I ultimately decided to use it in the hope that we will eventually be able to refer to each other in a familiar way, as the friends you seem to want us to be.*
>
> *Before that, however, I must address the unfortunate events that occurred just hours ago.*

I do not understand you. I do not understand why you get mad at me when I do something nice for your son. I did not hit you in his presence, as Mike did. I did not yell at him. I did not yell at you.

I made him a super-duper pedaling machine. That is all I did. I don't know why I have to feel bad about this.

I hope you will adjust your attitude toward me. I hope you do it soon.

I am, hopefully, your friend,
Edward

TUESDAY, OCTOBER 21

Let me make quick work of the perfunctory (I love the word "perfunctory") items, as there is so little to cover and so much time.

Wait. Strike that. Reverse it.

OK, then.

Woke up: 7:38 a.m. That makes 224 days out of 295 this year (because it's a leap year).

Yesterday's high temperature: sixty-one.

Yesterday's low temperature: thirty-seven.

Today's forecasted high: fifty-one. We shall see. Forecasts are notoriously off base.

Today's forecasted low: thirty-three. Again, we shall see.

Dreams: Not one that I can remember, for the first time in days.

My data: complete.

And, yes, I made a *Willy Wonka & the Chocolate Factory* reference. I am pretty funny sometimes, as I keep telling you.

— • —

I arrive at Dr. Buckley's office nineteen minutes and twenty-two seconds early. I am filled with anticipation to see her, which is an odd sensation for me. It's not that I don't like coming to see Dr. Buckley; on the contrary, I sometimes feel as though without her I would not push through. But it has been a long time since I had this many things I wished to discuss with her. Perhaps I never have. I don't keep track of that.

— • —

I scan the end tables filled with magazines, which are predictably scattered every which way by patients who are not courteous enough to put things back the way they found them. I would be lying if I said I didn't care—and I don't lie, except for that one time to Donna Middleton about the cost of the Blue Blaster—but I also find myself unwilling to sort through them. If I had concentration today, it would be focused squarely on my impending discussion with Dr. Buckley, but focus is beyond my reach. I sit and I stare straight ahead and I wait.

After a few moments, I look down to see where the *thump-thump-thump* sound is coming from, and it is coming from me, as my heel fires up and down like a piston, making a metronome sound on Dr. Buckley's carpeted floor.

— • —

At 9:57, Dr. Buckley guides a client out through the waiting room—she (the client) looks to be a fifty-something woman, lumpy and matronly, and she has been crying. My eyes dart away, out of an unwillingness to make eye contact with a stranger and out of deference to her pain. Soon, she is gone.

I look up and Dr. Buckley is giving me a "let's go" look.

I look at my watch.

9:57:08…9:57:09…9:57:10…

I stand up. I may need the extra two-plus minutes.

— • —

"How was your week, Edward?" Dr. Buckley asks.

"You won't believe it."

I've started where I never start, and Dr. Buckley sits up, attentive. "Try me."

"I have been having dreams that I remember vividly, and that never happens."

"Go on."

"I have started online dating."

"You have?"

"Yes, through Montana Personal Connect. I may be having a date soon."

"Well, that is something new."

"Yes. And I've become friends with a nine-year-old boy and his mother. At least, I think we're friends. I'm sure the boy and I are friends. With the mother, it's harder to say."

"Anything else?"

"I had another fight with my father."

"Well, Edward, that's not anything new, is it?"

"No, I guess it isn't."

"OK," she says. "Let's take these things one at a time. Let's start with the boy and his mother."

— • —

I tell Dr. Buckley everything: how Kyle came over and helped me paint the garage twice, the dream about losing my grip on him, the misunderstanding at the Billings Clinic emergency room, Mike's assault of Donna later that night, the chat on the doorstep early in the morning, the Blue Blaster, and Donna's tepid (I love the word "tepid") response to it.

She asks me to tell her more about the dreams, so I give her the rundown on the rest of them: the one with the naked woman I don't know, the one with Joy and the giant plasma screen, the one where Mike is coming after me with a baseball bat. I tell Dr. Buckley that I'm embarrassed to talk about the dreams where I am naked, but she says that it is all right, that I should go ahead and tell her.

"Edward, there is much we still don't know about dreams and the biological purpose they fill, but I think we can make some reasonable assumptions about yours."

"I don't like assumptions. I prefer facts."

"I know you do, but let's just go with this, OK?"

"Yes."

"You've had a big week. People have become part of your life and your consciousness in a way that they never really have before. Would you agree with that?"

"Yes."

"I think your dreams are probably rooted in that. You have made room for these people in your life, even in small ways. You take the time to correspond with the woman in Broadview, Joy. You have let Kyle help you paint, and you even made him a cool bicycle."

"Tricycle. Three wheels."

"OK, tricycle. The point is, they are in your sphere now. And that greatly increases the likelihood that they will also occupy places in your subconscious. Do you understand what I'm saying?"

"Yes."

"The dreams where you're naked, those are probably about vulnerability—about some latent fear of being laid bare in front of people. Does that make sense?"

"Yes."

"And the one with the man who attacked your neighbor..."

"That one I understand. He's in jail because of me. It's a revenge dream."

"Yes, I think so, although I would say that he's in jail because of him. Very good analysis. Now, I'd like to talk about Kyle."

"OK."

"Edward, what do you think you have in common with a nine-year-old boy?"

"I don't know."

"I really want you to think about this."

"OK." I draw a deep breath. "I like that he doesn't make things harder. He makes them more fun. Even when he wasn't painting the garage all that well, he was having fun. That made me have fun. And on the Blue Blaster—you should have seen it. He was riding all over the place and laughing and yelling. I can't remember the last time I saw anyone have that much fun."

"That's a good answer. Now, why do you suppose you've had more difficulty with Kyle's mom?"

"I don't know."

"Consider this: She is not nine years old. She is a grown-up woman who is raising a little boy on her own, and from what you've told me, she has had a very rough go of it. Is that fair to say?"

"Yes."

"You may enjoy the wonder of a child, Edward, but to this woman, you're not a child. You're a grown man. And this woman has had a lot of trouble with grown men."

"Yes."

"Do you understand why she would be leery of you? When you came to where she worked and were frantic about that boy, you probably represented a lot of bad memories and fears for her. I know you didn't know that, but do you see it now?"

"Yes."

"She felt closer to you after you called the police and saved her, but for someone who has been treated that way by men, Edward, trust can be difficult."

"Yes."

"Tread carefully, Edward. Do you understand what I'm saying?"

I understand. I understand Dr. Buckley more than I ever thought possible.

— • —

On the subject of Joy and Internet dating, Dr. Buckley's tone is less serious.

"What brought this on? I'm intrigued."

"Have you seen those eHarmony television ads? Everybody seems so ridiculously happy and in love."

"Yes, well, the television ads are trying to sell a product. They're not going to show desperately unhappy or lonely people."

"Do you think that's who does online dating?"

"I think there is a whole range of people out there, Edward. You just have to deal with them as they come. What do you think of Joy?"

"She's very pretty."

"Anything else?"

"Her grammar is atrocious."

"I think a high grammar standard may be a losing fight on the Internet."

"I think you're right."

"So what are you going to do?"

"I don't know. She thought it would be a good idea to meet, and I said I would like that. I haven't heard back from her yet. What do you think I ought to do?"

"Well, I'm on record as in favor of your getting out and being among people. You know that. I would simply say to protect yourself."

"What do you mean? Condoms?"

Dr. Buckley snorts out a laugh. "I'm sorry…That was funny. Yes, certainly, if it comes to that, but I hope that's not on the agenda for your first date."

"No."

"What I mean, Edward, is that you know what situations are dangerous for you, and you know when people are pushing your buttons. If you sense that danger, leave. There are plenty of fish in the Internet."

— • —

My usual Tuesday series of right turns delivers me into the Albertsons parking lot. On a Tuesday morning, when most of the rest of Billings is at work, my shopping goes easily: ground beef, spaghetti, spaghetti sauce, Banquet meals, DiGiorno pizza (supreme this week), twelve-pack of Diet Dr Pepper, corn flakes, milk, and ice cream.

The self-checkout stand is a breeze, and soon I'm back in the 1997 Toyota Camry, right-turning my way home.

At Grand Avenue and Eighth Street W., two blocks from where I'll turn off Grand for the final run home, Billings drops away into a bowl that leads downtown. This is my favorite view of the city, better even than the one from atop the Rimrocks. I can see the First Interstate Bank building cast against a backdrop of the canyon, called Sacrifice Cliff, which borders the Yellowstone River.

It's really pretty.

— • —

Back at home, I square away the groceries, and then I opt for an early lunch of Banquet Swedish meatballs. I don't want to eat too much, as I will be dining at my parents' house tonight, which I do monthly. I also don't want to eat too little, as I may be making an early exit. I can never tell at my parents' house.

It is often a torturous evening. My mother treats me like a child, and my father treats me like just another constituent, except when he's treating me like a failure and a disappointment. Given the events of the past week, it's not hard for me to imagine which version of him I will get tonight. Still, I won't know until I'm there. I remember what Dr. Buckley has said, again and again and again, when it comes to my father: Do what I can to control my own behavior and hope for the best from his. Dr. Buckley is a very logical woman.

— • —

At Montana Personal Connect, I see what has become a familiar sight:

Inbox (1).
I click the link.

Dear Edward,

Your SOOOO funny again. I think I can forgive you for not liking Garth Brooks.

Would you like to do something Friday night? Maybe we could meet in downtown Billings at that new wine bar on Broadway. Ive heard good things about it.

8 all right? I know I must seem pushy but I guess since its my idea, Id just throw it out there.

Let me know…

Joy

I write back:

Joy:

I would very much enjoy meeting you at the new wine bar Friday night. Can we please make it seven? That will give me time to get back home for Dragnet.

With regards,
Edward

— • —

My parents' house sits atop the Billings Rimrocks, giving them a view of the bustling city of 100,000 below. It is a huge home for just two people: 6,200 square feet, with stone floors, a kitchen with side-by-side Sub-Zero freezers, an indoor lap pool and sauna, and gardens for my mother to spend her days tending. On the south side of the house, the side that faces town, there are huge windows. I have heard my father, when leading visitors through the house, say that the windows allow him to always see "the city I love." At this altitude, I think it's more likely that the windows allow him to see his minions without their seeing him. This is a mean thing to think, and it's not so much conjecture as an informed opinion, but perhaps it would be better for me to wait for the facts.

I always feel foreboding when I drive to my parents' house, and it's not just because of my parents. When I make the drive up the Rimrocks along Twenty-Seventh Street, then turn west at the airport and ride two more miles to their turnoff, I have to make many left turns to get there, and those left turns—I prefer right turns—lead me out of my world and into theirs. Theirs is not the house I grew up in. When I was a young man, which I will concede was a long time ago, we lived in a nice three-bedroom house in West Billings. During the latter part of the 1990s, when I was still living there with my parents, my father made some fortuitous (I love the word "fortuitous") investments in technology, and then he got out of them before taking on the losses that other tech investors saw in early 2001.

Once I was out of the house and put into the place on Clark Avenue—because of the "Garth Brooks incident"—my father and mother sold that house and moved up here. It is their place. It is not mine.

At the wrought-iron gate, I press the call button. After a few moments, I hear my mother's voice.

"Yes?"

"It's Edward."

"Come on in, dear."

The gate opens. I feel like I want to throw up.

— • —

"So there's the hospital hero," my father bellows as I step into the foyer, with the last of the late-afternoon light hitting me from the skylight above.

"Hello, Father."

He sidles up to me but offers neither a handshake nor a hug. He is dressed in a pink-and-white golf shirt, impeccably pressed slacks, and penny loafers—no socks. My father has been rocking this look for thirty years. (I love the phrase "rocking this applicable noun.") From the smell wafting toward me, I am guessing that he's on his second scotch and soda. Maybe his third. I don't like to guess. I prefer…Well, never mind. It doesn't matter.

"How have you been, Edward?"

"Fine."

"Fine, eh?"

"Yes."

"You didn't seem too fine when I saw you last."

"It's OK now."

"I heard what happened."

"What?"

"You called the cops and got that boyfriend of hers busted."

"Did the police call you?"

"No, Edward. But I'm a goddamned county commissioner. I know things."

"Yes."

"Scumbag."

"What?"

"That guy. He's a scumbag."

"Yes, he is."

"Well, you did good on that. I have to give it to you, Edward."

"Thank you, Father."

"Come on in, then."

— • —

My mother is in the kitchen, scurrying from island to stove to refrigerator and back to island as she prepares dinner.

"There's my boy," she says as I come into her view, and she dashes over to squeeze my cheeks and coo at me. I hate this part.

"We're having your favorite: pork loin, grilled asparagus, rosemary potatoes."

"My favorite is spaghetti."

"But you like this, too."

"I guess."

"That's good." She's now away from me and back to her cooking. My mother is the sort of woman who is dressed to the nines at all times, even when cooking dinner. She has been this way for as long as I've known her, which is all of my life. When I was a child, I was not permitted to see her until she had showered and put on her makeup and fixed her hair. She was a lovely woman then—tall and lithe, dirty-blonde hair, everything in its place. You can still see that beauty in her, though at sixty-three she is fighting a losing battle against the hair, which is rapidly graying, and the waistline, which is expanding. Her clothes and nails and shoes, as ever, are flawless.

My father is in the dining room, staring out a window into the approaching dark.

"Cocksuckers," he says to no one.

"Ted," my mother scolds him.

"Ah, shit, Maureen, I'm sorry."

When my father drinks, as he is doing now, his incidence of curse words—the "shits" and "fucks" and, yes, even the "cocksuckers"—increases exponentially. It can be amusing to watch, if you're not the target of them.

"It's just this goddamned economic development thing. Those assholes are killing me on this."

I have been reading about this in the *Billings Herald-Gleaner*. The county's economic development council, on which my father and the two other county commissioners sit, has been trying to hire a new director. My father put forward the name of a friend of his, someone who worked with him in the oil business years ago. The man came up to Billings for an interview and did quite well— so well that he appeared to be a lock for the job. While in town, though, he was cited for drunk driving, and now the council is cutting him loose as a candidate. My father is his lone backer, and he and the other commissioners have been sniping at one another through the newspaper and television news programs.

I do not know who is right, as it doesn't really concern me, but I will note that my father often ends up on the other side of the fence from his fellow commissioners. Make of that what you will.

"Those assholes are so fucking high and mighty," my father says. "Dave blew a zero-point-eight—a zero-point-eight. One glass of wine before leaving the restaurant, and they're saying he's a drunk. Had those fucking cops stopped him two blocks later, he would have been fine. Now these guys are busting my balls over the whole thing."

"Well, Ted, why don't we just forget about it and have dinner?"

"Assholes."

"Ted!"

"Yeah, yeah, OK. Well, come on, Edward, let's eat."

— • —

My father is holding a forkful of pork loin, and he's jabbing it in the air toward me.

"Edward, what are your plans?"

"Plans?"

"Yes, plans. You know, those things that give some guidance to life. You do know what plans are, right?"

"Dear, please," my mother says. Her dinner is dissolving into a family quarrel. Again.

"Yes, Father, I know what plans are."

"Do you have any?"

"I'm not sure what you mean."

"Plans, Edward. Surely your plan is not to paint your garage every day between now and the end of time."

"You know about the garage?"

"I don't just know about it. I have seen it. All three iterations of it, in fact. What the hell is that about?"

"You've been by my house?"

"It's my house, Edward. Yes, I have been by. I've seen you up on that ladder, painting away. It's goddamned ridiculous. And I'll tell you this: I have half a mind not to pay that bill when it comes due. I'm not your goddamned bank."

I look at my mother, who isn't looking back at me. She isn't looking at either of us. And my father is wrong: Under the rules for my living, set up and overseen by my father after the "Garth Brooks incident," that's exactly what he is. He is my goddamned bank. I do not point this out, however. I try to defuse the situation with calm, which is difficult for me but something that Dr. Buckley endorses.

"It would have been nice if you had stopped and said hello."

"I was busy, Edward. I was on my way to somewhere else."

Clark Avenue is not on the way to somewhere else. It is not a thoroughfare. If my father were on his way to somewhere else, he would have been on Central or Broadwater or Grand, or maybe even Lewis. He would not have been on Clark.

"Three times?"

"Yes, Edward, three times. How come you're not answering my question?"

My mother speaks up. "Ted, just leave it be."

"Maureen, all I want is some answers from the boy." My father is sneering at me.

I look at him and say, "When I have some plans, Father, I will let you know."

— • —

After dinner, I politely decline dessert and bid my parents good-bye.

My mother comes over to me and wraps me in a hug. In my ear, she says softly, "He doesn't mean it. He's under a lot of stress right now."

On my way out, I stop at the entryway to the living room. My father is on the couch, drink in hand, staring.

"Good night, Father." He doesn't move or look up.

— • —

You know how on an airplane when it's coming down for a landing and your ears pop and your breathing slows down? That's how I feel as my Toyota Camry descends the Rimrocks on Twenty-Seventh Street. I have not been as high as an airplane, but it was too high for comfort.

— • —

Back at home, on my way in the front door, I fetch what little mail I've received out of the box. There are two coupons for local pizza places and a letter with the seal of Lambert, Slaughter & Lamb, Attorneys at Law.

There on the front stoop, I open the envelope.

October 21, 2008
Mr. Edward Stanton:

This letter is in regard to your actions at Billings Clinic on the morning of October 19, 2008. We wish to remind you that such action will not be tolerated by your benefactor, Mr. Edward M. Stanton Sr. Any further action that warrants police involvement or puts the reputation of your benefactor at risk will be cause for revisiting the arrangements made for you, up to and including the elimination of all payments and benefits.

Regards,
Jay L. Lamb

— • —

On the other end of the phone, I hear my mother's tired voice. "Stantons' residence."

"Mother, put Father on."

"Oh, hello, dear. Your father is asleep. He has had a difficult night."

"Put him on the phone."

"He's sleeping, dear."

"Put him on the goddamned phone," I bark at her.

My mother lets out a small yelp. I hear rustling in the background and her voice, urgent: "It's Edward. It's Edward."

"Edward?" My father sounds groggy.

I am now shouting. "I was just there. Why can't you talk to me? Why does it always have to be the goddamned lawyer?"

I slam the phone into its cradle.

— • —

Tonight's episode of *Dragnet* is the first one of the first season, called "The LSD Story," and it is one of my favorites.

Sergeant Joe Friday and Officer Bill Gannon go out on a call because a boy has been seen putting his head in holes and chewing the bark off trees. This strikes Sergeant Joe Friday and Officer Bill Gannon as peculiar behavior.

What they find is a boy named Benjy Carver, only nobody calls him that. He is known as "Blue Boy." His face is painted half blue and half yellow. And he has been taking lysergic acid diethylamide, better known as LSD. This presents a quandary for the cops, as the drug is not yet illegal in California.

Soon, Blue Boy is passing the drug all around West Holly-wood, and lots of kids are getting sick from it, including two nice teenage girls named Edna May and Sandra. After the Califor-nia Legislature finally makes LSD illegal, Edna May and Sandra help Sergeant Joe Friday and Officer Bill Gannon find Blue Boy. Unfortunately, Blue Boy is already dead, having consumed too much of his own product.

This episode of *Dragnet* is a morality tale.

I think I would have liked to have had a father like Sergeant Joe Friday. I couldn't have put one over on him—Sergeant Joe Friday is way too smart for that—but I think he would have tried to understand me and the things I do, and if he didn't approve, he would tell me himself. Sergeant Joe Friday never would have had a lawyer send me a letter. That's not how he does business.

But Sergeant Joe Friday never married and never had kids. The man who portrayed him, Jack Webb, married four times—which Sergeant Joe Friday would have never done, I'm sure—and had two children. Sergeant Joe Friday is also off the air, and Jack Webb has been dead for almost twenty-six years.

I am stuck with the father I have.

— • —

I now need six green office folders for my letters to my father.

Dear Father:

I can say without reservation that your treatment of me this evening was simply unacceptable. While I can appreci-ate that you are facing many pressures at work—although

I suspect that you are bringing them on yourself, in large measure—I cannot condone your ruining dinner and my chance to visit with Mother by hectoring me over painting the garage.

And yet, all of that paled in comparison to coming home to find a letter from your lawyer castigating me for the events of Saturday at Billings Clinic. I find it hard to believe that this is something that we couldn't have worked through on our own, without legal involvement.

I don't know what to do, Father. I don't know how to please you. I don't know if you know how I can.

As ever, I am your son,
Edward

WEDNESDAY, OCTOBER 22

When I wake up—at 7:40 a.m., the thirtieth time out of 296 days this year (because it's a leap year)—it's because the wind is whipping against the house, rattling windows. My data entered, I strain across the bed and pull aside the curtain on the bedroom window.

The lone white ash tree in the backyard, clinging to its last maroon leaves, is being bent by the high wind. I glance up at the sky, which is a foreboding gray.

I have two thoughts about this: First, I think that Montana in fall is about to deliver confirmation of just how off base a forecast can be. Second, I am glad that I have no plans to paint the garage today.

As the first droplets of rain crash into the window, it occurs to me that I ought to hurry and fetch the newspaper, or else the remainder of my data will be ruined.

— • —

At the kitchen table for breakfast, I'm choking down my eighty milligrams of fluoxetine. Here is something I did not tell Dr.

Buckley yesterday: When the dreams started, I thought perhaps that I should go off my medication, just to see if that would toggle the dreams away and bring back my peaceful sleep. I can only imagine what Dr. Buckley's reaction to that would have been. She would have asked me to think about all the trouble I had before we got my dosage right, about all the moments when I felt like an unwilling passenger in a car driven by a madman—only I was the madman.

She would have been right, too. The fluoxetine, in large measure, keeps day-to-day life from being more of a mess than it sometimes is. I get credit for some of that, and Dr. Buckley would not hesitate to give it to me. Using some of the coping strategies she has given me—closing my eyes, counting backward, visualizing the path out of danger—I have often averted situations that, before Dr. Buckley, would have escalated into horrible confrontations that my father would have had to defuse. I think it's those coping skills plus the medication that have done it for me. I wouldn't want to try life without either one.

Had I gone off my medication, Dr. Buckley's reaction would have been predictable. My father's would have been apocalyptic. (I love the word "apocalyptic.") If I think my father and his lawyer are acting badly now, I should try them after I've ditched my medication.

I have trouble enough. I down the last pill and get on with it.

— • —

Inbox (1).

I have been waiting for this.

I click the link.

Dear Edward,

Awesome! Seven p.m. it is at the wine bar. Your totally cracking me up with this Dragnet *stuff. You have to tell me all about it.*
I will see you Friday.

Joy

— • —

The wind and rain are complications I do not need today, but they will have to be dealt with. If I am to go on an Internet date, I will need new clothes. The ones I have are fine for painting the garage, or puttering around the yard, or seeing Dr. Buckley, but they are not acceptable Internet date clothes by a long shot. Today has to be the day for that. It is Wednesday. My date is Friday. Were I to wait a day to buy the clothes, I would not have time to return them if something were to go wrong, like a button falling off or a shoe not fitting or something else that I cannot anticipate. Logic demands that I try clothes on today, buy them today, try them on again tomorrow, and then hope for the best on Friday. I cannot do more than that.

And so it is that I will drive to Rimrock Mall, in the wind and the rain, and then deal with the crowds at the mall. These are not things I enjoy. Worse still, I have to make many left turns to get to Rimrock Mall. Given where this house is and where the mall is, I have no alternative.

— • —

600 HOURS OF EDWARD

Here are a few things you should know about Rimrock Mall so you'll understand why I am dreading today's visit there.

Rimrock Mall is the biggest mall in Montana. Because Billings is such a geographic oddity—at 100,000-plus people, it is the largest city in a 500-mile radius—it isn't just Billings people who come to the mall. I read somewhere, maybe in the *Billings Herald-Gleaner*, that half of Northern Wyoming does its monthly shopping in Billings, and it stands to reason that a good number of those people end up at Rimrock Mall.

If you walk through the Rimrock Mall parking lot on a weekend—I would rather not, but I am setting up a hypothetical statement—you will see license plates from all over Montana and Wyoming and even other places. Montana makes it easy to pick out where license plates are from: The first number is the county code, and the counties are numbered by the population size of the counties when the system went into effect. Yellowstone County plates have the number three on them, because it was the third-largest county, population-wise, back when the system started. It should be number one now, but that would make the people in Butte-Silver Bow County angry, so it stays at number three.

Anyway, when I am driving in Billings and someone in front of me makes a wrong or erratic turn, I get angry if I see a three on his license plate, as he is from here and should know better. If I see a twenty-seven—that's Richland County, an agrarian (I love the word "agrarian") outpost in far Eastern Montana—I don't get so mad. That's someone who perhaps doesn't spend much time in Billings, and I have to be a good person and remember that Billings can be confusing to outsiders.

I am dreading today's visit to Rimrock Mall.

— • —

At 9:00 a.m., I am sweeping the kitchen floor. The big department stores in Rimrock Mall won't be open for another hour, and I'd just as soon spend part of the day on housework and let everybody get to work before I venture out in the rain.

I'm bent over, straining to get the broom under the cabinets, when the phone rings. It startles me every time, because no call is ever expected. I have the phone for emergencies and so my parents can reach me. I have a pretty good idea which one this is, although I won't know for sure until I pick up the phone.

"Hello?"

"Edward." It's my father.

"Yes."

"Quite a stunt you pulled, calling me like that last night and yelling at me."

"Quite a stunt you pulled, Father."

He sighs heavily into the phone. "You may be right about that, Edward." And then, in an instant, he's no longer making a concession to me. "Of course, you forced my hand with that business at the hospital."

"That's over. It's a nonissue."

"You're sure about that?"

"Yes."

"Have you had any dealings with that woman or her boy?"

I do not like deception or equivocation, but clearly this is a question that demands the sort of answer former President Bill Clinton might offer.

"I don't see them."

"That's good. You understand my concern here, right?"

"No."

"You're a hard case, Edward."

"I am what you made me, Father."

"That's not fair."

"I don't think you can talk about fair."

My father now sounds exasperated. "You know what the funny part is, Edward? I called to apologize."

"I can think of something funnier."

"What's that?"

"You never managed to do it."

My father has hung up on me.

My heart is beating fast.

I've never stood up to him before, not like this.

I've either won a round or ensured that Father's lawyer is going to accumulate more billable hours.

— • —

The only bright spot of being at Rimrock Mall is that I know exactly where I am headed. That knowledge makes it easier to start the slog that begins at the front door near the food court and extends deep into the place. I am not here for pizza or for greasy Asian noodles. I make a left turn at the Starbucks kiosk and walk a diagonal line to the far wall, and then I walk toward Dillard's at the south end of the mall. I'm dodging baby carriages and listless teens who ought to be in school and slow-moving old people who come here to walk.

Dillard's looms like a beacon, an outpost of affordable, fashionable wear for men and women and even a big-and-tall section—the kind of place that will have something for my six-foot-four, 280-pound frame. I am almost there.

I'm just steps away when a middle-age woman in a pink T-shirt ("Beauty Queen") and too-tight gray sweats plows into me, spilling her supersize Orange Julius down the front of my pants.

"Jesus H. Christ on a Popsicle stick!" My father says that a lot. I am surprised to hear it come out of my mouth.

— • —

I race-walk into Dillard's, trying to look like someone who didn't have an accident in his pants. Judging from the stares I'm getting, I am failing. I duck into the big-and-tall department, which thankfully is just inside the door.

"Can I help…?" The sales person's smile disappears.

"Someone ran into me with an Orange Julius."

"Oh no."

"I'm here for some dress clothes, but I need jeans now." I rattle off my size to her, and she fetches a couple of possibilities, and then she leads me to a changing room.

After a few minutes of writhing out of my soaked jeans and into the two she has offered me, I make my pick: a pair of dark-blue Joseph Abboud jeans. Tag price: $65. My father will not be happy.

I emerge from the changing room and tell the woman that I'll wear the Abbouds out the door. She clips the scan tag, then smiles and says, "What else can I help you with today?"

— • —

My final haul looks like this: three button-down dress shirts (lavender, white with thick blue stripes, and white with thin brown-and-blue stripes). They are fine items of clothing, fitted Gold Label shirts from Roundtree and Yorke, and I found them at a closeout price. These $75 shirts are being sold for $17.50 (75 percent off).

I also have two pairs of trousers, blue and chino, also Roundtree and Yorke, and also on closeout, $20 apiece (again, 75 percent off).

I also have the most wonderful belt I have ever seen, one that reverses and thus is black or brown, whatever I need. Its cost: $35.

I also have a pair of brown, size twelve, Rockport lace-up dress shoes. Cost: $65.

I also have a blue suit with tiny little tan pinstripes. The name on the tag is George Foreman—"The same guy who does the grill!" the friendly saleswoman tells me. It looks good on me. Cost: $300.

Grand total: $492.50.

Holy shit!

— • —

As I'm making a left turn from the mall parking lot onto Twenty-Fourth Street W.—with the blessing of a left-turn arrow on the traffic light, I might add—the front of my 1997 Toyota Camry is clipped by a car making a right turn out of the strip mall directly across the street. The rain, now coming down in waves, is pelting my windshield so hard that I don't see the other driver, and by the time I bring the Camry to a stop, set the hazard lights, and climb out of the Camry, the car that hit me is long gone.

"Cocksucker," I yell after the car, which I can't see.

My new Joseph Abboud jeans are soaked.

— • —

I wait until I get home to inspect the damage. It's not bad: a small paint swap on the front right fender (my assailant's car was white), some scratching, a dent perceptible only if you run your hand along the fender, which I do.

But there is a principle involved. I had the right of way. The light favored me. What was that idiot in the white car doing? And why did he or she not stop? That's breaking the law.

Also, I will have to talk to my father about this and find out what he wants to do about repairing the Camry. I am not looking forward to that.

— • —

At 4:03 p.m., I hear a knock at the door. I look through the peephole and see Donna Middleton under an umbrella.

I open the door.

"Hello, Edward."

"Hello."

"Listen, I hate to sound pushy, but I'm getting soaked out here. Can I come in?"

"Um. OK."

I step back and open the door for Donna Middleton as she closes her umbrella.

"Leave that on the porch," I say.

"Yeah, OK," she says, and she sets the umbrella down.

She steps into the house and takes a sweeping look around the small living room. To her left are the two bedrooms, one of which I sleep in, the other of which holds my computer and desk. Dead ahead is the bathroom. To her right are the kitchen and the dining room. Through the kitchen and downstairs is the basement.

"This is a cute little house, Edward. You keep it so clean."

"Yes."

"Can I sit down?"

"Yes."

She picks the love seat along the west wall of the house. I pick the couch that runs perpendicular to it and the cushion farthest from her.

"Edward, I want to thank you properly for that…What is it called? That Blue Flash? Anyway, I want to thank you properly for that. You've made Kyle a very happy little boy."

"Blue Blaster."

"Blue Blaster! Yes," Donna Middleton says, laughing. "Anyway, Kyle has had so much fun on that thing. He's bummed that he can't ride it today in all this rain."

"Where is he?"

"At home, soothing himself by playing PlayStation Two. *Guitar Hero.* I had to get out of there. There is only so much 'Slow Ride' I'm willing to listen to."

"Foghat."

"Is that who it is?"

"Yes. I've never played *Guitar Hero.* But it's definitely Foghat."

"You should come over some time and play it. It's fun in small doses. I'm terrible at it."

"Does it have Matthew Sweet or R.E.M.?"

"I don't know."

"Those are my favorites."

"I like R.E.M. I haven't heard of Matthew Sweet, I don't think."

"He had that song 'Girlfriend.' That was his big hit."

"Nope, don't recognize it. Why do you like those guys so much?"

No one has ever asked me that question.

"I watched a lot of MTV several years ago. I liked the video for the R.E.M. song 'Losing My Religion' and—"

"That's a really good song."

"Yes. So I started listening to more of their songs, and Michael Stipe, their lead singer, uses really interesting word combinations."

"Interesting. What about the other guy?"

"Matthew Sweet?"

"Yeah."

"I don't know, I guess. He sings a lot of songs that are sullen, and I feel that way sometimes. He is also really good at melodies, and I like those. Do you think there's a chance that he is on *Guitar Hero*?"

"Well, it's Kyle's game. He could tell you everything that's on it, how well he scored, the words to the songs. Until that Blue Blaster showed up, *Guitar Hero* was just about all he did, other than sleeping, eating, and going to school."

I give Donna Middleton a half smile.

"Edward, can I ask you a question?"

"Yes."

"What do you do? Do you have a job?"

"No, I don't work. I do things around the house. I paint the garage. I build things. I keep track of the weather. I watch *Dragnet*. Things like that."

"How do you pay for everything?"

"My father does."

"Edward, I want to tell you something. That day at the hospital, your father told me about your condition. Does it bother you that I know?"

"No, I heard him tell you that."

"Is that why you don't work?"

"Jobs are hard for me. I'm good at the work, but it's hard to deal with bosses and coworkers sometimes. My therapist, Dr.

Buckley, and I have been working on that. Maybe someday I could have a job again."

"I talk to a therapist, too. Life is hard. Sometimes, it helps to talk about it, don't you think?"

"Yes."

— • —

For nearly an hour, Donna Middleton sits on my love seat and tells me about her therapist, about how she put herself through nursing school after Kyle was born, about how she lived at her parents' house in Laurel, and about how her mom helped raise Kyle. Kyle's dad was Donna's high school boyfriend. They had broken up after graduating from high school, and then they ran into each other at a bar several years later. She tells me about how one night changed everything for her. After she got pregnant, her old boyfriend would have nothing to do with her. That's when she knew she was going to have to do better for her boy.

"He looks so much like his father, and that is hard sometimes," Donna Middleton is telling me. "But he's such a sweet boy, and that's not like his father at all. He's the greatest gift of my life."

— • —

In that same hour, I tell Donna Middleton about my therapy, about my difficulties with my father, about how I came to live in this house. I do not tell her about the online dating, and I cannot explain why except to say that it doesn't seem right. I do tell her about the letters of complaint. This intrigues her.

"Any letters of complaint to me?" she says.

"Two."

She arches an eyebrow. "Can I read them?"

"No. They don't get read, and they don't get sent. They are a therapeutic tool."

"Interesting. And you write one of these letters every day?"

"Yes."

"Don't you ever run out of things to complain about?"

"Not yet."

— • —

Donna Middleton bids me good-bye. I open the door for her, and she gathers up the umbrella, opens it, and holds it tight against the wind and rain. I watch her look both ways on Clark Avenue, and then she dashes diagonally across the street and back to her house.

— • —

Tonight's *Dragnet* episode is called "The Big Explosion," the second installment of the first season of the color episodes. It originally aired on January 19, 1967, and it is one of my favorites.

Sergeant Joe Friday and Officer Bill Gannon are investigating the theft of 400 pounds of dynamite from a construction site. Because they are good police officers, they eventually trace the missing dynamite to a white supremacist named Donald Chapman, who borrowed a friend's car and stole the explosives. A witness saw the license number, which leads to the friend, who leads Sergeant Joe Friday and Officer Bill Gannon to Donald Chapman. You have to be tenacious (I love the word "tenacious") to be a cop.

This episode is interesting in another way. It is full of actors who went on to be members of the *Dragnet* ensemble and other Jack Webb projects. Kent McCord, who played Officer Jim Reed in *Adam-12*, is in it. So is Bobby Troup, who played Dr. Joe Early on *Emergency!* and who in real life was also a jazz pianist and married to Jack Webb's ex-wife Julie London. Don Dubbins plays the white supremacist, Donald Chapman.

Jack Webb saw the benefit of having friends and relying on them. I'm beginning to see that myself.

— • —

Before bed, I prepare another green office folder.

Unnamed motorist who hit me on 24th Street W.:

You made a lot of mistakes today. First, you turned against the light, clipping my 1997 Toyota Camry. Second, you left the scene of an accident without swapping insurance information, and that is a crime.

Why run? The damage is not much—so little, in fact, that I suspect my father will not opt to have it fixed, as the deductible will be charged to him. Had you been responsible about the situation, your insurance would have covered the damage. Now I am having to confront the likelihood of having to drive a dinged-up car. This is not fair to me.

Driving is not a right. It is a privilege. Unfortunately, you left the scene of an accident and will be able to keep driving. I hope that you don't affect other motorists the way you have affected me.

Finally, I would just like to add that you have confirmed the reason that I prefer right turns to left turns. Left turns, statistically, are more dangerous than right turns, especially on two-way streets, as 24th Street W. is. Had I been making a right turn, our paths would not have crossed, although that would not have mitigated against the fact that you were turning against the light.

Please, for your own sake and the sake of the many drivers who share the road with you, be more mindful of the situations you are in.

Regards,
Edward Stanton

THURSDAY, OCTOBER 23

I am in the driver's seat of a car. It's not my car. It is far bigger—a station wagon, from the looks of the inside. I look to my right, and Joy is sitting in the front seat with me. I reach up and tilt the rearview mirror so I can see behind me. Kyle is in the middle of the backseat, flanked to his left by his mother and to the right by Dr. Buckley. In the far back, in the foldout seats, are my mother and father. I scan every face, and each looks back placidly at me.

I look outside the car, and I see that we are on a bridge—it looks much like the one I have seen in Eastern Montana, on Interstate 94 near Terry, which spans a wide portion of the Yellowstone River. We are not moving.

"Sorry about that, everyone," I say as I put the car into gear. I nudge the gas, and the car slips off the road into nothingness, an empty space now occupying an area that I am sure held a road just a moment ago.

I look again to my right, and Joy's face is ashen.

"I'm sorry," I say.

— • —

My legs kick into the air, my involuntary response to the expecta-
tion of certain death. When I don't hit ground, my eyes open, and
I squint as I adjust to the absence of light.

From the nightstand, the green numbers of my digital clock
cut through the dark: It's 5:12 a.m. I take a deep breath as I wait
for my heartbeat to slow, and then I turn away from the clock and
clutch my spare pillow. I slip away again, this time into dreamless
sleep.

— • —

It is 11:51 a.m. when I awake again. My data isn't ruined—indeed,
it has a first-time-ever entry—but my erratic sleep has cut into
my day.

In the bathroom, I pee long—and I'm not talking about distance, but rather, time. This is something I do not keep data on.
First, it's gross. Second, my sleep is ordinarily so reliable—in 297
days this year (because it's a leap year), my wake-up time has been
in a four-minute range for 294 of them—that it has other physi-
ological benefits as well. Not to put too fine a point on it, but my
bathroom breaks are as predictable as my wake-up times.

In the living room, I peek through the front-window curtain
and see what yesterday's *Billings Herald-Gleaner* foretold: snow.
It's not much—a medium dusting that will be gone as soon as the
temperature gets into the high thirties, I would guess, though I
don't like to guess and will instead just wait and see what the facts
bear out—but it's snow, nonetheless. I can add a round of shoveling to my day.

— • —

Outfitted in snow boots, gloves, a hat, and a warm coat, I trudge out the back door, through the backyard gate, and to the garage, where I retrieve my snow shovel.

When I was in Los Angeles two years ago, I told the desk clerk at the Renaissance Hotel at Hollywood Boulevard and Highland Avenue that I was from Billings, Montana, and he performed a little mock shiver. They say that everyone is an actor in Hollywood.

"I couldn't live there," he said. "How do you handle the snow?"

I thought that was a misinformed statement. Billings's annual snowfall is 57.2 inches, which I will concede is a lot more than Hollywood gets, but it's also less than Great Falls (63.5 inches) or someplace like Syracuse, New York (115.6 inches). I thought I might tell him this, but he was already handing me the room key and inviting me to "please let us know if you need anything at all."

I might further have told him that I enjoy shoveling snow, thank you very much, and that's why I'm outside, bundled up and grinning.

I find great appeal in a freshly shoveled sidewalk and driveway. I love how the blade of the shovel forms beautiful, clean lines where the snow once was. I carefully line up the edge of the blade with the edge of the sidewalk, and then I push through to the end of the property boundary with one stroke, then line the blade up against the edge of the swath I've just created and repeat the process.

The driveway, being far wider than the sidewalk, requires several such swaths, and I push the snow out into the street, where the comings and goings on Clark Avenue will compress it and melt it away.

It takes me less than a half hour to clear away the accumulations that have been building all day. I'll probably have to come out again later, but I won't mind.

— • —

At lunch, I dine on a Banquet beef enchilada meal. I have missed breakfast in all of my sleeping, and my medication has been pushed off until now. I'm a little off when I finally take it—not light-headed but definitely aware that something is not quite right in my system. As I sit and shovel forkfuls of Spanish rice into my mouth, I can feel the medication take root, and my unease drifts away.

My father has made the front page of the *Billings Herald-Gleaner* again, under the headline "Stanton denounces Big Sky EDA board."

By MATT HAGENGRUBER of the *Herald-Gleaner* staff

Yellowstone County commissioner Ted Stanton, at odds with fellow commissioners and other members of the Big Sky Economic Development Agency advisory board since his pick for director fell through, criticized the panel Wednesday and signaled that the county faces a battle "for the soul" of its economic future.

"I think the voters and the businesspeople of this region are going to have to take a hard look at this group," Stanton said in an interview at his office. "I think when people really get into the meat of it, they're going to see that they've been underserved here. Yellowstone County deserves better."

The "meat," according to Stanton, is a series of decisions that have "stunted" economic growth in the county. Among them, he said, is the failed Promenade project that had been slated for the West End and would have brought approximately ninety retail stores in an outdoor, urban-style setting. Backers of the project pulled out last month, citing a contracting economy, but Stanton maintains that

Yellowstone County officials and the Big Sky EDA failed to come through with a promised package of tax incentives.

Stanton said his criticism of the board is unrelated to the candidacy of a friend, Dave Akers, for the economic development agency's director job. Akers, considered the front-runner for the job, was dropped from consideration after being arrested on suspicion of drunk driving two weeks ago.

"The way Dave was dealt with is emblematic of how the board works," Stanton said. "But it's immaterial to what's hurting development in this county."

Fellow commissioner Rolf Eklund was skeptical of Stanton's claims.

"Everybody knows what Ted's problem is," said Eklund, who frequently spars with Stanton in county meetings. "He's never made much of an effort to hide his agenda."

To be sure, Stanton has long been a divisive—but also beloved—figure on the Yellowstone County political scene...

Always needing a fight, my father seems to have found one. Perhaps that will put an end to the one he's having with me, at least for a while. I can always hope. I prefer facts.

— • —

After lunch, I step into the bedroom and consider the clothes I bought yesterday.

First, as I had determined, I need to try them all on and make sure everything is in order.

This takes a while, among all the slipping out of my work clothes, shimmying into the new items, looking myself over in the full-length mirror on my closet door, then shedding one set of new clothes for another.

The fits are all good, and the clothes hang nicely on a body that I know has gone doughy, especially in my thirties. At one point, I step forward to the mirror and press my face up close. A face changes imperceptibly day to day, but on close examination, I can see what has happened through the years. The creases across the bridge of my wide, flat nose are starting to deepen. My eyes are crinkling at the corners. My hair, which has been thinning at the temples for years, has turned gray on the sides.

I am beginning to look my age.

— • —

At 3:02 p.m., I hear the *rap-rap-rap* of knuckles against the front door. I've been in the computer room, reading up on Bobby Troup, one of Jack Webb's ensemble players. (Did you know that he wrote the theme song for *Route 66*? I didn't.)

I take the five steps to the front door and fling it open. Standing there on the front porch are Kyle and his mother, bundled up and beckoning me outside. Behind them, on the sidewalk leading up to the front door, is the Blue Blaster.

— • —

Donna Middleton and I are sitting on the front lawn, on folding chairs I dragged out of the garage. With the snow shovel, I've built a mound of loose snow in the middle of the sidewalk. The house I live in is the second to last one in the 600 block of Clark Avenue, and Kyle and the Blue Blaster are on the sidewalk at the corner of Clark and Seventh Street W., where the 700 block begins.

"Are you ready?" he shouts down to us.

Donna starts pumping her right fist in a forward-and-back motion and chants, "Go! Go! Go! Go!"

I pump my right fist in unison but do not chant.

Kyle settles into the Blue Blaster's seat, and then he starts pedaling furiously, his piston-like legs driving the glorified tricycle to a high speed. When he connects with the pile of snow, it's like a frozen explosion, the powdery snow blowing out in all directions.

"Awesome!" Kyle yells.

"Do it again," I say as I get up, grab the shovel, and start rebuilding the snow pile while Kyle wheels the Blue Blaster around and goes back to the corner.

Soon, his mother and I are chanting and fist pumping as Kyle blasts through another mound.

"I know what," Kyle says. "I'm going to ride around the block, and you guys make snowballs and try to hit me as I go by."

Donna fixes her boy with a wicked grin. "You're going down."

"No, you are," Kyle yells, and he and the Blue Blaster light out of there.

Donna and I drop to our knees in the front yard, scrounging up snow and forming it into perfectly round projectiles. As Kyle rounds the corner and bears down on us, we start flinging snowballs at him. A few connect, but mostly we miss, sending little snow skid marks across the sidewalk. He really is fast on that thing.

While Kyle wheels around the block for another pass, I have an idea. I slip over to the side of the house, where the snow is a little deeper from my neighbor's shoveling, and I mold a few snowballs. Perhaps if Kyle doesn't see where they're coming from, he'll be easier to tag.

I see him round the corner and come down the straightaway, and I cock my arm back, try to time my throw, and then let it go.

The snowball crashes against the back of Donna Middleton's head, spraying snow on her shoulders.

She pivots and faces me, her jaw slack.

I look back at her and want to say I'm sorry, but my mouth moves only a little and forms no words.

And then she throws a snowball at me, which explodes against my buttoned-up coat.

She starts laughing, and I throw one back. Now she's taking evasive action, running erratically in loops around the yard as I give chase. Kyle has left the Blue Blaster, and he's chasing her, too. We're throwing snowballs and chasing and laughing, and I cannot remember the last time I did any of these things.

— • —

That's not true. I can remember.

In November 1974, when I was five years old, my father took me on a business trip. We flew from Billings down to Denver on a Saturday—I remember the day clearly because there was no school, and it was the weekend before Thanksgiving. When we landed in Denver, my father hailed a cab that took us to a downtown hotel. It had been snowing in Denver, and downtown was mostly dead on a weekend. The gray of the day and the snow combined to give downtown Denver an eerie sort of pallor (I love the word "pallor"), one that was both appealing and a little creepy. After dinner, my father and I went outside and built a snowman on a deserted street corner, then pelted it with snowballs. It was fun.

The next morning, another cab took us to the International Harvester dealer in Denver, where my father signed the paperwork on a new red Paystar 5000. It must take an awful lot of paperwork to close a deal on such a purchase; I remember that we were there for a long while. I amused myself thumbing through glossy brochures that touted the latest in International Harvester machinery.

After that, we road-tripped in the new truck down to Midland, Texas, where the Mayhew Co. was waiting to put a drilling rig on the back of it. That's the earliest memory I have of being in a big truck with my father, and I have vivid memories of thinking that he had to be just about the coolest father in the world. He was in a good mood, too, honking the horn for children in passing cars who would hold up their right fists and pull down twice, asking for such an acknowledgment. I can't account for that good mood, because although I did not know it at the time, my father's life was in a shambles. The reason I was with him at all was that my mother had left him, something I didn't learn until years later, 1992, when my mother mentioned it in a fight with my father.

In Midland, we were met by Grandpa Sid and Grandma Mabel, who picked us up and drove us the seven hours back to Dallas for Thanksgiving. That day, we saw rookie quarterback Clint Longley come off the bench after Roger Staubach got hurt and lead the Dallas Cowboys to an incredible 24–23 victory over the Washington Redskins, still one of the most amazing finishes in Cowboys history. Longley hit Drew Pearson on a fifty-yard touchdown pass with twenty-eight seconds left to win the game.

"Teddy," my father said, "as long as you live, you'll never see another one like that." (On a Thanksgiving Day nineteen years later, I saw one even more amazing, in a bad way. Leon Lett slid into the ball after a blocked field goal attempt that would have given the Dallas Cowboys a victory over the Miami Dolphins. Miami recovered the ball, kicked again, and won. I wrote Leon

Lett four letters that week, castigating [I love the word "castigating"] him for his foolishness.)

Back in 1974, two days after Thanksgiving, my father and I were on a plane home to Billings. Mother met us at the airport. She had come home, never to leave my father again.

Things just work out sometimes. I don't know how or why. It would be easier if there were some hard data about these things.

— • —

"Edward," Kyle says to me. "Do you want to come over and play some *Guitar Hero*?"

We have thrown all the snowballs we wish to throw. What had been a pristine blanket of snow on the front yard is now full of three sizes of footprints and tiny valleys where snow was scooped up.

I don't want to play *Guitar Hero*. I don't want to go to Donna and Kyle's house. Why, I cannot explain. I also do not want to be rude. Dr. Buckley says it is OK for me to not want to do some things but that I don't have to "be abrupt" with people. She says one of the keys to getting along socially is being able to say no firmly and gracefully. I try this.

"No, thank you, not today."

"Oh." Kyle—and even Donna—looks a little sad. Saying no is hard. No wonder Dr. Buckley has spent so much time talking about it with me.

"But I have a large DiGiorno supreme pizza," I say. "Would you like to have dinner with me?"

"Can we, Mom?"

"Sure," Donna says. "Thank you, Edward. We'd be happy to."

We agree to meet back here in an hour. At the front door, I look back and watch Donna and Kyle cross the street, hand in hand.

— • —

"You don't have a lot of stuff, Edward." Kyle, changed out of his playing-in-the-snow clothes, is standing in the living room, looking around.

He is not entirely correct, but it's easy to see why he would think so. My furnishings are spare; when my father bought this house, he asked me how I would like to outfit it, and I asked for furniture from IKEA. For one thing, I like how modern it is—it is unadorned Swedish furniture. For another, IKEA furniture is all about utility. What Kyle sees as spare is actually furniture that allows me to make sure everything has its place. For yet another, IKEA furniture has to be assembled by the buyer, and I like putting things together. My father was not happy about the price—it costs a lot of money to have IKEA furniture shipped to Montana—but he let me have it.

"Watch this, Kyle," I say.

I show him how the small entertainment center holding my TV and stereo system, against the south wall of the living room, has lots of tiny compartments and how I've filled them with movies and compact discs and other things. I show him the coffee table, with still more compartments, where I have stored pens and paper clips and rubber bands and batteries and other things I need.

I take him into the computer room and show him the stackable storage containers, full of seasonal clothing and household items.

"Wow. I guess you do have some stuff. Do you have a PlayStation Two?"

"No."

"Do you have a Wii?"

"No."

"How do you have fun?"

Before today, that's a question that would have flummoxed me.

— • —

After dinner, Kyle is in the computer room, playing the only game I have on my computer: blackjack. I had spent a few minutes explaining how it worked, how he didn't want to exceed twenty-one with his cards. I showed him how he could split two cards of the same number and double his bet.

"But only do it with aces and eights," I said.

"Why?"

"Because with anything else, you're only building two bad hands. If you split two tens or two face cards, you've broken up a hand that will win most of the time. Same thing with two nines. With two sevens, often the best you can do is get two ties, and that's only if you draw tens on each one. And so on. Do you understand?"

"Not really."

"Just play. You'll figure it out."

Back in the living room, Donna tells me something. "Mike's going to be in court next week—Monday."

"Are you going to be there?"

"Yes."

"Will you be OK?"

"I don't know. But I will be there, for every court appearance and for the trial."

"Does Kyle know what happened?"

"Most of it. I couldn't hide the bruises, you know. I haven't told him about the choking." There is not much bruising to hide now. If I didn't know it had happened, I might not be able to see the damage at all.

"Maybe that's for the best."

"I think so," she says. "Part of the reason I'm going to court is for Kyle. The main thing is that I want Mike to know that he's not going to get the better of me. But it's also a reminder to me that I've done poorly in choosing who I let near my son. I won't make that mistake again."

Donna's eyes have a faraway look, as if she's seeing beyond my little living room on Clark Avenue. I sit quietly with her.

— • —

I had asked Donna and Kyle if they would like to stay and watch *Dragnet*, but Donna declined, as it's a school night for Kyle. Maybe some other time, she said.

Tonight's episode is called "The Kidnapping." It originally aired on January 26, 1967, and it is one of my favorites.

In the episode, a woman who owns a line of boutiques has been taken captive at her home. One of her store managers, in town for an audit, is sent by the abductor to a bank to get the $75,000 in ransom. Sergeant Joe Friday and Officer Bill Gannon are called in by the bank president, and once they determine that the store manager's story is on the level, they get her the $75,000 and enlist her help in catching the bad guy. She agrees to help, even though she admits that she doesn't really like her boss. The abduction ends when Sergeant Joe Friday wrestles the bad man to the ground on a freeway on-ramp. The store manager—played by Peggy Webber, who appeared in eight *Dragnet* episodes—is freed from the trunk of the car.

There are two lessons in this episode: First, Sergeant Joe Friday always gets his man. Second, don't mess with a determined woman.

— • —

Dear Father,

I had a memory today that made me both happy and sad. Do you remember our trip to Midland, Texas, in the new International Paystar 5000? Even though I now know that you were enduring a difficult time, I remember how happy you seemed to be, traveling with me and spending Thanksgiving with Grandpa Sid and Grandma Mabel and watching the Dallas Cowboys. Thinking of that made me happy.

We never have that kind of fun now. Thinking of that made me sad.

I hope we can have fun again sometime. I found out today that I still know how. Maybe you still know how, too.

Your son,
Edward

FRIDAY, OCTOBER 24

It's an odd and embarrassing thought that stirs me from sleep:

What if Joy wants to have sex with me tonight? This is not an eventuality I have planned for, and it seems so preposterous (I love the word "preposterous") that I am inclined to just lie back down and return to sleep.

And yet, I cannot. So I watch time peel off my digital clock in the darkness as I ponder this.

5:57...5:58...5:59...

I keep coming back to what Dr. Buckley said: "I hope that's not on the agenda for your first date." No, it's not. We don't have an agenda. We are meeting at the new wine bar downtown, the one on Broadway. Everything after that is uncertain—including, and especially, the question of whether we are having sex.

6:00...6:01...6:02...

I must make a confession: I have never had sex, at least not with another human being. I am thirty-nine years old, and so, yes, I have discovered self-satisfaction. There's no need to be excessively descriptive or gross about it. I read Dear Abby every morning in the *Billings Herald-Gleaner*, and I remember her saying something years ago about self-satisfaction: Half of men do it, and the other half lie when they say they don't do it. That's what

Dear Abby said, and that's good enough for me. Dear Abby is a very logical woman.

6:03...6:04...6:05...

Since I've never had sex, you can probably understand why I am wigging out about it. (I love the slang phrase "wigging out.") Setting aside the obvious questions—How does one arrive at the decision to have sex on a first date? Does one just say, "This is a delicious salad. I look forward to telling you more about it later, when we're having sex"?—I am uncomfortable with the idea. It seems like an irresponsible thing to do.

6:06...6:07...6:08...

Let's say for argument's sake that we were to have sex. This is a hypothetical situation. Where does it happen? Do we drive all the way back to Broadview and have sex at her house? We cannot have sex at this house; that simply is not a possibility. Among other potential problems, my father would be apoplectic if he found out. If Joy and I drive all the way back to Broadview, how do we have sex and leave enough time for me to get back to Billings to see tonight's episode of *Dragnet*? I don't see how it would be possible. I couldn't have sex with that kind of time pressure. I'm not sure I can have sex at all, seeing as how I never have had it. I'm simply saying that, even if the physical act of love were possible, I would not be able to concentrate on it knowing that I might miss *Dragnet*.

6:09...6:10...6:11...

So what? A hotel room? That still brings up the *Dragnet* problem. A nice hotel, like the Crowne Plaza, might be willing to put a videocassette player in the room, but then I would have to make sure to bring my *Dragnet* tape along, not knowing whether I would actually need it.

I think that would be awkward.

Joy: "Hi, Edward. Why do you have your *Dragnet* tape?"

Me: "Hi, Joy. I thought we might have sex, so I wanted to be ready. I can't miss *Dragnet*."

Also, the Crowne Plaza is not the sort of place that would rent us a room for the sole purpose of having sex. The sort of place that would rent us a room for sex—and I don't know how to find such a place—might not have a videocassette player to lend me. It would probably just want us to have sex and leave.

6:12...6:13...6:14...

It's settled. We're not having sex, even if Joy wants to. Even if I want to. There is just no way it can happen. I will have to apply the lessons I've learned from Dr. Buckley about saying no to this situation. I can say no to sex with Joy while still treating her with dignity and grace.

I should practice this.

"Sex? I'm ever so sorry, Joy, but it's just not possible tonight. I do hope you understand."

"Under normal circumstances, Joy, I would love to have sex with you, but it's simply not a good night tonight."

"I am appreciative of the offer, but I cannot. Perhaps I could take a rain check."

Yes, any of those will work.

If she's aggressive and grabs my wiener, though, I may have to come up with another plan. I have seen that sort of thing happen on late-night cable television, and I think it's prudent that I be ready for it.

— • —

Here is something I did not know until today: Almost twenty minutes of thinking about nothing other than sex ruins you for sleep. I grab my pen and notebook and groggily record 5:57 a.m. in the space I have made for today, and my data is complete.

— • —

While I am eating corn flakes and waiting to hear the thump of the *Billings Herald-Gleaner* on the doorstep, I plot a plan for tonight—one that, as I have decided, does not include sex.

I want to try to be romantic, but I have been reading some online-dating advice columns, and if there is a single piece of counsel that comes through consistently about first dates, it is this: Do not make grand gestures. A first date is about building a little bit of trust and rapport and walking away from it wanting to have a second date. Some of the columns I have read say no flowers on a first date. Others say that a single red rose is a nice touch. I would like to give Joy a single red rose.

I have also decided, on my own, to burn a CD for Joy of some of my favorite songs, especially by R.E.M. and Matthew Sweet. I am not putting overt (I love the word "overt") love songs on the CD. I do not want to come on too strong with Joy. I will tell her that the CD is just some of the music I like and that I hope she likes it, too. I will not be trying to send any kind of message with the CD.

Finally, I will go to get my hair cut today. I have new clothes for my online date. A fresh haircut will complete the look.

It's a good plan, I think.

At 6:33, the newspaper lands on the doorstep. I rinse out my bowl in the sink, cross the living room, open the door, and pick up the paper. The forecast is calling for a high of forty-seven, which should be enough to melt away this snow if it comes true—but I won't know until tomorrow, as forecasts are notoriously off base.

Inside, I write down the figures from yesterday, and my data is complete.

— • —

Mixing a CD for Joy is more difficult than I had imagined. The R.E.M. songs go pretty well, and I end up choosing ten from across their catalog of albums:

1. "Radio Free Europe," *Murmur*
2. "So. Central Rain," *Reckoning*
3. "Driver 8," *Fables of the Reconstruction*
4. "Begin the Begin," *Lifes Rich Pageant*
5. "Disturbance at the Heron House," *Document*
6. "World Leader Pretend," *Green*
7. "Half a World Away," *Out of Time*
8. "Find the River," *Automatic for the People*
9. "Electrolite," *New Adventures in Hi-Fi*
10. "Man-Sized Wreath," *Accelerate*

I skip the albums *Monster*, *Up*, *Reveal*, and *Around the Sun* because, although I like some songs on each of those albums, they are not as good as the others. That's my opinion. It's not fact, although a lot of people agree with me.

Finding ten Matthew Sweet songs is a harder chore. Don't get me wrong, I can find ten that I like, but I can't necessarily find ones that I think someone else would like. Matthew Sweet can be a real downer.

I end up choosing six:

1. "I've Been Waiting," *Girlfriend*
2. "Devil with the Green Eyes," *Altered Beast*
3. "Superdeformed," *Son of Altered Beast*
4. "Come to California," *Blue Sky on Mars*
5. "I Should Never Have Let You Know," *In Reverse*
6. "Wait," *Kimi Ga Suki* (the Japanese album)

It's a fine collection of songs. I think if Joy for some reason decides that she doesn't want it, my disappointment will be soothed by the fact that I will get to keep it.

— • —

At 10:00 a.m., I walk in the door at the Great Clips haircutters on Grand Avenue. There is no line. Most of the rest of Billings is at work.

I have had this stylist before. Her name is Heather, and she is very pretty, with big blue eyes and long, blonde, straight hair. One thing about her, though, is that her attitude varies wildly. She recognizes me and smiles and invites me back to the chair.

"The usual?" she asks.

"Yes."

This is an easy job for Heather. My hair does not need styling. It needs to be cut, and she quickly does it.

"What're you up to today?" she asks.

"I have an online date."

"Cool."

"Yes."

"I haven't had a date in for-ev-er," she says, drawing out the syllables, and then she starts telling me about what a disaster her last date was and how she swore off men but can't stay away for long and that she wishes me luck and just be a gentleman and it will all work out just fine.

Heather is fun to listen to when she feels good, like she does today.

— • —

On the way back home, I stop at the Albertsons on Grand and Thirteenth Street W. and buy a single red rose from the floral department. The nice lady who works there wraps it loosely in a cellophane cone and pops a small container of water onto the stem to keep it looking fresh.

I am nearly ready for my 7:00 p.m. date.

It is 10:57 a.m.

— • —

While it's true that I am feeling a bit overeager—an odd sensation for me—it's also true that I do have some other chores.

For one thing, I have to eat lunch. I will not have much, in case Joy wants to eat tonight at the wine bar downtown. It's not just a wine bar. I have been reading up on it, and apparently, the place—it is called Bin 119—has very good food, too, including something called lobster mac 'n' cheese. I don't know if that sounds good or not. I don't have seafood very often—only at my monthly dinner with my parents, and not at every one of those. I've had lots of mac 'n' cheese; it was one of my favorites when I was a child, with the box of noodles and the powdered cheese that would turn gooey when mixed with butter and milk. I do not think that kind of mac 'n' cheese would taste good with lobster. But that's just my opinion. It's not necessarily a fact.

I have spaghetti for lunch.

— • —

At 5:00 p.m., I start trying on all of my new clothes again. I have two purposes. First, I need to ensure, again, that none of it is defective. If there's a zipper that doesn't work or a button hanging by a thread or a small tear at the corner of a pocket, now is the time to know. Second, I need to choose what I'm wearing tonight.

In the end, I choose the George Foreman pinstripe suit and the white shirt with blue stripes, with no tie. I think it looks dressy, yet easygoing. I also think I look too round and puffy. This is not something I thought about before I decided to look for dates on the Internet, but now that I am an active Internet dater, I may have to incorporate some belly control into my daily routine. I could start doing sit-ups. That would give me something new to count and whip my stomach into shape. The thought of this makes me happy.

It is 5:37 p.m. and I am dressed for my 7:00 p.m. Internet date with Joy from Broadview.

— • —

After putting the mix CD in my front coat pocket—and then checking twice more to make sure it is there—I decide to do some last-minute brushing up on Internet dating, just so I know as much as possible about what will happen tonight.

On one website, I find an article called "Everything You Need to Know Before You Go on That Online Date." At first, I am not interested, as the article plainly says that it is written for women over forty, but then I remember that Joy is forty-one and I think that it might benefit me to consider things from her perspective.

By the time I finish reading the article, however, I wonder why any woman would ever want to go on an Internet date. The person who wrote this article does not seem to like dating or to expect much from it. She says that men don't want to date older women and that the only way a man will show genuine interest in someone is by stalking her, which alarms me, because I don't want to stalk anybody.

Finally, the writer suggests buying the book *He's Just Not That Into You*, by Greg Behrendt. She says that it will reveal everything about men and what they think.

Regardless of what happens tonight, I must read this book. I would be very interested to know my feelings about dating women.

I immediately go to Amazon.com and order it.

I think I now know more about Internet dating than I want to know. I hope Joy hasn't seen this article. Why would she come?

— • —

It is very easy to get from the house on Clark Avenue to the wine bar downtown. After backing out of the driveway, I head east on Clark down to Sixth Avenue W., make a right turn, then an immediate right on Yellowstone Avenue, then a right on Seventh Street W., pass by Clark Avenue, and then make a right on Lewis Avenue.

I have driven in a circle, but I also have taken all right turns.

Lewis rides down through the tree-lined neighborhoods of central Billings, crosses Division Street and becomes Fourth Avenue N. downtown. At the corner of Fourth and Broadway,

I can see the big *Billings Herald-Gleaner* building, where people are inside compiling the things I'll need tomorrow, including my weather data and Dear Abby.

I turn right on Broadway, cross over Third and Second Avenues, and pull into a diagonal parking spot across from the wine bar.

As I shut off the ignition, the digital clock in my Toyota Camry flips over to 7:00 p.m.

— • —

Bin 119 is impressive, and busy.

Joy does not seem to be here yet.

I find an open table at the far end of the place, and I sit down facing the door, so I can see her when she comes in.

It's a very nice table—very modern, with leather-bound seats. I like it. The soft lighting and dark-wood decor remind me of Dr. Buckley's office, and I like that, too.

I look at my watch. It's 7:03.

I may have to prepare myself for the possibility that Joy is not as punctual as I am. If I work hard at it, I'm sure I can do this. Dr. Buckley says that all people have things they are good at and not so good at and that if I like someone, I should appreciate his or her good points and forgive the bad. This makes sense to me. Dr. Buckley is a very logical woman.

At 7:05, a server comes by and asks if I would like a menu or to order a drink. I tell her that I'm expecting someone and will wait, thank you.

Five minutes isn't too late, right? That can be the difference between a well-set clock and a haphazardly set one. While I don't understand why anyone would want a clock that doesn't tell exactly the correct time, I know that some people don't give such things a lot of thought. Maybe Joy is one of those people.

I read somewhere that giving someone fifteen minutes of leeway on an appointment is the polite thing to do, and so I resolve that I will give Joy until 7:15 before I start to become annoyed at her.

On the other hand, I remember that when Jimmy Johnson was the coach of the Dallas Cowboys, he considered a player late to a team meeting if that player wasn't in the room five minutes early, and he would dock the player's pay. Jimmy Johnson would not tolerate someone's being fifteen minutes late, and he won two Super Bowls. Clearly, there is politeness, and then there is what works.

At 7:11, the server asks again if I want something to drink. I decline. Also, I am annoyed. I can't help it.

At 7:13, I see Joy at the door. She looks just like her picture—striking. She's tall, too, maybe close to six feet tall. I like that. She is wearing a white dress with big brown-and-blue swirlies—paisleys, I think they are called—that comes down to about the middle of her calves. She looks very nice.

I start to raise my hand to flag her down, but she sees me first and smiles.

She's walking back here toward the table.

Holy shit!

"Edward, I'm so happy to meet you," she says, offering a handshake as she sits down.

I accept and try to remember to shake firmly.

"Have you been waiting long?"

I look down at my watch: 7:13:57…7:13:58…7:13:59…

"Fourteen minutes. We were supposed to meet at seven, correct?"

"Yes. I am so sorry. I left Broadview early so I could get here in plenty of time, and then there was a big wreck on Highway

3—a really bad one—and that slowed me down, and then when I got down here, I had a really hard time finding a place to park. It's busy here on a Friday night."

"I parked right across the street."

"Oh?"

"Yes."

"Well, Edward, I'm glad I'm here now." She looks me over. "I like your suit."

"Yes."

I reach down on the bench seat beside me and pick up the rose, which I've been hiding. I set it on the table across from Joy. "This is for you," I say.

She picks it up. "Thank you so much. It's beautiful. You're so sweet."

The server comes by again to drop off menus and take our drink order. Joy orders a Gewurztraminer, which appears to be some sort of wine. I order a glass of water. I've never had wine, and I don't drink alcohol. Or, at least, I haven't.

"You're not having wine?"

"No."

"I love Gewurztraminer. I like sweeter wines—Rieslings and chardonnays. Not so much red wines. Are you sure you don't want to try it?"

"I'll try it, I guess." When the server walks by, I ask her to bring me a glass of Gewurztraminer. Even if I don't end up liking the wine, I sure like the word.

"We didn't really talk about eating, but this menu looks yummy," Joy says. "Would you like to have something to eat?"

"Yes."

When the server comes back with the Gewurztraminers and the water, she asks us if we would like something to eat. Joy orders the lobster mac 'n' cheese. I order a Caesar salad with grilled chicken.

"A salad?" Joy says. "You're going to make me look like a pig for ordering a big, hot meal."

"I'm interested to see your mac 'n' cheese. I can't decide if it sounds good."

"I've heard that it's fantastic. Would you like a bite when it comes?"

"No. I couldn't do that."

— • —

Over dinner, Joy asks me a few questions but mostly talks about herself. She is surprised when she asks what I do for a living and I say "nothing." I then tell her that I'm living on my investments, which is a little white lie. I'm living on my father's investments.

She launches into a story about growing up on a farm outside Broadview and how her parents were mean to her and her and brothers and how eventually she ended up living in town with her aunt and uncle, who were very nice people and—

The Gewurztraminer makes me belch. It's not loud, but it interrupts her story.

"I burped," I say.

"Yes, well," Joy says, looking momentarily annoyed, and then she's off and talking again. I like listening to her. Her story doesn't have a lot of structure—she jumps around a lot in time and place and goes on little side stories called tangents—but she is so demonstrative in telling the story that I just shovel salad into my mouth and listen.

"Edward, I'm sorry, I'm dominating the conversation," she says. "I'd like to hear what you think of all this."

"I think it's nice that your aunt and uncle took care of you."

"No, I mean about this," she says, waving her right hand in a parabola over the table.

"It's good food."

"No, about us, about being here," she says. "Were you nervous? I was."

I think about her question for a few seconds before answering.

"I guess I was a little nervous. I woke up really early this morning, at five fifty-seven. I usually wake up at one of four times—seven thirty-seven, seven thirty-eight, seven thirty-nine, or seven forty—but today I woke up at five fifty-seven thinking about tonight."

"What were you thinking about?"

"I was wondering if we were going to have sex."

"What?"

"I wasn't planning on it, but I wondered what would happen if we did."

Joy looks cross. "We are not having sex."

"I know. That's what I decided, too."

"Well, I'm glad."

"I just don't see how it could happen. I would miss *Dragnet*."

"That's not the only reason it's not going to happen. And listen, I read up on *Dragnet*. Why do you keep talking about a forty-year-old TV show?"

"I always watch *Dragnet*, every night at ten."

I look down at my watch. It's 8:04.

"I'm very uncomfortable with this conversation," Joy says.

"I'm sorry."

"I can't believe you brought up sex. That's really out of line."

"I was just being honest about what I was thinking of, because you asked me."

"I don't know. I'm really uncomfortable. I think I'm going to go."

Joy flags down the server and asks for a box for her lobster mac 'n' cheese and for separate checks. When they arrive, she puts cash on the table to cover her check, and then she stands up.

"Well, it's a long drive back to Broadview," she says. "I'll talk to you soon." And she pivots and walks out.

I reach into the breast pocket of my suit jacket to fish out my wallet, and I realize that I never gave her the mix CD.

— • —

By the time I get home, I have replayed the whole scene in my head, and I am frantic. Joy thought I wanted to have sex with her, and she wigged out. I didn't want to have sex with her. I told her that. She didn't understand what I was saying.

And then there was that last line: "I'll talk to you soon."

She's just not that into me.

— • —

I make a bold decision: I am not going to watch *Dragnet* tonight. I don't have the energy for it.

It's too bad, too, because the fourth episode of the first season, "The Interrogation," is not just one of my favorites, it is my favorite. Kent McCord plays a rookie cop named Paul Culver who is mistaken for a liquor store robber while on undercover duty, and Sergeant Joe Friday and Officer Bill Gannon, now working in internal affairs, try to wring the truth out of him: Did he rob that liquor store or not?

In this episode, which originally aired on February 9, 1967, Sergeant Joe Friday gives a speech that I think should be printed out and passed out to anyone who wants to be a policeman. It goes on for several minutes, and it never gets boring. Paul Culver sits rapt (I love the word "rapt") as Sergeant Joe Friday tells him that being a cop is hard work, that people don't treat cops very well, that he will never make very much money, that his uniform will get torn up by bad guys, and that he will write as many words in his career as there are in a library. He tells Paul Culver that he will see things that break his heart and that bad people will try to do bad things to him.

None of it sounds very appealing, but Sergeant Joe Friday says he is proud to be a cop, and in the end, Paul Culver is proud to be a cop, too. Sergeant Joe Friday convinced him that he ought to stick with it, even though Culver got agitated when he was falsely accused of a crime.

Sergeant Joe Friday always says exactly what he wants to say. I wish I were he tonight.

— • —

I also take a pass on writing my letter of complaint. I don't know who the target should be.

Is it I for chasing Joy away? Is it the vintner of the Gewurztraminer for making me burp? Is it Joy for showing up late and overreacting? Is it I for thinking that she overreacted?

I lack the clarity for a letter of complaint.

Internet dating has wrecked all of the things that I rely on.

SATURDAY, OCTOBER 25

Here are today's numbers:
  Woke up: 7:37 (seventeenth time this year out of 299 days, because it's a leap year).
  Yesterday's high temperature: forty-four degrees.
  Yesterday's low temperature: twenty-four degrees.
  Today's forecasted high temperature: forty-eight degrees.
  But forecasts, as you know by now, are notoriously off base. I shall wait for the facts, which I prefer.
  Here's a fact: I hate online dating.

— • —

After breakfast, I log on to Montana Personal Connect one last time to wipe out my account, and I see this:
  Inbox (1).
  I click the link.

  Edward:

  I wanted you to know that I am not feeling "the click" factor with you. I dont really know how to explain it but I feel as though we would not be compatable because I felt at Bin 119 that you were not interested in learning anything about me. When I was telling you about my uncle adopting me you said "I burped" and then didn't follow up on anything about what I was saying regarding just getting to know me. I guess I feel shut down with you and I dont enjoy feeling that way. I am not saying I wouldn't want to be friends but I dont want to date. Its a different level and I dont feel it with you.

I can't really put my finger on it and this is just a lame example of what I am trying to say but I am a very intuitive, sensitive (clearly), sensual and "musical" kind of person and you are more a "TV guy" and not as much of those things...and I have met men who are and I am looking more for that because around gardeners I open up and blossom and that's how I like to experience life.

When you brought up sex, that freaked me out also but Im willing to give you the benefit of the doubt that your nervous about meeting. I was too.

Anyway those are my thoughts and I share them with you with respect and I hope you will understand that this is a gift, to share anything is a gift...and my hope is you will treat it as such. But thats up to you.

I just don't see us being more than friends and since we live so far apart I dont see that either.

Sorry.

Joy

I don't keep records on such things, but surely 9:12 a.m. is the earliest I've ever written a letter of complaint. I prepare a new green office folder, put a tab titled "Joy" on it, and sit down at the computer to type.

Joy:

Thank you for your e-mail of the twenty-fifth. Please allow me to retort.
First, I don't know what "the click" factor is.
Second, I burped because of the wine, which I'd never had before and you were insistent that I try.
Third, you spelled "compatible" wrong.
Fourth, you need to learn how to use apostrophes correctly and consistently.
Fifth, I was listening to your story.
Sixth, I don't know what a "TV guy" is.
Seventh, your note doesn't feel much like a gift.
Eighth, why say you don't see us being more than friends and then say you don't see that, either? It makes no sense.

Regards,
Edward Stanton

I print out the letter and file it away, then come back to the computer, pull up Montana Personal Connect again and see this: Inbox (1).

Edward:

I had high hopes for this. I really did. Dating men in Broadview is so hard because there are only a limited number of cool places to go here and I always run into

*someone. I am an extremely private person and so I gen-
erally like not being around town and the rumor mill.
Also I meant to tell you this last night but didn't and
I feel I should now: my first name is actually Annette.
I didn't want to have my real name for my e-mail so I
created this account with my middle name. I figure that
anyone reasonable will understand and believe me it has
kept me safe.*

Annette

I go back to my files, pull Joy's folder, take out the tab, and
add this to the "Joy" that's already there: "aka, Annette."
Then it's back to the computer for another letter.

Annette:

*I am flabbergasted by this latest revelation. I was
honest about my name. Why couldn't you do the same?
Frankly, I find that our correspondence has taken an ugly
turn. Please refrain from contacting me further.*

Regards,
Edward Stanton

I file the second letter, then put the green office folder back in
the filing cabinet and return to the computer.
Inbox (1).
Holy shit!

Edward:

The guy Ive been writing to didn't show up last night. All in all, you seemed like a nice guy but not easy to talk to in person...for whatever reason. I don't like having to work this hard at something. Im sorry if my perceptions sting and they may be inaccurate as hell, I'll give you that.

I don't have it in me to wait for you to show up... and that you never commented or supported me on anything that I said about my life was very revealing that you thought you were the only one nervous or needing to feel put at ease. I gave you that, you didn't. It made me sad and angry a bit because I thought more of you.

Annette

I retrieve the green office folder yet again.

Annette:

I do not know why you insist on continuing to write to me. Your complaints are heading into bizarre territory now. Dr. Buckley says that when I start to feel overwhelmed or out of control, I should take a deep breath and focus on a path out of the chaos. I rather think you should take that advice now.

Regards,
Edward Stanton

Annette, or Joy, or whoever she is, writes three more times, and my green office folder begins to fill up.

Edward:

I was going to write and see if we could work something out but I think that it is better to let it go. I think that at this point, any making up would just lead to more of the same kind of misunderstanding and "drama." I think your substantial, kind-hearted, sweet, beautiful in your own way, and so much more you will never know. But I cant go into something this emotional. My last boyfriend, whom I dearly loved and completely supported through so much stuff, took it and then he slammed another girl just a few short months ago. Therefore, I am looking for a less dramatic deal right now.

Annette

Annette:

My head is swimming. You're looking for a less dramatic deal? Somehow, I find that hard to believe.

Regards,
Edward Stanton

Edward:

I wish you would write back. I need to know what your thinking about all of this. Maybe there's a way we could start over. I don't know. Write me back and lets talk about it.

Annette

Annette:

*I think it's funny—not funny "ha-ha," but just funny—
that I'm the one with a mental illness.*

Regards,
Edward Stanton

Edward:

*Your an asshole. I pour out my heart to you and you
say nothing. Good-bye, looser.*

Annette

Annette:

Good-bye. And it's "loser."

Regards,
Edward Stanton

I put the green office folder called "Joy—aka, Annette"
away for the last time. It's nearly noon, and I'm headed back
to bed.

— • —

I stir at 6:03 p.m. and pad into the kitchen for dinner. In addition
to all the other ways in which this thing with Joy-Annette went
sideways, my meal schedule is fouled up. I didn't have lunch, and
now it's dinnertime. Consequently, I will have one extra meal in
the house when I return to the grocery store next week. These are
complications I do not need.

I cook my Banquet fried chicken dinner in the microwave and try to, as Dr. Buckley says, find a route back to normalcy.

I can't see that road.

— • —

At 10:00, I play tonight's episode of *Dragnet*.

I am irritated that I have missed the fourth episode of the first season, "The Interrogation," as it is my favorite of all ninety-eight color episodes. But I decide that sticking to my schedule is more important than making up the lost ground. As it turns out, I will see "The Interrogation" again on January 4, 2009, as I reset from the beginning of these series on the first day of every year. That is not so far away now.

The fifth episode of the first season is called "The Masked Bandits," and it is one of my favorites. It originally aired on February 16, 1967, and involves a gang of young punks who wear red masks and hold up cocktail lounges.

One of the punks is a seventeen-year-old kid named Larry Hubbert (played by Ron Russell, in his only *Dragnet* appearance). Larry is married to an older woman named Edna (played by Virginia Vincent, who made six *Dragnet* appearances). Edna took Larry in when his parents left town, and she wants what is best for him, even though he wants to rob cocktail joints.

At one point in the episode, Edna tells Sergeant Joe Friday that she's as entitled to love as anybody is. Sergeant Joe Friday doesn't disagree.

I don't, either, but I have news for Edna Hubbert: love isn't easy to find.

SUNDAY, OCTOBER 26

Do you know that gauzy feeling that comes from having not too little sleep but too much? Everything seems a little fuzzy, there is a faint headache, and things seem to move in slow motion but still too fast. That's how I feel today at 7:37 a.m., when I wake up. It's the eighteenth time in 300 days this year (because it's a leap year) and the second morning in a row for that time. Of the range of my four most common wake-up times—7:37, 7:38, 7:39, and 7:40—7:37 is the least frequent of the bunch. Maybe 7:37 is staging a rally.

I record my waking time, and my data is complete.

— • —

I'm still agitated and flummoxed by Joy-Annette's behavior yesterday. She seemed nice in our initial e-mails, if a bit sloppy and unfamiliar with proper punctuation. She even seemed nice at our abbreviated dinner, until the misunderstanding about sex. When she left so abruptly, I thought that it was my fault, even though she had asked me what I was nervous about and I answered her honestly, which I thought is what I should do.

But yesterday, she was not nice. I will tell Dr. Buckley about it, and I will bet that she will agree with my assessment. After yesterday, I am no longer even sure that it was my fault that our dinner ended so quickly. Joy-Annette's messages to me were erratic. First, she said that I was selfish when I burped. Then she said I wasn't supportive. Then she said she can't invest in something so emotional. Then she said maybe if I wrote back, we could try again. Then she called me an asshole.

That hurt my feelings.

Now I'm quite sure that I don't know what Joy-Annette wants, and I wonder if it's a woman thing or just a Joy-Annette thing. Dr. Buckley is a woman, and I don't think she would treat someone this way. It must be a Joy-Annette thing.

As I'm considering all of this, I find that my thoughts are drifting back to something that happened a long time ago.

When I was at Billings West High School—class of 1987—I didn't have many friends. I didn't have any friends, unless you count Mr. Withers, but he was a teacher. I kept to myself and did well in most of my classes, though I liked wood shop the best, partly because of Mr. Withers and partly because I was exceptional at it. "Exceptional" is Mr. Withers's word. I love that word.

One day during my junior year, a really pretty girl in my English class, Lisa Edgington, started talking to me. I didn't really know what to say back. She asked me if I thought she was pretty, and I said that I did. That kind of embarrassed me. She told me that she thought I was cute, and that really embarrassed me.

She told me that she wanted me to meet her after school, over near the football field. I said that I would.

A few hours later, I was at the football field. She was there, too. She asked me if I wanted to kiss her. I felt blood rush to my face, and I asked her not to tease me. She said, "No, really, do you want to kiss me?" I said I did. And she let me. Then I heard laughing. A bunch of kids from school were under the bleachers, pointing at us.

"Let's get out of here," Lisa Edgington said to them, and she ran off with them, laughing. They went to the parking lot and climbed into a car and left.

The next day at school, a lot of people were pointing and laughing at me. When I passed by her locker, Lisa Edgington wouldn't even look at me. In English class, she didn't talk to me.

The laughing went on for a week, at least. Lisa Edgington's silence went on longer than that, until graduation, and then I never saw her again. One day, a boy asked me in wood shop, "Hey, Edward, are you going to hump Lisa Edgington?" Mr. Withers overheard it and pulled that boy into his office and yelled at him. That boy came back to his seat red faced, and he never said another word to me.

Is Joy-Annette like Lisa Edgington, only grown up?

I don't know.

— • —

Joy-Annette has said good-bye, and I have written her my last letter of complaint and filed away the green office folder with her name on it, and yet she continues to affect me. I am not happy about this.

Today, for example, the Dallas Cowboys are playing against the Tampa Bay Buccaneers, and it is almost game time before I remember to pull on my authentic white Tony Romo Dallas Cowboys jersey. I like the white jersey better than the blue one, but whatever jersey the Dallas Cowboys are wearing on a given Sunday is the one I choose.

Tony Romo is still hurt by a broken pinkie finger, and I am dubious about the Dallas Cowboys' chances without him, given what I have seen so far from his backup, Brad Johnson. The Tampa Bay Buccaneers are a good team. The Dallas Cowboys are supposed to be a good team, but I just don't know if that's true unless Tony Romo is playing.

— • —

A few hours later, I have an odd sensation: The Cowboys won 13–9, but I have no joy about it. The Cowboys have won 298 times in the regular season since the first game I remember, that 1974 Thanksgiving game in which Clint Longley rescued the team after Roger Staubach got hurt, and I've been happy every single time. Today, I'm glad they won, but I'm not happy. I'm not sad, the way I would be if the Dallas Cowboys had added to their 210 regular-season losses since Thanksgiving 1974, but I'm definitely not happy.

First, it was a terrible game. The Dallas Cowboys gained only 172 yards of offense, and I heard the announcer say that was the fewest yards Dallas had ever accumulated in a victory. Tony Romo accounts for way more than 172 yards a game all by himself.

Second, Brad Johnson, again, did not look good. To his credit, he did not throw any interceptions, but he also seemed unable to pass the ball very far down the field. As it will be at least a couple of more weeks before Tony Romo is back, I cannot be confident that the Dallas Cowboys will be able to win like this again without him.

It seems that the only reason the Dallas Cowboys won is that the Tampa Bay Buccaneers apparently have just as many problems as the Cowboys do, and I also heard the announcer say this.

Tampa Bay kept driving down deep into the Dallas Cowboys' end of the field but came away with just three field goals. It's hard to win that way, harder even than winning with only 172 yards of offense.

— • —

I skip lunch, putting me two meals behind my weekly plan. I find it difficult to care about this anymore.

Here's what I don't get about Joy-Annette: What did she expect when she wrote that first note to me yesterday? I don't know. Dr. Buckley and I have talked about my tendency to get defensive when I am challenged by someone, especially my father, and as I go and dig out my first letter in response to her, I see that I was defensive. But isn't defense what is called for when someone is making accusations against you? Further, I did not send a response to Joy-Annette, so she did not know that I had become defensive. Her increasingly erratic notes to me just got angrier, until she called me an "asshole" and a "looser." That was an uncalled-for personal attack.

I will take this up with Dr. Buckley on Tuesday. I wish I didn't have to wait.

— • —

That sensation that I felt after I woke up, I just remembered what it's called: lethargy. I love the word "lethargy," but I hate the feeling.

That's not true. Hate is an intense, burning, blinding dislike. I think it is reckless to use words in an imprecise way, the way Joy-Annette uses them. I don't hate lethargy. I just would prefer to not experience it.

I pull out my tattered copy of *Roget's Thesaurus*. I'm curious if I might at least have the opportunity to expand my vocabulary in the wake of this regrettable interaction with Joy-Annette.

Under "lethargy," I find the word "torpor." I look up that word, and I see it described as "a deficiency in mental and physical alertness and activity," and I realize that this definition is exactly what I feel today. Just above "torpor" is the word "torpidness," which is the state of being in torpor.

I have two excellent new words and decide that I should be thankful for that, even if I am still flummoxed by Joy-Annette.

— • —

At 6:04 p.m., I hear a knock at the front door. A peep through the spyglass shows that it is Donna Middleton.

I open the door.

"Hi, Edward."

"Hi, Donna."

"Haven't seen you outside much lately."

"Yeah. It's torpor."

"What's that?"

"A deficiency in mental and physical alertness and activity. I'm in a state of torpidness."

"I've never heard it described in quite that way."

"Yes."

Donna Middleton looks down, then back up at me. "Listen, Edward, I just got off work and have to go pick Kyle up at my folks' house, but I wanted to ask a favor."

"Yes."

"Do you remember how I told you that Mike has a court appearance tomorrow?"

"Yes."

"I was wondering if you'd consider coming with me."

"To court?"

"Yes."

Before I can answer, she's talking again. "Look, I really feel bad asking you, but I don't know where else to go. I'd like to keep my parents away from it—they mean well, but there's just too much hassle. They worry about Kyle and they worry about me, and I can't deal with all those questions and judgments right now. But I also don't want to go alone. So even though it's asking a lot, and you'd be well within your rights to say no, I'm asking: Will you go to court with me?"

My mind flashes on the dream of Mike swinging a baseball bat at my head, but I beat back that thought. They won't let Mike have a baseball bat in the courtroom. That would be against protocol.

"I'll go. I used to work there."

"At the courthouse?"

"Yes. In the clerk of court's office."

"That's great. You'll go?"

"Yes."

"Thank you so much, Edward. I appreciate this more than I can say. The hearing is at nine thirty in the morning. Why don't you come over around nine and we'll go?"

"No, you come over here. I have to drive."

— • —

Tonight's episode of *Dragnet*, the sixth of the first season of color episodes, is called "The Bank Examiner Swindle," and it's one of my favorites.

In "The Bank Examiner Swindle," which originally aired on February 23, 1967, Sergeant Joe Friday and Officer Bill Gannon are called in to investigate a series of scams in which elderly people are approached by two men pretending to be bank examiners who say that they're trying to catch thieving tellers. The fake examiners ask the old people to withdraw their money from the bank and give it to them, and they say that they will mark the bills, redeposit them, and then find out which tellers are lifting those bills. As you've probably surmised, the fake examiners don't do that. They just take the money.

Sergeant Joe Friday and Officer Bill Gannon end up running a ruse. Officer Bill Gannon poses as the son of an elderly woman who is targeted by the phony bank examiners, and he gives the men the money. Sergeant Joe Friday then busts in from the kitchen with a gun and puts them under arrest.

Sergeant Joe Friday always gets his man. He also would never be thrown off by the smooth talking of a con man. Not for the first time, I wish I were a lot more like Sergeant Joe Friday and a lot less like I really am.

— • —

After *Dragnet*, I prepare a new green office folder for my files.

Dr. Neil Clark Warren:

I have an issue to take up with you, sir. Your ubiquitous advertising of eHarmony fails to come clean on two points:

First, you can't find matches for everyone. You certainly could not for me, and thus I ended up having to pursue online dating through Montana Personal Connect.

Second, you portray online dating as a wonderland in which happy couples come together as soul mates who have every little thing in common. You ascribe this to your twenty-nine levels of compatibility, but I must say, sir, that I ascribe it to your living in a fantasy world.

I did not find a soul mate. On your site, I found nothing. On Montana Personal Connect, I found an erratic woman who was progressively hostile toward me, culminating in her calling me an "asshole" and a "looser." Her poor spelling skills aside, I found those comments to be demeaning and hurtful.

In short, my online dating experience was not enjoyable. Had I never seen your ads, I might not have been prompted to try online dating. I can safely say that had I not tried online dating, I would not be in the torpor that I'm currently experiencing.

I ask you to reconsider your advertising campaign and choose an approach that is more honest about what online dating is really like. I would think that a clinical psychologist of thirty-five years, as you profess to be on your website, would be interested in honesty above all. I know that my own psychologist, Dr. Buckley, values truth and honesty. I trust her. You, I don't trust.

Regards,
Edward Stanton

MONDAY, OCTOBER 27

Donna's knock on the front door comes promptly at 9:00 a.m. I'm impressed by her punctuality. I've been up since 7:38 a.m., eating my breakfast of corn flakes, taking my eighty milligrams of fluoxetine, reading the *Billings Herald-Gleaner*, and canceling my membership to Montana Personal Connect, which I had neglected to do in the flurry of messages from Joy-Annette on Saturday. I had been skittish about logging on, for fear of finding yet another message from Joy-Annette, but there was none.

I answer the door and see Donna Middleton standing there, looking more formal than I've ever seen her. She's in a pair of brown slacks, a blue knit two-piece top, a long leather coat, and dress shoes (flats, I think they are called). Her dark-brown hair is swept back in a ponytail, and her face is made up. She looks very pretty.

"Hello," I say.

"Hi, Edward. Are you ready to go?"

"I am. My data is complete."

— • —

On the short drive downtown, Donna Middleton is silent. I am not supposed to take my eyes off the road, but I can see that she is gripping both hands, making her knuckles look like small white rocks popping through her skin.

"Are you nervous?" I ask.

"No," she says. "Determined."

We're driving along Lewis Avenue, past bungalows and churches. Although this is one of Billings's well-traveled secondary thoroughfares, it's mostly quiet at this hour. Children have headed off to school. Those who work nine-to-five jobs are already at them. We see a few walkers and a few elderly drivers. Other than that, Lewis is ours.

"What's happening today, the arraignment?" I ask.

"Yes."

"It should be a short appearance. Arraignments usually are."

"I hope so."

"A lot of times, victims don't attend arraignments." I don't know if Donna Middleton is looking for a way out of this trip to court, but if she needs one, I want to provide it.

"I'm going to be there," she says, "every time he is."

— • —

The Yellowstone County Courthouse is one of the distinctive buildings in the Billings skyline. To be fair to other skylines, Billings's isn't that impressive. Despite its prodigious growth over the past decade or so, Billings remains in many ways the small cow town that it started as in 1882.

The courthouse is an eight-story granite building, and it sits on the southeast corner of Third Avenue N. and North Twenty-

Seventh Street. Among downtown buildings, I would say that only the Crowne Plaza Hotel, the Wells Fargo building (which is next door to the courthouse), and the First Interstate Bank building rival the courthouse in terms of distinctiveness. When I worked at the courthouse, I was proud to come to work every day at so important a building.

We park in the garage attached to the Wells Fargo building, then walk across Second Avenue N. to the courthouse.

Donna tells me that the hearing will be in Department 1. That's Judge Alan Robeson's courtroom, I tell her.

"Is that good?" she asks.

"That's very good. Judge Robeson is a wise, logical person."

"Good."

We ride the elevator up to the fifth floor, where Judge Robeson's courtroom is (Room 506, technically).

It's 9:21 a.m. It won't be long now.

— • —

For first court appearances, those who are charged with crimes generally don't show up in person. It's often done by video from the county jail. For arraignments, however, where formal charges are presented and bond is haggled out by the prosecutor and defense attorney, the accused often does show up.

The district courts in Yellowstone County are austere places. (I love the word "austere.") The furniture dates from the 1960s and is built for function, not style. The gallery, of which we're a part, sits on five rows of benches that look like church pews. The rows are divided by an aisle down the middle that leads to the lectern in front of the judge. When we came in, Donna chose a spot in the front row of the gallery.

There are two tables, one for the defense and the other for the prosecutor. The judge sits on an elevated stand called a dais, flanked by the witness stand and a court reporter. The jury box today is full of inmates wearing the distinctive orange jumpsuit of the county jail. Their hands are shackled in front of them, connected to a waist chain. Their feet are shackled, too. Mike is one of them, and he stares at Donna Middleton in her seat and at me next to her. I look away and focus on the symbols behind Judge Robeson's bench—the Montana and US flags and the state of Montana seal directly behind him. Donna, I hope, is also looking away.

Criminal hearings are a cattle call of arraignments, changes of pleas, violations of parole, and the like. The judges work through the caseload deliberately but quickly, handling upward of twenty cases in a couple of hours, and sometimes faster.

Mike's case is the fourteenth of the seventeen that Judge Robeson is dealing with today. When the case comes up, Mike is led from the jury box by two armed guards. As he shuffles to the lectern, he fixes a gaze on Donna, and she reaches down and grabs my hand and squeezes. It hurts. I glance at her and see that she is returning Mike's withering stare.

The hearing is as I told Donna that it would be.

First, the prosecution requests that the charges—violation of a restraining order and a felony charge of assault—be served. This is called "requesting leave to file." Judge Robeson waves his hand, and the prosecutor steps up to Mike and his defender and hands them the charging document.

The defense attorney, Sean Lambert, says, "We'll waive a reading, Your Honor."

Judge Robeson peers down over the top of his glasses at Mike. "Do you understand the charges, Mr. Simpson?"

"Yeah," Mike says.

"That's 'Yes, Your Honor,'" Judge Robeson corrects him.

"Yes, Your Honor."

"And your plea to the first charge, violation of a protective order?"

"Not guilty, Your Honor."

"And your plea to the second charge, felony assault?"

"Not guilty, Your Honor."

Now begins the haggling over bail. The prosecutor—I don't recognize him—says, "The people are seeking bail in the amount of twenty-five thousand dollars, Your Honor Mr. Simpson blatantly disregarded a restraining order against him, appeared at the complainant's home, engaged her in an argument that became physical, and choked her. We feel that the gravity of the situation and Mr. Simpson's clear disregard for a legal order of restraint merit this bond."

Donna Middleton is again gripping my hand.

"And you, Mr. Lambert?" Judge Robeson says, gesturing at the defense attorney, Sean Lambert.

"A few points, Your Honor," Sean Lambert says. "Mr. Simpson is not a flight risk. He is a small-business owner, the operator and sole employee of a growing concern. He has no prior criminal record. He looks forward to a swift adjudication of this case. He is eager to get back to work and get his affairs in order before trial. He has no intention of sullying the process, but twenty-five thousand dollars is too steep. We ask for a five-thousand-dollar bond."

Donna Middleton tightens her grip beyond what I thought possible, and my hand begins to hurt.

"Mr. Lambert, I'm not interested in helping your client get his affairs in order," Judge Robeson says. "In the view of this court and this community, restraining orders are legal documents to be honored, not suggestions that can be disregarded on a whim. Perhaps Mr. Simpson should have thought of that before landing in this mess. Bond is set at twenty thousand dollars. We'll be back here in two weeks to set a trial date and to sort out any motions by counsel. Next case."

Judge Robeson bangs his gavel.

Donna Middleton loosens her grip.

"Is that it?" she asks.

"That's it."

"Why only felony assault? I thought he was going to kill me."

"It's a balancing act. In the time I worked here, I saw only a few attempted-murder cases. Intent is difficult to prove. The prosecutor picked the charge that he thinks he can win, if the case goes to trial."

"What do you mean, *if*?"

"Often, there will be a—" My words fall off a cliff as I see Mike Simpson lunging at Donna as he's being led away.

"That your new man, bitch?" he snarls as Donna drops to the floor, screaming. "I'll fucking kill you both. You're dead."

Donna is on her back, her feet pushing at the floor in an attempt to scramble away from Mike. She's screaming and crying and slamming backward into the rows of seats, then dropping down and shimmying beneath them. The two sheriff's deputies tackle Mike, working him down to the floor in front of me. At one point, he cranes his neck out of the scrum, his veins bulging, his face red, and he looks straight at me, gasping, "You're dead."

Judge Robeson is standing up and banging away with his gavel. "No bail! Denied!" Judge Robeson yells. "Get him out of here."

As quickly as it all unfolded, the chaos is over. Deputies subdue Mike Simpson, and then they pull him to his feet and whisk him out of a side door in the courtroom, where he will be taken by a secure elevator downstairs and back to jail. The room is now full of wide eyes and open mouths and the whimpering cries of Donna Middleton, who is balled up in the corner.

— • —

Downstairs, on the first floor of the courthouse, I sit on a wooden bench and wait for Donna to emerge from the restroom. She has been in there a long time. For a while, it looked like she might not leave the corner she wedged herself into upstairs. Finally, the sheriff's deputies coaxed her to her feet and led her down here, where I wait.

"Hi, Edward."

I'm startled by the voice. I look up and see Lloyd Graeve, one of my former coworkers in the clerk of court's office. Though it has been several years since I have seen him, Lloyd looks the same to me: a head of floppy black hair, wire-rim glasses, a friendly grin. He has been with the clerk's office for years and does an excellent job.

"Hi, Lloyd."

"I saw you up there in Robeson's courtroom. Hell of a scene, huh?" Lloyd would have been seated at the spot reserved for clerks; I had not spotted him earlier.

"Hell of a scene," I agree.

"What are you doing here? I haven't seen you since...well, since...you know."

"That guy, the one who caused the commotion, he attacked my neighbor."

"You're here with her?"

"Yes."

"Why?"

"I saw it. I called the cops. She asked me to be here."

"Wow."

"Yes."

"You're probably going to have to be a witness at the trial, if there is one."

I hadn't thought of that until now. And yet I know that there's no way the prosecutor won't talk to an eyewitness to the attack.

"Yes."

"So maybe I'll see you again, eh?"

"Maybe."

Lloyd lingers silently for a few seconds, and then he says, "We miss you around here, Edward."

"You do?"

"You were good at the work. We could use that right now."

"I couldn't work here."

Lloyd laughs. "Yeah, I know what you mean. A certain boss hasn't gotten any better at the job since you left. But, hey, there's an election in a few days. There's always hope."

"Well, good luck, then."

"Take care, Edward."

— • —

When Donna emerges from the restroom, I can see that she has made a brave attempt at pulling herself together. She no longer looks disheveled, and her hair is brushed. But the makeup stains and her still-trembling bottom lip betray what she has been through.

"Are you OK?" I ask.

"Can you just hold my arm and get me out of here?" Donna says, limply offering up her right forearm, which I gently take in my left hand. I then guide her toward the door that will lead us out onto North Twenty-Seventh Street.

A few minutes later, as we're riding the elevator to the floor I parked on, Donna says, so faintly that I can barely hear her, "This is going to be harder than I thought."

From the parking garage, I can see that it's raining. The forecast didn't say anything about this. I never know what's coming anymore, it seems. That's a bad thing when you prefer facts.

— • —

We arrive back at the house at 11:53 a.m. It has been a silent drive. Donna stared straight ahead, and so did I. My job was easy: see the road and drive the car home. Hers is much harder. I don't know if she knows where the road is or where it leads.

"Edward," she says, as I set the parking brake, "would it be OK if I stayed here until Kyle comes home?"

"Yes. I could make some lunch."

"I don't think I can eat. I just don't want to be alone."

"OK."

"Edward, if I'd had any idea that was going to happen, I wouldn't have asked you to come."

"It's OK."

"But I'm so glad you did."

She's crying again, but not too much. Donna Middleton is tough. Tougher than Mike Simpson, that's for sure.

— • —

Inside, Donna urges me to go ahead and make lunch, which I do. Today is a spaghetti day.

As I'm stirring the meat sauce and waiting for the noodles to soften, Donna leaves the couch and comes into the kitchen.

"What did you mean when you said *if* Mike's case goes to trial?"

In my time in the clerk of court's office, I saw it again and again. Even in criminal cases like the one Mike is involved in, prosecutors and defense attorneys will meet and come up with a plea agreement. Sometimes, it's because the prosecutors have a sure case and can get what they want without going to trial. Sometimes, it's the opposite way, and the defense uses its leverage to force a deal out of the prosecutor.

"The goal, for prosecutors and defense attorneys, is often to not have a trial."

"Why?"

"A jury trial is not a sure thing, for either side. Lawyers like sure things. I would not be surprised, given the facts in this case, if the prosecutors press for a plea agreement that ensures that Mike is punished without having to go to the time and expense of a jury trial. They have a real good case against him, especially after what happened today. They might not need a trial."

"But what if I want a jury trial?"

"You can tell the prosecutor that. They do listen and take those things into account."

"I want a jury to make him suffer."

"But what if a jury doesn't make him suffer? What if it lets him go free? The prosecutor will probably ask you to consider that."

Donna is silent. I go back to stirring the meat sauce.

"Are you wondering why I would have been with a guy like that?"

"No."

"You're not?"

"I figured you would tell me if you wanted." I have learned this from Dr. Buckley, who never pushes me to talk about something before I am ready.

"I'd like to. Do you have the time?"

"Yes."

Donna says she met Mike Simpson a little more than a year ago. He had been in the emergency room with a friend of his. They had been out riding motorcycles, and the friend crashed. It was pretty bad, from what Donna said—broken ribs and pelvis, bad scars from where his skin scraped along the road. Donna had attended to him, and Mike came around a few days later with some roses as a thank-you, and from there, it went.

"He was a really great guy, in the beginning," Donna says. "And he was good to Kyle. I waited a long time to let them meet. I'd made that mistake with other guys, and I wasn't going to this time."

"What changed?"

"Little things, at first. He would call me, a lot. At first, I thought he was being attentive. Later, I wondered if he was keeping tabs on me."

"Was he?"

"Yeah. He'd make little snide remarks about things, like he knew where I had been. He'd get insane if he saw me talking to another guy. Hello? I work in a hospital. There are a lot of guys there."

"Do you think that's why he got so angry with me?"

"Probably. He's very jealous."

"Are you scared?"

"I am, yes. Are you?"

"I would be if Judge Robeson hadn't revoked his bail."

"That's right," Donna says, her eyes suddenly brightening at the memory. "He isn't going anywhere."

I hold my right hand up, as I did several days ago for Kyle. Donna slaps it in high-five style.

— • —

Later, we're in the living room, she on the love seat and I on the couch, and Donna is telling me about her final days with Mike.

"I knew at the end of August I was going to leave. We'd had another fight, and they were growing more frequent now. As we were talking in the kitchen, Mike pulled out a pocketknife and started flicking it to the linoleum near my feet, making it stand up on the blade. He kept reaching down and grabbing it, then flicking it back."

I feel a tingle in my spine as I imagine that.

"Yeah," she says, apparently seeing my reaction. "It was spooky. He never made what I would call an overt threat. But he was definitely threatening.

"Anyway, after that, I started to lay the groundwork for my exit. I rented the house we're in now. I moved some money into my parents' bank account. I had a bag packed and hidden deep in my closet, ready to go in a moment when I was ready."

"I know he hit you."

She looks surprised. "You do?"

"Yes. Kyle told me."

"Oh."

She's silent again. "That was the worst," she says, finally, "that he punched me right there, right in front of Kyle. I think it shocked even Mike. I didn't say anything. I just walked into the bedroom, got the bag out of the closet, took Kyle by the hand and left. Mike didn't even chase after us."

"You did the right thing."

"I know."

At 2:18 p.m., for the first time since we left the Yellowstone County Courthouse, the steely resolve has returned to Donna Middleton's eyes.

— • —

At 2:51 p.m., Donna is looking expectantly out my front window for Kyle's arrival from school.

"So," I say, "I went on an online date last week."

Donna wheels around. "Really?"

"Yes."

"How was it?"

"Terrible."

"Why terrible?"

I tell her why. I even tell her about the Gewurztraminer burp and the preoccupation with the notion of first-date sex. I tell her about the bizarre series of e-mails from Joy-Annette and the return series of letters of complaint that are now in my files. She laughs at that. I'm not sure why it's funny, but I don't mind.

"Well, Edward, I'm sorry you had a bad online date. Women can be weird—weirder than men sometimes."

"What do you mean?"

"Well, take this Joy-Annette person. She pretty clearly enjoys creating drama."

Donna Middleton is a very logical woman.

"I think you're right," I say.

"I don't understand women like that," Donna says.

"Neither do I."

"Dating is hard, Edward. It's hard with the so-called traditional ways of meeting people, and it's hard on the Internet. Can you imagine being on a rocky seashore and looking at thousands of rocks in the hopes of finding one pearl?"

"Yes."

"That's what dating is."

"I don't think I want to do it anymore."

Donna laughs again. "You're not the first person to say that, and you won't be the last."

— • —

At 3:03 p.m., Donna spots Kyle trudging up the sidewalk toward their house.

"Edward, again, thanks so much," she says as she heads to the door.

"OK."

"I'll see you soon."

"OK."

And she's out the door, splashing across the rain-soaked street to see her son.

I don't keep data on such things, but it seems to me that every day Donna Middleton has been at this house, something extraordinary has happened.

— • —

Tonight's episode of *Dragnet*, the seventh of the first season of color episodes, is called "The Hammer," and it is one of my favorites.

In this one, which originally aired on March 2, 1967, Sergeant Joe Friday and Officer Bill Gannon are called to an apartment house where a man has been murdered, bludgeoned with a hammer. By piecing together details and talking with the apartment house's residents, the cops zero in on two suspects—a teenage boy and his girlfriend—who are detained in Arizona on a warrant.

The suspects are mouthy. The boy answers all of Sergeant Joe Friday and Officer Bill Gannon's questions by reciting state capitals. He even says that the capital of Nevada is Reno. Officer Bill Gannon, who can track down criminals and win geography bees, corrects him and points out that the capital of Nevada is Carson City.

The girl, Camille Gearhardt, tells Sergeant Joe Friday that his eyes are nice—for a cop.

He then tells her that her mother probably had a good bark. Sergeant Joe Friday doesn't suffer fools gladly.

One of the things I like best about this episode is that it doesn't just show how a crime is solved. It also shows how crime affects the people who witness it or know the victim. The death of the man at the apartment leaves his best friend without a companion.

Tonight, I am thinking a lot about crime and why it happens and what it does to people. I am flummoxed.

— • —

Mike Simpson:

I did not think it was possible to detest you more than I did that night that you tried to choke Donna Middleton in her driveway. Today, in court, you elevated things to the level of hate. I hate you. It's not a word I use lightly.

If there is any upside to your horrible outburst today, it is that Judge Alan Robeson saw with his own eyes what a horrible person you truly are and denied you bail accordingly. While I cannot know how long you will remain behind bars—I can only guess, and I prefer facts—I do know that Donna Middleton is going on with her life without you and your controlling, deceitful, harmful ways.

She is much the better for it. While that will no doubt make you angry, it makes her family—and especially her boy—happy. And I am happy for them.

Regards,
Edward Stanton

I print out the letter and place it in the green office folder I prepared days ago, taking the time to alter the tab so that it reads "Mike Simpson" and not just "Mike."

I hope it's the last time that I ever have to take it out of the filing cabinet.

TUESDAY, OCTOBER 28

I am in a room that is empty save for a table and three cardboard boxes—one red, one blue, one yellow.

I walk over to the table and lift the lid on the red box, and Mike Simpson's head pops up.

"What if I don't go to jail, Edward?" Mike Simpson's head says to me. "What then?"

And now I am in another room, also empty, save for three doors on the wall across from me. They are marked with a 1, a 2, and a 3.

I walk over and open door number 1. Mike Simpson is standing behind it.

"What then, Edward?"

And now I am in yet another room, this one filled with people of different sizes and shapes, yet all of them with Mike Simpson's anvil-like head, all of which whip around to look at me.

"What then, Edward?" they say in unison. "I will kill you, that's what then. You're dead."

— • —

And now I am awake, my heart thumping loudly against my sternum. It's 6:45 a.m. I don't dare return to sleep for fear of seeing that face again. I reach for my notebook and record the time, and my data is complete.

— • —

The rain, it says here in the *Billings Herald-Gleaner*, will linger through the week, a prospect that is neither here nor there to me. I am interested in the facts of the situation, and the only facts about the weather that today's *Herald-Gleaner* can provide are yesterday's high and low temperatures and precipitation. I record them in my notebook, and my data is complete.

I remember when I was attending school at Billings West High School, during my junior-year English class, I had a teacher who would talk endlessly about symbolism in literature. She said that rain in a scene always portended (I love the word "portended") a parting of ways. And yet I have years' worth of data on the weather patterns here in Billings that suggest it's not true. Rain is caused by cloud droplets that become too big for the clouds to hold. Water vapor below the clouds condenses into these droplets, which then fall from the sky. That has nothing to do with the parting of ways. The science of the matter is that it's always raining somewhere on Earth, and while there may also always be parting of ways on Earth, that's a coincidence, not science.

This teacher also told us that a move east portended disaster. She justified this by quoting Horace Greeley, who famously said, "Go West, young man." I think if she had just thought of all the people who have gone east to New York and hit it big, she might have realized the folly of what she was teaching us. It was Frank Sinatra who said that if you can make it in New York, you can make it anywhere. You take Horace Greeley. I'll take Frank Sinatra. He was the chairman, after all.

I take the last couple of big bites of corn flakes, pop the fluoxetine into my mouth, wash it down with orange juice, and head off to the shower. Today is important. Dr. Buckley awaits.

— • —

This trip to Dr. Buckley's office will require some packing first.

I printed out Joy-Annette's increasingly belligerent e-mail messages as they came in, and they are stacked neatly on my office desk. I pull up my Word files on the computer and print out my letters of complaint back to Joy-Annette. I don't trust myself to tell the whole story accurately, as it flusters me, and so I've decided to let Dr. Buckley read everything for herself. I look forward to hearing what she thinks.

I fold the papers and put them into a briefcase. Then I open the briefcase and make sure I can find them easily. I then decide that I should segregate the papers, putting Joy-Annette's notes in one compartment and my letters in another. I close the briefcase. Then I open it again and make sure that I know which compartment is which. I close the briefcase. Then I open it again and check one last time.

I'm looking forward to seeing Dr. Buckley today.

Of course, it's only 8:32 a.m. Mike's visage started my day far too early.

I check the briefcase one more time.

— • —

An hour and twenty-three minutes later, I am in Dr. Buckley's office. The past week's patients have left me much to clean up. On every end table, the magazines are ridiculously out of order.

I stack them again, chronologically within a given title and then alphabetically by title.

I am unable to sit down. I'm fidgety. I used to feel this way a lot, especially before I started seeing Dr. Buckley and she helped figure out the proper dosage of my fluoxetine. I have no ready answer for why such jumpiness has returned today, but perhaps Dr. Buckley will have some ideas.

I look at my watch, and it's 9:59:51.

If I don't start on time today, I will be very upset.

9:59:54...9:59:55...9:59:56...

Dr. Buckley's door opens, and I barrel down the hallway, crashing into the distinguished-looking gentleman who is exiting her office.

I look down at my watch.

10:00:04...10:00:05...10:00:06...

"Cocksucker," I say, scolding myself for my tardiness.

— • —

"Edward, I need you to take it real slow now."

Dr. Buckley's voice is low and soothing. She never loses her temper with me, even when I push her to exasperation, as I have today. After I ran into that man and then shouted a very bad word, I could hear her on the other side of the door, apologizing profusely to him and assuring him that I was not referring to him as a cocksucker. She didn't actually say the word "cocksucker," but it was obvious that was the word causing consternation.

When Dr. Buckley comes back in, I start talking very fast before she even sits down. My brain is moving faster than my mouth, and I am making little sense, I am afraid.

"Slow down, now," Dr. Buckley says.

"I went on that online date, and it was a complete disaster. I couldn't…she was…I was worried…"

"Breathe and slow down."

This is a technique that Dr. Buckley used often in the early days of my coming to see her, when we were meeting every couple of days to work through my problems. I was often frantic back then. After my fluoxetine dosage settled in at eighty milligrams and took effect in my body, we didn't have to do this so much, and we were able to dial back our sessions to once a week. I can see in Dr. Buckley's face that she is surprised that we're in this mode again.

"Are you breathing better?" she asks.

"Yes, I think so."

"Are you ready to talk?"

"Yes."

"OK, then. Let's take these one at a time."

— • —

We start with Joy-Annette and the disastrous online date. I bring Dr. Buckley up to speed on all that happened since my last appointment, including the clothes-buying trip ("My husband has those slacks," she says at one point. "They look good."), the anxiety about sex, the Gewurztraminer-fueled burp, and the abrupt end to the date.

I only allude to the flurry of e-mail and my own unsent responses. Rather than tell about them, I reach into the briefcase and hand her the printouts.

Dr. Buckley reads quickly but also intently. At several points, I can see her brow furrow. At those junctures, I wonder what part of the correspondence she is reading, and I hope that it isn't mine.

"Edward, I think you've learned something about dating in general, but online dating in particular," Dr. Buckley finally says.

"What?"

"It can be difficult to find the right person, no matter the circumstance. I'm not willing to say whether online dating is inferior or superior to dating the old-fashioned way, whatever that is, but it's different in one important way."

"What's that?"

"You're missing a dimension of the person that you get when the first interaction is face-to-face. What I'm talking about here is a vibe. Do you know what I mean?"

"I think so. A vibe is hard to quantify."

"Yes, it is. But that innate feeling you get about someone else is important. Online dating delays that. I'm not saying that's a bad thing, in and of itself. But it happens. Do you follow me?"

"Yes. I didn't get a good vibe from Joy-Annette. Did you in reading her notes?"

"No, but I don't dislike her. I feel sorry for her."

"Why?"

"She's clearly dealing with some issues that stretch beyond dating and beyond you, Edward. There's unhappiness there."

I hadn't considered that, and now I feel bad that I've been harboring such hostile thoughts toward Joy-Annette. I'm not being fair.

"What have you taken from your online dating experience, Edward?"

I think for a few seconds before answering. "I don't think I want to do it again. There's too much torpidity when it goes poorly."

"But what about if it goes well?"

"I don't know. I haven't experienced that. Are you saying that you think I should try it again?"

Dr. Buckley shakes her head. "I'm not saying that. That's your decision, Edward. I'm saying that you have made the decision to let people into your life—"

"I don't recall making that decision."

"Well, it wasn't an occasion. But it happened just the same. Look at what we're talking about."

"Yes, that's true."

"As I was saying, you have made the decision to let people into your life. Part of that involves being disappointed by them sometimes. Part of that involves being thrilled by them sometimes. It's up to you to decide whether the risk is worth the reward."

"I guess I'm thinking that it's not."

"Have you ever heard the phrase 'You have to kiss a lot of frogs to find a prince'?"

"Yes."

"Do you know what it means?"

"Yes, but Donna Middleton said it was that I had to turn over a lot of rocks on the beach before I find a pearl."

"Donna Middleton is a very logical woman," Dr. Buckley says.

— • —

Next, we talk about Donna Middleton and the fracas at the courthouse yesterday. There was a news brief on the second page of the Local & State section in today's *Billings Herald-Gleaner* about it, and Dr. Buckley says that she saw it.

"Partner and family member assault is a terrible thing," she says. From my years in the clerk of court's office, I know it by the initials used by people in jurisprudence—PFMA.

"I think she's very brave to confront him like that," she says.

"She is."

"Edward, have you spoken with your father about this?"

"I don't think he would be happy that I have become friends with Donna."

"He might not. But I think he might have some good advice."

"He'll just yell at me."

"Perhaps you should give him more credit than that. We've talked many times about your father and how to interact with him. What, in this case, do you think the best approach would be?"

"Deference."

"Why do you say so?"

"I should appeal to his protective and analytical instincts. If I defer to his wisdom about a situation, he's more likely to share it with me." I have repeated, verbatim, what Dr. Buckley has counseled me to do on many occasions with my father. I have been less successful in actually following through with him.

"Word for word, Edward. Word for word."

— • —

We finish our session with a brief discussion about goals for the coming week. This is a fairly regular aspect of my weekly session with Dr. Buckley. I say "fairly regular" because it is sometimes superseded (I love the word "superseded") by some emergency on my part, but in an average week, as most of them have been up until lately, we finish with a goals session. I wonder if I shouldn't be keeping track of when we set goals and when we don't, then shake off that thought as Dr. Buckley starts in.

"You've made real progress, I think," Dr. Buckley says. "Do you think so?"

"Yes, I guess. It has been a hard, frustrating week."

"But you're still here."

"Yes."

"And you've taken some steps outside your comfort zone, away from full-time solitude and into some fellowship with others. How do you feel about that?"

"Mixed emotions, I guess."

"Are they so mixed that you are unwilling to keep going?"

"No."

"OK, then. Here's your goal: What's the next step? How will the next seven days be different for you from the past seven? Let's find out, OK?"

"OK."

Dr. Buckley is up and opening her office door. "Until next week, Edward."

I walk out the office door, down the hall, and out the door into the foyer of the medical arts building. I can see through the glass doors that front the parking lot that it's raining hard now.

— • —

At the Albertsons on Thirteenth Street W. and Grand Avenue, I have my cart and I begin to make my weekly pattern: spaghetti and sauce in the soup-and-pasta aisle, ground beef in the meat department, corn flakes in the cereal aisle, milk in the dairy, Diet Dr Pepper in the soda aisle, DiGiorno pizza and Banquet frozen meals and ice cream in the freezer compartments. Under optimal conditions, with no other customers or pallets of yet-to-be-unloaded food blocking my way, I can get from the store to the self-checkout area in six minutes.

After taking down the corn flakes and putting them in the cart, I stop and consider my haul: three packages of ground beef, three packages of spaghetti, three jars of Newman's Own spaghetti sauce, and one box of corn flakes. These make up the basis of my weekly diet, and they are my favorite foods.

In the soda aisle, I bypass the Diet Dr Pepper. I think this week that I would like a twelve-pack of Barq's root beer, which I load into the cart.

In the dairy case, I reach for the 2 percent half gallon of milk, not the skim as usual.

In the frozen-food aisle, I bypass the Banquet meals entirely, and the pizza, too. Instead, I select a few Lean Cuisine microwavable dinners—sweet and sour chicken, enchiladas *suiza*, pepperoni pizza, and Swedish meatballs. I eschew (I love the word "eschew") Dreyer's vanilla ice cream for a pint of Häagen-Dazs chocolate sorbet. I saw myself in the mirror before I went on my date with Joy-Annette, and I think I could stand to take in fewer calories.

I then backtrack to the meat department and select what appears to be a very fine New York steak. In produce, which I never visit, I pick out a Caesar salad in a bag.

The whole exercise exhilarates me. I don't even know how to cook a steak, but surely there is a website that can tell me.

I roll my cart toward the front of the store, to one of two open checkout stands, both jammed with customers. My shopping spree took eighteen minutes. It's OK, I think. Today, I am happy, and I can wait a few minutes more to talk to an actual person.

— • —

I'm nervous on the drive home. The rain is coming down even harder than when I went into Albertsons, and the thump of fat raindrops against the windows reminds me of last week, when that car hit me as I was turning left onto Twenty-Fourth Street W.

From Albertsons to home is all right turns, thank goodness, but you never know with other drivers.

I'm relieved when I pull into the driveway without incident. As the garage is not attached to the house, I'm facing a small fight through the rain with the groceries, regardless of whether I leave the car exposed or pull it into the garage. I opt for the former, then scramble out of the car, dash around to the back, unlock the trunk, and start wrestling with the plastic bags.

I can nearly scoop them all up, but the bulkiness of the box of Barq's root beer is too much for me. I stand there in the rain for a minute or two, trying to find the grip that will allow me to move all of the bags toward the front door.

Finally, I get it. I'm holding on to the carrying latch on the box of root beer with just three fingers, and I begin shuffling toward the door. Halfway across the front yard, the root beer box rips apart and slips from my grasp, landing with a metallic thud. A few cans roll toward the sidewalk, propelled along by the slight crown of the yard. One can has blown apart from the fall and is spraying warm, carbonated root beer.

"Holy shit!" I say, and drop the bags of groceries.

"Edward, let me give you a hand." It's Donna, splashing toward me from across the street in a yellow raincoat.

"Thanks."

I collect the groceries again, while she chases down the cans of root beer. I waddle to the door in a half-run, and she's behind me with an armful of soda cans. I set one bag down and retrieve the keys from my pocket, then unlock the door, gather up the bag, and hustle inside. Donna is right behind me. Tracking rain and mud through the house, we herd the groceries into the dining room and set them on the table.

"Whew," Donna says. "I think that one can's a goner, Edward. Sorry about that."

"It's OK."

I start pulling groceries from the bags and organizing them to be put away.

"Do you need help?" Donna asks.

"No, I can do this."

She looks back into the tramped-through living room. "Oh, Edward, we made a big mess in there."

"Yes."

"Do you have a vacuum cleaner and some cleaning supplies?"

"Yes, in the hall closet."

"OK," Donna says. "You put away the groceries, and I'll clean the floor."

— • —

By 12:45, we're finished—the groceries put away, the living room carpet looking as if nobody had ever walked on it, let alone tracked mud and water across it—and we're enjoying some of what Donna has dubbed The Root Beer That Tried to Get Away. She's having hers in a glass, with ice. I'm drinking from the can, as I prefer my soda at room temperature.

At 12:47, there is a knock on the door.

I set my can of root beer down on the coffee table. I have no coasters, which started as a rebellion against my parents but now is just one of those idiosyncrasies that Dr. Buckley occasionally counsels me about; I can imagine her now, saying, "How, exactly, does not having coasters figure into your image of yourself, Edward?"

At the door, I look through the peephole. I can see the distinctive blue outfit of the US Postal Service. He's late today. It must be because of the rain. I open the door.

"Edward Stanton?" he asks. He has been coming to this house for as long as I have lived here.

"Yes."

"Registered letter. I need a signature."

I sign where he has indicated, and he hands me a white business envelope.

The sender: Lambert, Slaughter & Lamb, Attorneys at Law.

"Oh no."

"What is it?" Donna asks.

"A letter from my father's lawyer."

"What about?"

"I don't know. It can't be good."

I open the letter, peeling away a corner of the envelope, and then sliding my right index finger through the top of the envelope like a crude blade.

October 27, 2008
Mr. Edward Stanton:

Your benefactor and I would like to talk with you about recent events and their possible bearing on your benefactor's continued support of you. Please extend us the courtesy of meeting at 9:00 a.m., Wednesday, October 29, at the law offices of Lambert, Slaughter & Lamb, 2600 First Avenue N., Suite 303.

We look forward to meeting with you.

Regards,
Jay L. Lamb

"It's not good," I say.

"Can I see it?"

I hand the letter to Donna, who reads it quickly.

"This is so weird," she says. "Your father uses a lawyer to talk with you?"

"Sometimes."

"Why does the lawyer refer to him as your benefactor?"

"I guess it's a lawyerly way of putting things."

"Why can't your father just call you up or come by?"

I shrug. That would be nice. That also would never happen. I shouldn't say that, I guess. I don't know what will ever happen, as those things haven't happened yet, and until then, it's all conjecture. I prefer facts. The fact is, my father has never just dropped by.

"What's it about?"

"I don't know. It could be anything."

"He seemed like a nice man when…well, that day at the clinic."

"He is when he wants to be."

"Are you going to go?"

I shrug. "I have to."

— • —

Donna is preparing to leave. She puts her raincoat back on—the pelting continues outside—and turns and faces me.

"Are you OK, Edward?"

"Yes."

"I enjoyed hanging out with you."

"Me, too."

She smiles at me.

"Edward, can I ask you a question?"

"Yes."

"Would it be all right if I kissed you on the cheek?"

I've never been asked this before.

"OK," I say.

She puts her hands on my shoulders and tiptoes up to me, gently placing her lips against my left cheek. She smells good. I close my eyes.

After she finishes, she releases me.

"Thank you, Edward."

She opens the door, steps through, and closes it behind her.

— • —

Tonight, at 10:00, I settle into the couch and watch *Dragnet*. The episode, the eighth of the first season of color episodes, originally aired on March 9, 1967, and it is one of my favorites. It is called "The Candy Store Robberies."

In this one, Sergeant Joe Friday and Officer Bill Gannon investigate a string of armed robberies at a chain of downtown candy stores in Los Angeles. For a while, the robberies seem to follow a pattern, but then the robber or robbers—Sergeant Joe Friday and Officer Bill Gannon aren't sure about the number— hit a store that he or they have robbed before. Rolling stakeouts finally break open the case, and two transient men are arrested. It turns out that one of them found a gun, and they have both been using it, hitting the candy stores when they need some cash for liquor. They are actually gentle men, the gun notwithstanding (I love the word "notwithstanding"), and they have become friends because neither can read.

Their crimes are serious, but Sergeant Joe Friday and Officer Bill Gannon have empathy for the men just the same. I think this episode is just as much about friendship as it is about the unraveling of a crime.

Friendship, I'm finding out, is a good thing.

— • —

The sixth green office folder holding letters of complaint to my father gathers another one.

Dear Father,

I was most disappointed to receive the registered letter from your attorney, Jay L. Lamb, today. It was a dark moment in what had been, for me, a day of breakthroughs and greater understanding.

I am left to wonder if you and I will ever have a similar breakthrough. I am inclined to defer to your wisdom on so many things. I wonder if you will ever talk to me yourself or come over and have a Barq's root beer with me, instead of having your lawyer write to me.

But wondering is not much different from conjecture. Neither one deals in facts.

So here is a fact: I will continue to hope that we might do better.

As ever, I am your son,
Edward

WEDNESDAY, OCTOBER 29

I awake with a start at 7:40 a.m. I'm propped up in bed, my fore-arms flat against the mattress, my elbows holding me up. I can remember only the faintest outline of a dream: My father, ahead of me, walking along a road I don't recognize. He keeps the same, steady pace, occasionally looking back and waving me to come along. I walk as fast as I can and never catch up to him.

I find the dream both comforting and threatening. I cannot reconcile these two things in my mind, and as my alertness grows, my grasp on the dream loosens.

It's no use.

I record my awakening time, the thirty-first time in 303 days this year (because it's a leap year) that I've been up at 7:40 a.m. My data is complete. And, as is made plain by the clock, my morning meeting will be upon me soon.

— • —

I shower quickly, not savoring the hot water as I generally do. It's cold today; I could feel that when I threw off the covers and climbed out of bed. How cold, I do not know and won't know until tomorrow. The *Billings Herald-Gleaner* awaits on the stoop.

I step out of the shower and dry off quickly, then slip into my terry cloth robe. I'll have to eat a quick bowl of corn flakes. I can't say that I'm particularly hungry, as my appetite is being affected by the fact that I have to be at my father's lawyer's office. I also cannot imagine facing that on an empty stomach.

At the front door, I stop and sweep the newspaper off the porch. I am in a hurry this morning, but I can complete my data. I see that the forecast calls for snow flurries today. It seems that the TV weatherman, Kent Shaw, whose smiling face is on the weather page every day, and I have a similar sense of things. The difference is that he states his forecast as if it's fact. I know better. I shall wait for tomorrow for the facts.

I eat spoonfuls of cereal as I thumb through the newspaper. The *Billings Herald-Gleaner* is the only newspaper I have read consistently in my life, and I like it, although there are some things that bother me about it. I don't start at the front of the newspaper and look at every page in succession; I would be surprised if many people do, but I can't really know without taking a scientific survey of the *Billings Herald-Gleaner*'s readers, and I just don't have time for that.

First, I go to the weather page (I have already been there today and recorded yesterday's high and low temperatures and precipitation, and my data is complete). Then I skip over to Dear Abby (the headline today: "Husband Should Ditch Secretary"), and this is one of the things that bothers me about the newspaper: The page with Dear Abby is in different places on different days. Sometimes, it's with the front section. Sometimes, it's with the Local & State section. And sometimes, it is with the Sports section. Every day, I have to check the index on the front page of the newspaper to find out where it is. And that brings up another thing I dislike about the *Herald-Gleaner*: The index always says something like "4C" or "8A." The letters mean nothing to me. I want the *Herald-Gleaner* to tell me what section to turn to, whether it's Local & State or Sports or the front section. I am flummoxed by the *Herald-Gleaner*'s fixation on alphabetizing.

Finally, I turn to the Opinion page. This is my recreational reading, as my father often turns up on the Opinion page—sometimes because a letter writer mentions him, for good or for bad, and sometimes because the *Herald-Gleaner* editorial board mentions him, and that's almost always for bad. My father refers to the *Herald-Gleaner* editorial board as "that full-of-shit, left-wing league of loons." My father has a creative way of putting words together sometimes. The *Herald-Gleaner* editorial board, so far as I can tell, has never called my father anything that mean, although I could only guess at what its members say privately about him, and I don't like guessing. I prefer facts. And it is a fact that the *Herald-Gleaner* editorial board is generally not supportive of my father as a county commissioner. It routinely criticizes his positions and has, in every election, endorsed his opponent. Today, as it turns out, a small editorial, with the headline "Stanton Misses Again," takes him to task.

> *The Big Sky Economic Development Authority has yet to select a new executive director, but it made a smart move by moving on from candidate Dave Akers after his drunk-driving arrest while in Billings for his interview with the group. We can only hope that Akers's most ardent supporter, Yellowstone County commissioner Ted Stanton, realizes the wisdom in moving on and ceases his incessant criticism of fellow board members.*
>
> *The* Herald-Gleaner *has been up front about the ways in which we consider Commissioner Stanton's stewardship of*

the county to be lacking, but we would be remiss if we didn't
also acknowledge his keen political gifts and the value of his
experience in business and finance. The county's residents
are often well served by that expertise. Nobody is served by
his banging the drum—and berating his peers—on behalf of
a man who will not get the job to which he aspires.

— • —

The waiting area outside Jay L. Lamb's office is pristine. Unlike Dr. Buckley's waiting room, which is often in various stages of dishevelment and has such magazines as *People* and *Sports Illustrated*, Jay L. Lamb's is polished and almost antiseptic. The furniture is modern—steel and glass and hard plastic. I find it uncomfortable and unwelcoming. The magazine titles are not the breezy reads favored by Dr. Buckley; they are such things as *Kiplinger's* and *Inc.* and *Portfolio*. It seems that the biggest story in each has something to do with investing.

"Mr. Lamb says you can go in now," says the receptionist, who is perfectly made up, perfectly coiffed, and has perfectly angular facial features. She is a good match with the furniture.

I stand up and check my watch. It's 9:03 a.m. I walk through the office door to the immediate left of her desk. As I push it open, I draw in a big breath.

— • —

"Sit down, Mr. Stanton," Jay L. Lamb says.

I hesitate for a moment, as Mr. Stanton is standing just off Jay L. Lamb's right shoulder. Jay L. Lamb is sitting behind an expansive glass-topped desk. Then I realize that he is talking to me.

I sit. The chairs in here are just as uncomfortable as the ones outside.

"Hello, Edward."

"Hello, Father."

Jay L. Lamb clears his throat as if to speak, but my father cuts him off.

"What were you doing at the courthouse Monday?"

"How did you know I was there?"

"Cut the shit, Edward. We've been over this before. I know things."

Yes, but that doesn't make sense. My father's job, aside from being at the courthouse, has nothing to do with court cases. We didn't cross paths when I was there. Lloyd Graeve isn't a friend of my father's, so far as I know.

Wait. Lambert, Slaughter & Lamb, Attorneys at Law. Sean Lambert. Mike Simpson's defense attorney. That has to be it.

"I was there with a friend."

"Who's your friend?"

"My neighbor."

"What is your neighbor's name?"

"Donna Middleton."

"You were at the county courthouse with Donna Middleton, the woman who not two weeks ago asked me to have you stay away from her and her little boy?"

Now Jay L. Lamb speaks. "On October twenty-first, you were sent a letter warning you about the outburst at Billings Clinic. Your father, in mitigating that situation for you, told you to leave that family alone."

"What do you mean by 'leave alone'?" I ask.

"You know goddamned well what he means," my father says.

"She is my friend. Circumstances changed after that day at Billings Clinic."

"I am not interested in what has changed, Edward. I am interested in knowing why it is that you continually defy me, continually land in situations that you must be rescued from, and continually make this situation more difficult than it has to be."

"What do you mean by 'this situation'?"

"Smarting off is not going to help you here, Edward."

"I'm not smarting off. I'm asking you a question. What is the situation?"

"You know damned well what it is."

"I know that you can't talk to me about anything without your lawyer," I say, waving my hand dismissively at Jay L. Lamb.

"That's not what this is about."

"How can it not be about that? Where are we, Father? We're in your lawyer's office."

"There are legal aspects of our arrangement, Edward, and that's the reason for the lawyer."

"But whether or not I am friends with Donna Middleton is not part of our arrangement. You're just bossing me around because you can."

"I'm trying to protect you, goddamn it."

"You're trying to protect you is what it seems like to me."

— • —

It goes on like that for a while, until my father and I begin to run out of angry words. At 9:22, Jay L. Lamb starts talking.

"Mr. Stanton," he says, again addressing me. "I have drawn up a memorandum of understanding. Our wish is that you sign it and your father signs it, and it will constitute the basis of your father's continuing support of you. You should understand that any breach of this memorandum of understanding could be viewed as a sufficient reason to withdraw that financial support."

I ask to see the memorandum. Among the codicils (I love the word "codicil," although not so much today):

I am to not have contact with Donna Middleton or her son except as is "reasonably neighborly." ("Giving a wave from your driveway is OK," Jay L. Lamb says. "Traveling together, eating together, any sort of extended social interaction is not.")

I am to live within my monthly budget of $1,200, not counting household utility costs and property taxes. Any overage is to be paid by me to my father.

I am to clear with my father all household improvements or alterations before embarking on them. ("You're not going to paint that garage every damned year," my father says. "Shows what you know," I reply. "I paint it every other year.")

So long as I adhere to these rules, Jay L. Lamb says, I am permitted to live in the house on Clark Avenue "until the end of my natural life."

"Can I ask something?" I say.

"Go ahead," Jay L. Lamb replies.

"This part about living within my budget, does it mean from this day forward?"

My father's eyes zero in on me. "Is there something I need to know?"

"There are some bills coming."

"What kind of bills?"

"I bought some clothes. About five hundred dollars' worth. I am wearing some of them today." I have on the tan slacks and lavender shirt that I bought at Dillard's, plus the shoes and the belt.

My father says nothing.

"And two hundred and twenty-one dollars and ninety-five cents from Home Depot."

"You bought two hundred and twenty dollars' worth of paint?"

"The paint was another purchase."

"What the hell was the two-twenty for?"

"A project."

"What kind of project?"

"A big tricycle."

"What?"

"Like a Green Machine. Do you remember mine?"

"No. What the hell is this about?"

"I made it for Donna's son."

"You what?" My father has come around the desk to face me.

"It's already done. He has it. No bringing it back now." I am trying not to smile as my father grows angrier by the second.

"This, Edward, is why you're signing this goddamned document."

"Maybe I will. Maybe I won't."

"You will."

"Also, someone hit the car."

"When?"

"Last week, outside Rimrock Mall."

"Did you get insurance information from them?"

"He or she drove off."

"Well, Jesus Christ. How bad is it?"

"It's hard to tell that anything happened."

"Forget it, then. No way I'm paying a five-hundred-dollar deductible and seeing my rates jacked up. Now then, is that it?"

"Yes, I think so."

"Then sign the document."

"And if I don't?"

"You can start looking for somewhere else to live and a way to pay your bills, starting today," my father says. "Because the gravy train will be gone."

"Yes, Father, you're all heart," I say. "Anyone can see that."

It's like a flash of lightning my father is so quick as he back-hands me across the bridge of the nose. I haven't even compre-hended what has happened when I feel the sharp sting spread across my face. My eyes are watering, and the tinny taste of blood seeps into my mouth from my sinuses.

"Jesus Christ, Ted," Jay L. Lamb shouts, jumping up and grab-bing my father by the shoulders. My father slumps backward and sits down on Jay L. Lamb's glass desk.

I rub the back of my right hand across my eyes to clear away the tears that filled my eyes from the force of the blow. Then I dab under my nostrils and see little spots of blood.

"I strongly suggest that you sign and leave. We're not going to have this here," Jay L. Lamb says to me.

"You're paid to give advice to him, not me," I say. "Give me a pen."

— • —

Before I leave Jay L. Lamb's office, I say one last thing.

"I saw your good review in today's *Billings Herald-Gleaner*, Father."

He fixes me with a haggard stare. "Go home, Edward. We've had enough bullshit for one day."

— • —

On the drive home, I see that wispy flakes of snow have started to fall, dissolving as they hit the ground.

I cannot believe what has happened. My father has always yelled at me and ridiculed me. He has never hit me, not until today. My father has broken my heart.

I hate him. Hate is not a word to be used lightly. I consider this, and then I stick with it. I hate my father.

— • —

I can see Donna Middleton in her front yard when I pull up into the driveway at home. I step out of the car, and she gives a big wave and shouts, "How are you?"

I don't look at her. I give a half wave back, walk briskly to the front door, open it, and go in.

— • —

By 10:00 p.m., I am exhausted. I have spent the day since I arrived back home alternately sleeping and stomping angrily around the house and, at times, crying. I am not ashamed. Crying does not make me a baby. Crying comes from many sources and has many causes: anger, frustration, sadness, lack of sleep. I think I am suffering from all four, and I think that is why I have been crying.

It's time for *Dragnet*, and although I don't have much energy for it, I've already skipped one episode of the first season, and to miss another would put me horribly off track. I cue up the tape and press play.

Tonight's episode, the ninth of the first season of the color episodes, is called "The Fur Burglary." It originally aired on March 16, 1967, and it is one of my favorites.

In it, a furrier by the name of Emile Hartman (played by Henry Corden, who appeared in two episodes of *Dragnet* and nearly every popular TV show of the '60s and '70s) has been wiped out by burglars. Sergeant Joe Friday and Officer Bill Gannon are called in to investigate, and they soon determine that they will have to pose as buyers in hopes that the burglars will attempt to sell the furs. Emile Hartman teaches Officer Bill Gannon how to be a connoisseur of fine fur, giving him a vocabulary that includes such terms as "gamey" and "split skins."

Eventually, Sergeant Joe Friday and Officer Bill Gannon arrest the men responsible and get the furs back to Emile Hartman, saving his business.

I suppose when something is taken from you, it can be a lucky break to have men like Sergeant Joe Friday and Officer Bill Gannon to get it back.

There are not enough men like those two to go around.

— • —

As you may have guessed, I already have a green office folder for the man who does my father's bidding, Jay L. Lamb. I should write to my father, but I just don't know what I could say to a man I suddenly do not know.

Mr. Lamb:

I must again voice my objections to your interference in affairs that should be handled within my family. I realize that you serve at my father's whims, but I am left to wonder if $350 an hour is really worth intruding where you do not belong and are not welcome. For me, the answer is clearly no, and after the events of today, I would think that any reasonable person would come to the same conclusion. You will have to make peace with that question yourself.

At any rate, I very much resent your attempts to provide me with legal counsel. Should I require the assistance of an attorney, you can be sure that I will choose someone who is not a toady for a frustrated, spiteful, violent man.

In other words, I will not choose you.

While I would like to be able to say that this letter concludes our interaction, I know that this is not up to me, but rather to my father. I am hopeful that we will not have any more such episodes, but hope is not a reliable emotion. I shall wait for the facts to emerge.

In the meantime, I bid you good day, until I can bid you good riddance.

Regards,
Edward Stanton

THURSDAY, OCTOBER 30

My waking hours on the 303rd day of the year (because it is a leap year) begin with a 7:14 a.m. phone call.

"Hello?"

"Edward?" It is my mother. My mother never calls me at this hour.

"Mother?"

"Edward," she says, and I can hear a wobble in her voice, "you need to come to St. V's. Something has happened to your father."

"What?"

"Just come, Edward. St. V's emergency room." She hangs up.

My data will have to wait.

— • —

St. V's is what people in Billings call St. Vincent Healthcare. There are two main hospitals in Billings, St. V's and Billings Clinic. They sit side by side in the hospital district downtown. Billings, because it is the largest city in a 500-mile radius, is where many of the people in Montana and northern Wyoming come for hospital services. If you have an extremely serious medical condition, you might have to go to Denver or Salt Lake City or Seattle, but the

Billings hospitals can handle most anything else. My father is at St. V's, so maybe he doesn't have an extremely serious medical condition. He is also in the emergency room, so maybe he does. I try not to think of this on the drive over, because it's just conjecture. I prefer facts.

I've moved quickly. After my mother hung up the phone, I pulled on a pair of blue jeans. I can wear my 1999 R.E.M. *Up* tour T-shirt to the hospital. At 7:29, I pull into the St. V's parking lot and cross the street to the emergency department. I am not wearing a coat. It's cold.

My mother is sitting in the waiting room. So is Jay L. Lamb. I hadn't imagined that I would see him again so soon.

"Edward, come sit down," my mother says when she sees me. She is calm in a way that I find eerie, but I can see that she has been crying. Her makeup is splotchy from her tears.

I sit next to my mother.

Jay L. Lamb nods to acknowledge me, but I do not return it.

"Edward, your father collapsed this morning," my mother says.

"I don't understand."

"He was going to hit golf balls and he collapsed."

"He was playing golf? In these temperatures?"

"Edward, that's not important. He collapsed. Someone saw him. They got help to him. He's..." My mother is crying again.

"He's inside," Jay L. Lamb says. "They're doing what they can."

He wraps an arm around my mother's shoulders, and she leans into his chest, sobbing.

I clasp my hands in front of me, lean forward, and stare at the floor. And I wait.

— • —

It is not a long wait in terms of time, but it seems endless. It occurs to me again that time can be an illusion, even though it is also a fact. My mother continues to sob, and Jay L. Lamb continues to comfort her. "He has a good team in there," he says. She cries some more. I keep my eyes on the floor.

At 7:58, the emergency room doctor, a young-looking man with a mop of swept-back black hair and round wire-rim glasses, emerges with a grim look on his face. Beside me, my mother starts quaking.

"Mrs. Stanton, gentlemen," he says to us. "I am so sorry. We did everything we could, but we just could not revive him."

My mother wails. Jay L. Lamb clutches her tightly.

"He appears to have suffered a massive heart attack. The lab work will tell us for sure. I am so sorry."

"He's dead?" The voice is mine, and yet it seems to be coming from outside me.

"Yes. I'm sorry."

My mother wails again, sobbing, "No, no, no, no."

The young doctor reaches out and clasps her hand.

My mother sniffles and gurgles and turns her head from Jay L. Lamb's chest to face the doctor. "I want to see him."

— • —

My father's body is in an empty room in the emergency department. Although I recognize him, it's not really him. Gone is the brightness and color in his face and the way his expressiveness added to it. He is pale. His chest, stripped free of his ever-present golf shirt, shows the trauma of the attempts to save him— the compression from CPR, the use of the defibrillator paddles. His ordinarily well-kept graying hair is mussed and tangled and wet. In life, my father could be found where there was chatter and aroma and motion. Here, it smells of cleaning fluid, we're standing still, and no one is saying a word.

He is gone.

My mother, sturdier now than she was just minutes ago, steps to the edge of the gurney and strokes my father's face, then bends down and kisses his cheek.

"Jay," she says softly, "will you take care of everything?"

"I will. Shall I give you a ride home?"

"No," I say. "I will take her home."

— • —

My mother is mostly silent on the climb up the Rimrocks along Twenty-Seventh Street. As we hit the straightaway atop the rock, heading toward my parents'—my mother's—house, she says, "I can't believe it."

"I can't, either."

"Edward, your father is gone."

"I know."

She looks out the window at the farmland speeding by. Up here, yesterday's snow still lies sprinkled on the ground.

"I don't know what to do," she says.

— • —

The house, which always seemed to me to be ridiculously large for just two people, seems cavernous without my father in it. I had my troubles with him—never more so than the last time I saw him, an occasion that now fills me with regret—but I loved his outsized personality and the way he could fill a room with his laugh and his voice.

There are many empty spaces in this house now, and I do not know who can fill them. Not my mother. Certainly not me.

"Would you like some breakfast?" my mother asks.

"Mother, you don't have to cook."

"I would like to."

I nod. "Breakfast would be good."

— • —

My mother cooks and tells me what happened this morning. My father, figuring he could get in a few buckets of practice balls before the rain picked up again today, had left the house around 6:00 a.m. and headed down the hill to the Yegen Golf Club in the West End.

He didn't even make it out of the parking lot. He collapsed right beside his car. Someone called 911, the ambulance showed up, the golf pro called my mother, and she called Jay L. Lamb, who came to pick her up and take her to St. V's. From there, she called me. In a two-hour window, my father went from eager golfer to dead.

I am numb at the thought of this.

My mother places a plate of over-easy eggs, bacon, and toast on the kitchen's breakfast nook and waves me over. Her cooking is marvelous, as it has always been. I pick at the food. In fits and starts, my mother talks.

"He loved us."

I nod.

"He loved you especially."

This is not true, but now doesn't seem like the time to say so. When my Grandpa Sid, who had been sick for many years, died in 2003 and my Grandma Mabel followed just three weeks later, I remember that my father was given to extolling virtues that his parents never possessed. Dr. Buckley told me that it was part of his grieving process, a sort of "deification," she said, to help him think of them in the best possible way. Dr. Buckley assured me that, as my father went through the process of grappling with the loss of his parents, he would come to acknowledge their attributes and their faults. "We all have both," she said.

She turned out to be right, too. Dr. Buckley is a very logical woman.

I will not interfere with my mother's deification of my father. Her grieving has begun.

I wonder when mine will.

— • —

By 10:00 a.m., my mother has begun to wane and says she wants to go to sleep. She asks me to stay, and I say I will. Whatever plans I had—I can't remember what they were—have gone by the wayside.

At 11:11, when she is fast asleep, the phone rings. I pick it up. "Yes?"

"Hello. Could I please speak to Maureen Stanton?"

"She is asleep right now."

"This is Matt Hagengruber with the *Herald-Gleaner*. May I ask who I'm speaking with?"

"Edward."

"Edward Stanton?"

"Yes."

"You are Ted Stanton's son?"

"Yes."

"Edward, I'm sorry to hear about your father's death. Would you mind if I asked you a few questions?"

"Yes."

"I can ask a few questions?"

"No."

"Would it be all right if I called later to talk with your mother?"

"Yes."

"Thank you for your time."

I hang up the phone.

The calls come all afternoon like that, some from friends of my parents (I know none of those people), some from the radio and TV stations. Those are all variations on the call from Matt Hagengruber, and I tell each of them the same thing: they are welcome to call back later and see if my mother wishes to talk.

The only exception is the stupid woman from the TV station who asks for "Mrs. STAINton." I tell her never to call back again. I would like to say the same thing to Jay L. Lamb, who calls at 2:58 p.m., but I think my mother would like to talk to him. I write down the message.

All the while, my grieving mother sleeps.

— • —

I spend my off-the-phone time in my father's office, where I find a shelf full of photo albums that span the days when my parents met, long before I came along, to present day. I notice something else: Along about the time that I graduated from Billings West High School in 1987, I started disappearing from the rows of photographs. By the late 1990s, around the time of the "Garth Brooks incident," I was gone entirely.

In the past decade of family life as captured by a camera's lens, the Stanton family is my father and my mother and their trips together (I recognize France and Egypt and London among the photos). Edward Stanton Jr. is nowhere to be seen.

And yet today, Edward Stanton Sr. is dead, and I am in his office.

I never really understood the concept of irony, but this situation may be it.

— • —

At 4:40, my mother emerges from sleep. She comes downstairs in her robe. She looks tired, which is to be expected. She looks older than she did when she left me several hours ago, which is shocking.

I tell her about the calls from the media and that they will be back, hoping to speak with her. She sighs. "I'll have Jay make some sort of statement."

I tell her about Jay's call and request for a callback.

I tell her that her friends are worried.

I tell her that I am OK.

And I tell her good-bye, that I have things to do at home.

"You're a good boy, Edward," she says to me, her thirty-nine-year-old son. "I will give you a call tonight and let you know about the arrangements for your father."

— • —

I thought that I might be able to breathe if I could just get out of that house. But here I am now, waiting to make a right turn at Twenty-Seventh Street and Sixth Avenue, and I can't find any air.

At Division, where I take a left turn that will lead me to Clark Avenue and home, I feel the tears sliding down my face. Soon, I can't see the road.

"I will not deify my father," I say, but no one is here to answer.

— • —

At home, I work calmly and silently in the kitchen, gathering the things I will need. They fit into two plastic bags left over from some long-ago trip to Albertsons. I walk the bags out of the kitchen, out the back door, through the backyard, and into the alley behind the house, where I drop them into the big city-owned trash receptacles.

It's the remaining root beer, the salad in a bag, the half-eaten sorbet, the uncooked steak, and every Lean Cuisine meal I bought. I should have known better than to change my routine. The only worthwhile things in life are those that you can rely on. Change brings uncertainty. Change brings chaos. These are things I do not need.

— • —

Tonight's episode of *Dragnet* is called "The Jade Story." It is the tenth episode of the first season, and it is one of my favorites.

In "The Jade Story," which originally aired on March 23, 1967, Sergeant Joe Friday and Officer Bill Gannon are called in to investigate the theft of nearly $200,000 worth of jade from a wealthy woman's safe. Even today, $200,000 is considered a lot of money; in 1967, it was an extraordinary amount, the equivalent of about $1.2 million in today's dollars.

As Sergeant Joe Friday and Officer Bill Gannon investigate, many things about the story told by the jade's owner, Francine Graham, don't add up. They do some more digging and discover that Francine Graham had long since sold many of the pieces that she claims were stolen. Confronted with this, she confesses and says that, when he died, her husband left her with no insurance and little in the way of liquid assets. She slowly unloaded the jade to maintain her lifestyle, until she could do so no longer.

I have seen this episode four times a year since recording it in 2000, and I had seen it many times before that, although I didn't count my viewings back then. Today is the first time that this episode has left me worried.

My father, like Francine Graham's husband, is dead. Unlike Francine Graham's husband, my father has left my mother no jade to sell off to maintain her lifestyle.

— • —

When *Dragnet* is over, I head into my bedroom and retrieve five thick green office folders and one less encumbered one, which I carry into the next room, where my desk and computer sit. I spend several minutes counting and organizing and thumbing through the sheets of paper, occasionally stopping to read one. I then turn on the computer and pull up Microsoft Word to compose a letter.

Dear Father,

This will be the final letter I write to you. Even if I sent my letters of complaint, which I have not done since what you call the "Garth Brooks incident," this one would not get a stamp. There is no mail service wherever you have gone.

I have counted 178 letters of complaint to you over the past eight years. This will make 179. This one is notably different from the others in one way: The complaint lies with me, not with you. I never could find a way to make you proud of me, and at some point, I think I stopped trying. When you were here, I blamed you for that. I think now that the failure is mine.

The 178 previous letters of complaint are full of indignation about ways in which you slighted me or made me feel bad or disregarded me, and while I remember many of the instances and feel justified for the things I said, what difference does it make now? You are gone. I am here. I thought maybe someday we would reach an understanding. Now we never will. These are facts, and I accept them. I've always said I prefer facts, and that means I have to prefer them even on a day like today.

Had I known that it would end up this way, I would not have taunted you yesterday in Jay L. Lamb's office. It occurs to me that death is a funny thing—not funny in a laughter sort of way, but in a twisty sort of way. It's the people who are left behind who have to grapple with the regret. The one who is gone is just gone. I don't think that is fair. Wherever you are, Father, I hope you have regret about what happened yesterday.

Finally, I will close with the hope that you have taken care of Mother now that you are no longer here. She misses you. That's also a fact. She is deifying you, which I will not do. I am not a bad son. I am bad at pretending things are different from what is obvious.

You weren't a deity. You were my father. I love you.

And I am, as ever, your son,
Edward

I put my father's 179th letter in the third green folder, then reach into my pocket and pull out a picture that I took from one of the albums in my father's office.

It's from Easter 1976. We had made a family trip to Texas and went to Six Flags. My father is younger in it than I am now, with a head of bushy brown hair. He and I are mugging for the camera. The grins on our faces are huge. I can't remember ever grinning like that. And yet I have photographic proof, and so I know it happened.

I place the picture in with my father's letters. Then I clutch them to my chest, and I rock slowly in my chair.

FRIDAY, OCTOBER 31

On the 305th day of the year (because it's a leap year), I awake at 7:38 a.m., the 225th time this year that I have done so. It is my most common waking time, and yet today is the most uncommon of days. It is the first full day of my life that my father has been dead. I consider whether this is something I ought to add to my data sheets. I think it is.

I reach for my notebook and make my notations, and my data is complete.

— • —

As I could have predicted—although I didn't, and thus have no proof that I could have done it—my father's death is front-page news in this morning's *Billings Herald-Gleaner*. I begin reading the article on the walk from the front door to the dining room, and then I sit down and finish it.

By MATT HAGENGRUBER of the *Herald-Gleaner* staff
Longtime Yellowstone County commissioner Ted Stan-ton, one of the most powerful and divisive politicians in the

region, died suddenly Thursday after collapsing at a West End golf course. He was sixty-four.

Stanton's death sent shock waves through the Yellowstone County political structure, rattling allies and foes alike, who noted that the county has lost a persuasive, at times bare-knuckled advocate for growth and business development.

One of Stanton's frequent opponents, fellow commissioner Rolf Eklund, said his presence would be greatly missed.

"While I often didn't see eye to eye with Ted on how the county should proceed, I always credited the depth of his vision and his powerful commitment to his ideals," said Eklund, who was elected to the county commission in 1996, four years after Stanton. "He was gifted and strong and a real advocate for this county's prosperity. I will miss him."

Stanton, a native of Texas who came to Montana in the mid-1960s as a young oil executive, broke onto the political scene in 1980, winning election to one of the two Ward 5 seats as a Billings city councilman. He worked tirelessly to move the council toward pro-business positions, and his advocacy for growth can be seen in the city's persistent expansion to the west.

On the council, he also flashed the combative style that, in many ways, defined his public image. In 1984, he challenged a popular mayor, Stephen Benoit, and emerged with a surprising victory by promising prosperity for a city that, at the time, was being lashed by collapsing home prices and the fallout from the energy bust.

"He was, perhaps, a more driving, ambitious politician than we had seen," said Benoit, reached for comment in Largo, Fla., where he now lives. "You have to remember

that Billings, at that time, was still a fairly sleepy town. But I give Ted Stanton credit: he ran a tough, hard, clean race, and he won."

Stanton, however, chafed at Billings's form of city government, which empowers not the mayor but the city administrator, and in his eight years in the post, he clashed repeatedly with a succession of city managers. But there was one constant: the city administrators came and went, and Stanton remained standing.

In 1992, he ran for an open seat on the county commission, winning handily against three other candidates.

"I look at it like this," Stanton said in a 1993 interview, soon after joining the commission. "I could have stuck around city government for a while, trying to get through to a bunch of knuckleheads whose eye was on negotiating the length of a lunch break with the police union. Or I could go somewhere that would allow me to help make the whole region a better place to live and do business. It was an easy decision."

While Stanton's rough-and-tumble style didn't always sit well with fellow politicians, he was beloved among the business community in Yellowstone County, and he ran unopposed for reelection in 1994, 2000, and 2006.

"If you go stand on the corner of Twenty-Fourth Street and Monad Road and look south and west, that's all Ted Stanton," said Billings developer Cody Clines, referring to the corridor of restaurants, auto dealerships, and big-box stores that drive much of the region's commerce. "It's his vision that made that happen. He'll be missed."

Stanton, a Republican, had one notable misstep, where he broke with his base of support and nearly paid a high *political toll for doing so. He became an advocate for instituting a local-option sales tax in Yellowstone County, which he contended would allow the county to extract revenue from tourists passing through the region. He endured backlash from many quarters, particularly from constituents who endorse Montana's no-sales-tax status. Stanton was heavily criticized in the press.*

"They're just not ready for it," Stanton said in a 2006 profile by the Herald-Gleaner, one of his frequent sparring partners over the years. "I accept that. I don't agree with it. But I accept it. It doesn't detract one iota from what I'm trying to accomplish around here."

Stanton, a graduate of Texas Christian University in Fort Worth, is survived by his wife of forty years, Maureen, and an adult son, Edward Jr. Funeral arrangements are pending, said lawyer and family friend Jay L. Lamb.

"Maureen and the family appreciate all the kind thoughts and gestures at this difficult time," Lamb said in a statement released by his firm. "Ted Stanton's adult life was dedicated to making Yellowstone County and Billings a better place, and his family feels secure knowing that he did so and that he touched so many lives in the process."

I eat my cereal and chase my daily dose of fluoxetine with a glass of orange juice.

— • —

At 9:07 a.m., my mother calls.

"Edward, how did you sleep?"

"I slept."

"Yes, so did I. I…I'm having a hard time believing this has happened."

"It was in the newspaper."

"I saw that. It was a nice write-up, don't you think?"

"Yes."

"It fixated a bit too much on his political fights. It made your father seem like a combative man."

"Yes."

"I miss him so much." I can hear her voice breaking.

"I know."

"So," she says, regaining her composure, "Jay has made the arrangements. We're going to have a very small, private funeral tomorrow afternoon at two. It'll be you, me, Jay, and some of your father's associates. I don't want anything big and public. I don't think I can handle that right now. Jay says there will be some sort of public memorial in the near future."

"Where will the funeral be?"

"The Terrace Gardens Cemeteries on Thirty-Fourth. Do you know where that is?"

"Yes."

"We'll have a small gathering here at the house after. I would like you to be here."

"OK."

"Monday morning, we're to meet in Jay's office and go over the will and such. Can you be there?"

"Yes."

"Nine a.m."

"OK."

"Edward, I'm so lonely. Could you come up here today?"

"Yes."

We say our good-byes and hang up, and I look again at the newspaper. Yesterday had a high of forty-nine and a low of thirty-one, with 0.2 inches of rain, all of which I record in my notebook to complete my data.

Today looks to be similarly wet, which I'll know for sure tomorrow instead of having to rely on a forecast today.

The forecast for tomorrow, the day of my father's funeral, is for freezing rain.

— • —

At the wrought-iron gate outside my parents'—my mother's—house, I press the call button.

"Yes?"

"It's me, Mother."

"Come on in."

The gate opens, and I guide my Camry down the drive. I can see that my father's Cadillac DTS has been retrieved from the Yegen Golf Club parking lot and brought back here. My father gets a new Cadillac every two years. I can remember his telling me one time, years ago when I was just a little boy, that a Cadillac "is the greatest negotiating tool ever made."

"When they see you coming in a Cadillac, they know two things," he said. "First, that you know quality. And second, that you don't need their deal. You know why? Because you're driving a goddamned Cadillac, that's why."

My father loves Cadillacs.

(It occurs to me now that I am going to have to learn to refer to my father in the past tense rather than the present. He got a new Cadillac every two years. He loved Cadillacs. Past tense.)

I park the car, and I can see my mother standing in the open doorway, waiting for me to come inside. Her hand gestures tell me to hurry, as it's starting to rain.

— • —

My mother sets a glass filled with ice and Coca-Cola in front of me. I'm sitting on a couch in the den. She had asked me if I wanted a soda, and I had said yes. This is what I got. I make the quick decision to just let it pass. It's my fault for not specifying. I don't like Coke. I don't like my soda chilled.

Aside from her bloodshot eyes, my mother seems to have moved on in one way. She is again the perfectly put-together woman I've known all my life: every hair in place, exquisite clothing, smart shoes, makeup just so. It's the eyes that betray her. I suppose there's no way to cover those up.

She is pacing the room, making random observations that I have to resist the urge to comment on so I don't come across as snarky. (I love the word "snarky.") I am relying on every strategy for patience that I ever learned from Dr. Buckley.

"If it weren't for Jay, I don't know how I'd make it through this."

(I would like to try it without Jay.)

"Such happy memories." She is reaching out and lightly touching a face mask that is on the wall, one of the mementos of a trip to Africa.

(I wasn't there.)

"He wasn't from here, but he lived for this place."

(Some thought that he made sure this place lived for him.)

"Edward," she says, turning to me. "What is your favorite memory of your father?"

This is an easy question.

"Thanksgiving 1974. We drove down to Midland, then had Thanksgiving dinner with Grandpa Sid and Grandma Mabel. We watched the Cowboys win."

"I wasn't there, was I?"

"No."

Mother suddenly looks hurt and angry. "That's your favorite memory, one that doesn't include me, one when our marriage was coming apart?"

I realize that I have stepped in it.

"You asked me about my memory of him. Not of you and him."

"Edward, your father was cheating on me. Did you know that? He was cheating on me with one of the women in his office, and I told him that I was leaving and that he should think about our future together. And this—*this*—is your memory." My mother is definitely angry.

"I did not know that. It doesn't affect what I remember."

"Oh, really? What's so special about Thanksgiving and football?"

Now I'm angry.

"Football is all I had with him. It's the only way he could stand to be in a room with me, is if we were watching football."

"That's not true. That is a horrible thing to say about your father."

"It is! It is true."

"I don't know why," my mother says, her voice cracking and tears welling in her eyes, "you can't remember something that isn't so painful for me, something from later on, when he was such a good man who didn't fool around anymore. Why can't you remember all of the good things he did here, the things he accomplished, the honors he was given?"

"Because I was never a part of that. Who among your friends now knows me? No one. How many of those awards dinners did I go to? Not a single one. What do I have to remember about all of that?"

"Edward! You talk as if we're ashamed of you."

"You are, aren't you?"

"No." She is indignant.

"Who did you hide away in a house on Clark Avenue? Who is invited here only once a month for a dinner that no one really wants to have anyway? Who gets letters from a lawyer when Father wishes to speak to me?"

It angers me all the more that my mother would pretend that these things haven't happened.

"What are you talking about? I always gave you love, always," she says. "You're mad."

"No, Mother, I'm developmentally disabled. But that doesn't mean I'm crazy."

I stand up from the couch and stalk toward the front door, and then I turn back.

"You sit around here and pretend that father was a god all you want, Mother. I will not."

I open the door, step through, and then slam it behind me.

I stop on the front step to catch my breath. I can hear my mother crying on the other side of the door.

— • —

Donna Middleton is sitting on the front step of the house on Clark. I pull into the driveway, set the brake, turn off the ignition, and climb out.

"Edward, I heard the news about your father. I am so, so sorry." She is walking across the lawn toward me, and when she reaches me, she presses her hands against my cheeks. Her hands are warm.

"I can't talk to you," I say.

"It's hard, I know your family is going through a terrible time, but I just—"

I grasp her hands and pull them away from me. "I cannot talk to you."

I push past her to the front door and disappear inside the house. My father's house. My father is dead. I don't know whose house this is.

— • —

At 2:01 p.m., the phone rings.

"Hello?"

"Edward, this is Ruth Buckley."

"Yes."

"I read the news about your father today. I'm so sorry."

"Yes."

"How are you doing?"

"OK, I guess."

"Would you like me to set aside some time for you today? If you need it, I can do it."

"I think I will be OK."

"You're sure?"

"Yes."

"Edward, death can be a very a difficult thing to handle. If you need to talk, at any time, you call me. Do you have all of my numbers?"

"Yes."

"Edward, are you certain that you're handling this?"

"Yes. I know the stages of grief."

"Where do you think you are?"

"I'm not in denial. It happened. I know that. It was in the newspaper. I'm always in isolation. I don't feel angry, except a little bit at my mother, who is deifying my father—"

"Many people do that immediately after the death of a loved one."

"Yes. I'm not bargaining. I don't think I'm depressed. I haven't accepted it yet. I guess I would have to say that I'm dealing with it."

"OK. That's good."

"Yes."

"Call me if you need anything. And I do mean anything."

"I will."

"Good-bye, Edward. I will see you Tuesday, if not sooner."

"Good-bye, Dr. Buckley."

— • —

The phone rings again at 6:17 p.m. as I'm clearing away the dishes from my spaghetti dinner.

"Hello?"

"Edward."

"Hello, Mother."

"Edward, I want to apologize for yelling at you."

"OK."

"I feel so crazy sometimes. This can't be happening."

"You're not crazy, Mother. And it is happening."

"I know. Will you still be at the funeral tomorrow?"

"I will be there."

"Thank you."

"Mother?"

"Yes."

"I'm sorry for yelling, too."

— • —

It is Halloween, but no one comes to the door. This is as I planned. On Halloween, I turn off all the lights and put my car in the garage, and it seems for all appearances that I am not home. That is so much easier than telling eager children at the door that, no, I have no candy for them. Children get sad when you say such a thing to them, and that is difficult enough. But some adults, they get violently angry. That I do not need.

Kyle, I guess, is off enjoying Halloween in Laurel, at his grandparents' house. I watched through a tiny slit in the curtain as he walked out to the car earlier today with his overnight bag, accompanied by Donna in her nurse's scrubs. Jay L. Lamb's "memorandum of understanding" said nothing about watching my friends from the living room of the house I live in, and even if it had, I would like to see him prove that I did it.

— • —

Tonight's episode of *Dragnet*, the eleventh of the first season, is called "The Big Shooting," and it's one of my favorites. It originally aired on March 30, 1967.

In this episode, Sergeant Joe Friday and Officer Bill Gannon investigate the shooting of a police officer, but they are hindered by two things: The cop, who survives the shooting, has a mental blackout about what happened. Also, there are no other eyewitnesses to the shooting.

For months, Sergeant Joe Friday and Officer Bill Gannon keep at it, slowly accumulating clues and evidence about the shooter and his cohort. (I love the word "cohort.") Finally, one of Sergeant Joe Friday's informants lets him know where the men can be found. Sergeant Joe Friday and Officer Bill Gannon bust in on them in a cheap motel and take them downtown. They still don't have an eyewitness who can identify the men. But Sergeant Joe Friday has an idea.

He dresses the amnesiac cop in his uniform and has him stand at the door when the men are interrogated. Thinking that they had killed the cop and now worried that he will identify him, they get spooked and admit to the shooting. Once again, Sergeant Joe Friday gets his men.

I would like to be lucky enough to not remember those who take things away from me.

— • —

Tonight, I need a new green office folder.

Dear Mother:

Although you have apologized to me and I have for-given you for the events of today, I feel that I must make it clear to you that there is much you either don't know or don't want to know about your now-dead husband, my father.

I am not making these things up. You may think that Father hung the moon—which is an idiom, as no one has the physical capability to actually hang a moon. But my memories of him are mostly of being marginalized and being unable to please him. That makes me very sad now that I will never see him again.

In Jay L. Lamb's statement in the Herald-Gleaner *article, he referred to "Maureen and the family." I should not have to point out to you that "the family" is I. It is you and I now. Father is gone. And while I realize that you are in the denial-and-isolation stage of grief, I do hope that you can deal with it in a brisk manner. I would like to be your friend and your child. I could manage only one of those things with my father.*

I am, your son,
Edward

SATURDAY, NOVEMBER 1

On the second full day of my life without my father, and the 306th day of the year (because it is a leap year), we are going to bury him. It is this strange custom that sits in the forefront of my mind when I awake at 7:42 a.m. Why do we bury those who die? Where did that come from?

I am lucky to live in an age when I can learn the answers to such questions as easily as climbing out of bed and going into the next room. To run the word "death" through an Internet search engine is to traffic in websites and pictures that educate and horrify.

I learn that we have not advanced so far from the days of the Neanderthals, when it comes to matters of disposing of the dead. They, too, buried the people who expired, and though Neanderthals were crude people, they did not bury carelessly. Bodies were tenderly placed in holes, sometimes in a fetal position, as if returning the person to child form, and sometimes in a recumbent position, presumably for a safe, comfortable trip to wherever the Neanderthals thought their dead were going. What happens to us beyond death is more than my fact-loving mind wishes to contemplate.

When this land I live in now belonged to the Indians, a body was often left out in the open for birds and scavengers to feast on. The Absarokes would place their dead bodies in trees or on scaffolds, and then they would come along to collect the bones for burial later. If you consider the culture of the Indian, it makes sense. The tribes were and are great stewards of the land and the animals who roam it. They would use every part of a buffalo and honor the animal in the hunt. It makes sense, then, that they would not let their own bodies decay without replenishing nature. I find myself liking the Absarokes' approach.

The Egyptians preserved their dead. The Romans and the Greeks burned theirs, a practice that did not catch on here in America until the nineteenth century. Nowadays, cremation is considered an environmentally friendly way of disposing of the dead, rather than taking up acreage in a cemetery. I can only imagine what my father might have said to this option; he detested environmentalists.

I also learn things I did not want to know about death. I learn about a man named Budd Dwyer, a politician like my father. Budd Dwyer got railroaded in an ethics investigation in Pennsylvania, showed up at a press conference in 1987, made a short speech, and then shot himself on live television. I saw the whole thing on video. I wish I had not.

Later today, we will bid my father farewell and ask that he rest in peace. I hope he does. I don't know what the afterlife is, or if there is one—this is a question I don't ponder long, as it challenges my preference for facts like nothing else. If there is an afterlife, I hope Budd Dwyer, treated so poorly while he was here, is having a good time and will be nice to my father. They were both Republicans. They should get along.

— • —

My father was not a religious man, but he saw great political value in going to church. If you belong to the right church in Billings— or anywhere else, I suppose, but I can't say for sure, as I don't live anywhere else—you can cut a few business deals while hearing the Good Word.

In Billings, the church my father chose is First Congregational. Father always said his favorite part of First Church, as it is known, is the rich diversity of its people. Yet when I was a child and a teenager, it wasn't difficult to realize that the only people he spent much time talking with were the six or seven developers who were also members—all middle-aged, white, rich men.

Whatever the roots of that longtime association, it explains why today, at 2:05, the Reverend Heron James of First Congregational has stepped forward to deliver the eulogy.

"Friends, welcome. We are here today to remember and say good-bye to a great man in the history of Billings, one who lifted the city and people he loved to a more prosperous place..."

My mother and I are sitting side by side, in front of my father's closed casket. To her left is the ever-present Jay L. Lamb. I turn my head and scan the other faces and see that my mother was not kidding when she said it would be a small gathering: I see the Billings mayor, Kevin Hammel, and one, two, three, four, five city council members, and my father's two fellow county commissioners, Rolf Eklund and Craig Hashbarger.

"...Ted Stanton was not a man who would settle for good enough, not when better than ever was so close to our reach..."

When I turn my head the other way, to the right, I see someone I missed on the first pass: Dave Akers, my father's buddy and the subject of the last political fight of his life. He is standing apart from the huddled crowd, which has jammed under the awning so as not to get pelted by the frigid rain falling outside. He looks sad and wan (I love the word "wan"), the way my mother did that first day.

"...so allow yourself this moment of sadness to mourn the loss of a true original, but let yourself be happy from now on that we were privileged to know him..."

I feel uncomfortable. How could I be my father's son and yet not know a single person, other than my mother or Jay L. Lamb (a dubious one, at that), who is here to mark his life? Whose fault is that? I'm not wise enough to know that answer. I hope it is mine. At least I still have a chance to rectify it.

"...Amen."

As the small band pushes forward to place roses upon my father's casket before it is lowered into the ground, I walk ninety degrees to my right, out from under the awning, into the rain that slaps my face, and between the rows of those who, like my father, are gone.

— • —

Two hundred yards away, I take cover under a tree. My hair is drenched, and I grip my head at the temples with both hands and sweep my fingers through, wringing water onto my collar.

I am standing over the resting spot of a family:

CLAUDE T. BOONE
1906–1954
Beloved father

AGNES MILLER BOONE
1910–1987
Beloved mother

RANCE LEROY BOONE
1930–1992
Devoted son

I slump down to the base of the tree, the backside of my black slacks landing in the mud. The tears that I so dislike are fighting my best attempts to tamp them down, until finally, I can't fight them anymore.

— • —

By the time I arrive at my parents'—my mother's—house, the reception is going full bore. Many of the Billings, Yellowstone County, and Montana power players are here, and they have broken into clumps of animated conversation, talking about whatever it is that political power players talk about.

There are more people here than were at the funeral. My mother attempts to introduce me to many of them—the mayor, then a youngish couple who I learn are neighbors, then one of my dad's old colleagues with Standard Oil. Inevitably, my mother gets diverted to other matters—food or drink or the beckoning call of some politico. Soon enough, I am left to wander through the house alone, trying (and it's difficult) to smile at the strangers who acknowledge me with a glance.

Three times, I am asked how I knew my father. The first time, it just seems absurd, but I answer, if only to see the questioner's chagrin. (I love the word "chagrin.") The second, I am insulted, but I answer again, testily. The third, I do not answer, but instead pivot and walk to the staircase, ascending out of the low roar in the main part of the house, until I find the guest bedroom—where I've never stayed—and close the door and welcome the silence.

This room is unlike the rest of the house. When my father built this place, he commissioned a contemporary style, with lots of glass and steel and sharp angles. The furniture through the house is comfortable but not welcoming, if you can understand what I am driving at. But this room seems much more like one you might find in an old, warm farmhouse—a big, poufy bed, warm colors, old-style wallpaper, bucolic (I love the word "bucolic") vistas framed and placed on the wall. I can tell that my mother got her hands on this room when it came time to decorate. My mother is the sort of person who would want a guest to be comfortable. My father was the sort of person who would want a guest to check out his new set of golf clubs.

I lay myself down on the bed and close my eyes, and soon, I am adrift in late-afternoon sleep.

— • —

"Edward. Edward, wake up." My mother is shaking me on the shoulder. "Edward."

My head feels as though it's filled with sand, and I have a hard time getting my eyes to focus.

"Edward, wake up."

"I'm awake. What time is it?"

"It's six."

I look down at my watch and wait for the digital figures to emerge from the blur. It's 5:57.

"Edward, we're going to do some toasts to your father. You should come down."

That sounds positively dreadful, but I am climbing out of the bed.

"I will be right there."

— • —

By the time I've put myself back together—re-tucked the shirt that escaped in my sleep, wet down my hair to get it in place, had a nice long pee—and trundled downstairs, the toasts have begun. Jay L. Lamb is holding the floor now.

"Ted Stanton wasn't just my client. He was my best friend. I always knew where I stood with him, I could always trust his instincts about things, and I could always rely on him. Ted, I know you're in a better place. I will miss you, buddy."

One by one, my father's colleagues stand and offer remembrances.

Some are funny:

"It must have been '94 or '95," Craig Hashbarger says, "but ol' Ted, he knew the animal trainer with the circus that came through—hell, you guys know, Ted knew damned near the whole country, it seemed—and he talked this guy into letting him bring a lion into the commissioners' meeting. Ted said, 'I want you to meet my new adviser. Anything you have to say to me, say to him first.'"

Laughter ripples through the room.

"The thing is, with Ted, damn—he might have been serious!"

More laughter.

Some are touching:

"When Mary got sick, Ted and Maureen were always there with whatever we needed, often before we knew we needed it,"

James Grimes, one of the biggest developers in town, is saying. "At his own expense, he chartered a jet to take us to Seattle for that last attempt at saving her life. I don't think we would have had the chance otherwise—that's how touch-and-go everything was at that point. A better friend, I never had."

Some are what Dr. Buckley would call self-indulgent:

"Ted always told me I was a fool to want to be mayor, and a lot of times, I think he's right," Kevin Hammel is saying. It's well known in Billings that Mayor Hammel is a climber; he has half a dozen defeats in races for higher office that would give him more money and more power. In fact, it seems that the only political race he can win is for mayor of Billings—perhaps because those who live here figure they can keep an eye on him and that he can't mess things up too much.

"So maybe he's given me another gift, by opening up this seat on the county commission..."

An "ugh" goes up in the room, and I hear, though I can't place the sources, "Sit down, Kevin," and "Cut that guy off."

As the toasts seem to be winding down, my mother steps forward and says, "I want you all to know how much your love and support mean right now. We"—and now she's looking at me, smiling—"are fortunate to know you, and Ted was fortunate to have had you in his life. Thank you ever so much for this lovely tribute to him."

And now my mother is shocking me, because she is actually saying, aloud, in front of these people, "Edward, please say a few words."

I can see Jay L. Lamb, and he looks as though he wants to dig a hole in the stone floor of this house and climb into it.

"Mother..." I say in protest.

"Just a few words, dear."

I step out of the gathered throng. I can hear my heart throbbing as if it is in my cranium. And then I am surprised to hear words leaving my mouth.

"I…I can't think of a funny story about my father."

Everybody is looking at me.

"I liked to watch Dallas Cowboys games with him."

There is now a bit of laughter, and someone says, jokingly, "Ted, watch the Cowboys? Never!"

"I'm not good at public speaking," I continue. "When I have thought of my father since he died, I think of the words to a song I like. It is by Matthew Sweet."

I see quizzical looks on the faces in front of me.

I recite the lyrics to "Life Without You." It is a song about loss and helplessness, and that's how I feel about my father. I say the words quickly, because I am not a public speaker and I don't feel comfortable. When I look up as I'm talking, I see people looking at me in quizzical ways. I don't like this, so I don't look up anymore.

When I finish, the room is silent. Maybe I should have tried harder to tell a funny story. The governor is looking at me as if I'm a loon. And my mother's shoulders are heaving as she tries to muffle her cries.

— • —

My father's death hasn't changed one thing: I am always relieved to be out of his house and back in mine. I decided to leave after Dave Akers approached Rolf Eklund, my father's county commission colleague, and poked a finger in his chest as they argued. After the brief scuffle was quelled and my mother had tried her best to act as if the gathering hadn't been marred, I decided that I should go.

So I did.

— • —

At 10:00, I cue up tonight's episode of *Dragnet*. It is the twelfth installment of the first season of color episodes, called "The Hit-and-Run Driver," and it is one of my favorites.

In this episode, which originally aired on April 6, 1967, Sergeant Joe Friday and Officer Bill Gannon track down an executive named Clayton Fillmore (played by Robert Clarke) who clipped an old woman and an old man in a crosswalk, killing them. By the time the cops catch up to him the next day, they suspect that he was drunk, but they can't prove it. Clayton Fillmore is a cavalier man—he doesn't care that the old people are dead, and his wife is about to leave him because he disregards her. But somehow, he gets off with a suspended sentence.

Soon enough, however, he drives drunk again. He has a bad crash, killing two teenage girls and critically injuring a couple. His wife, who decided to stay with him, is also hurt, and Clayton Fillmore loses his legs.

I think that is what is called karma, although karma is difficult to prove. Like Sergeant Joe Friday, I prefer facts.

— • —

After *Dragnet*, I prepare yet another green office folder.

God:

I have to admit something: It feels odd to be writing to something or someone that I don't know exists. I do not mean to be disrespectful. I believe in science, I believe in things that I can witness, I believe in things that can be empirically proved. The Judeo-Christian image of God—or even the ones revered by Muslims or Buddhists or Taoists—is not something that can be proved in that way. I hope you understand my hesitancy about this, assuming you exist to understand it. I don't like to assume. I prefer facts.

Despite all of that, it would give me some comfort to believe that you exist, especially at this difficult time for me and my mother. I hope you do exist. Even though hope is as intangible as belief, I am not hostile to it. Hope gives me comfort.

So here is my hope: That you will take care of my father. That you will let him know that I am trying hard to forgive him, even though I will not deify him like my mother does. That you will let him know that I love him. That you will let him know that we miss him.

I realize that this is not a letter of complaint. I hope you understand. I don't feel like complaining today, though there is much I could complain about. I'm just looking for some peace. It has been a hard week. It was a hard week before my father died. It's harder now.

I have one more hope, God, if you have the time or inclination: Could you see your way clear to send some peace our way?

With regards,
Edward Stanton

SUNDAY, NOVEMBER 2

When I awake at 7:37 a.m. for the nineteenth time this year (because it's a leap year), I quickly note two things:

First, this will be the third full day without my father. I make the notation in my notebook accordingly.

Second, this day will bring the first Dallas Cowboys game of my life without him.

Given how much I like to count things, how much I like the Cowboys, and how much my father liked the Cowboys, I think I have found a new entry for my data sheets. I make the proper notations, and for now, my data is complete.

— • —

Since my father bought this house for me to live in eight years ago—eight years and 106 days ago—he and I have not watched as many Dallas Cowboys games together as we did before, when we lived in the same house. I should have thought to count the games we've watched together in those years, but the instances have been erratic, and I am not as interested in random happenings as I am in patterns. I do spend every Thanksgiving Day at my parents' house—my mother's house now—and the Dallas Cowboys always play on Thanksgiving, so those games would account for the majority of the games we have shared in the past eight years and 106 days.

Dallas Cowboys games on Thanksgiving Day are a pattern, and so it should not surprise you that I do keep track of those. In the eight games that the Dallas Cowboys have played on Thanksgiving Day since my father bought this house for me to live in, the Cowboys have won four and lost four. That is a .500 record, and it's not very good, at least for the Dallas Cowboys. I assume that even with my father now dead, I will spend the upcoming Thanksgiving Day at my parents' house—now my mother's house—and will see the Dallas Cowboys play the Seattle Seahawks, who stink. The Dallas Cowboys ought to win that game, although at this point it's all conjecture. I prefer facts.

I guess what I am saying is this: I have seen a lot of Dallas Cowboys games with my father, even when you factor in the relatively few of them in the past eight years and 106 days. It will be odd to think that he is no longer here, on the day that the Dallas Cowboys play the New York Giants, who don't stink at all. I wish my father were here. He hated the New York Giants.

— • —

I take my morning newspaper—which tells me that yesterday's high was thirty-one and yesterday's low was nineteen—with my corn flakes, my orange juice, and my fluoxetine. The *Billings Herald-Gleaner* also tells me that today's high will be forty-one and the low will be thirty-three, but that's not as valuable to me as the first two numbers. The first two numbers are facts; the other two are just a forecast. I prefer facts.

Judging by the *Billings Herald-Gleaner*, there is a lot of interest in the presidential race, which will be voted upon Tuesday, two days from today. I have not been paying a whole lot of attention to the presidential race, if you must know. Politics of any sort are hard to be interested in when you care about facts as much as I do. Presidential candidates often seem much more interested in what is known as "spin"—that is, the twisting of facts to support a position beneficial to them. This is actually praiseworthy in politics. It is considered an art form. I cannot understand that, and so rather than letting it make me crazy (a word I do not love, yet one that is accurate when I allow myself to fret about politics), I simply tune it out. I have been alive for the presidencies of seven of the forty-three presidents in this country's history—Nixon, Ford, Carter, Reagan, Bush, Clinton, and Bush the younger—and as far as I can tell, not one of them has made much of a difference in the important things I care about: the high and low temperatures, *Dragnet*, Dallas Cowboys football, R.E.M., or Matthew Sweet. Although, you could make the argument that the Republican presidents inspire angrier music from R.E.M. If you wish to make that argument, I will not dispute it.

Much of the attention on this presidential race is on a man named Barack Obama, who apparently would become the first black president in United States history—although a lot of people seem to think he is an Arab. I don't care if he's an Arab or if he's black. It's not like the forty-three white men who have been president have all been great shakes. (I love the slang term "great shakes.")

— • —

Because the Dallas Cowboys' game does not start until 2:15 p.m., I have decided to embark on a project this morning. I am going to rate the ten greatest Dallas Cowboys games I saw with my father. I think it will be fun to count something like that, and I like remembering good times with my father.

I am not going to include Super Bowl victories among the ten greatest games. Let's face it: The Dallas Cowboys have won five Super Bowls, and so that would take up almost half of my list right there. I wouldn't count the Dallas Cowboys' first Super Bowl victory, 24–3 over the Miami Dolphins in Super Bowl VI, as I was too young to have a memory of the game. I feel confident that my father watched it, as he loved the Dallas Cowboys, and because I was just a little boy, barely three years old (I was three years and seven days old on January 16, 1972, when Super Bowl VI was played), there is a good chance I was with him, but I don't know for sure. It's conjecture. I prefer facts.

— • —

After clearing away the breakfast dishes, I head into the spare bedroom and fire up the computer. My project flows quickly.

TEN MOST MEMORABLE COWBOYS GAMES
A memoir of football-watching with my father
By Edward M. Stanton Jr.

Game number 1: November 28, 1974
Result: Dallas Cowboys, 24; Washington Redskins, 23
What happened: Rookie quarterback Clint Longley, playing in place of the injured Roger Staubach, threw a fifty-yard touchdown pass to Drew Pearson with twenty-eight seconds remaining to beat the hated Washington Redskins and keep them from clinching a playoff berth. Clint Longley also had a thirty-five-yard touchdown pass to Billy Joe DuPree.

Why I remember it: We watched the game in Texas, with my Grandpa Sid and Grandma Mabel. My father and I had been on a road trip together, and we had Thanksgiving dinner, and we saw the Dallas Cowboys win. This is the first game I remember watching with my father. He told me after the game, "Teddy, as long as you live, you'll never see another one like that." I didn't like my old nickname, Teddy, but I didn't mind that day.

Game number 2: December 28, 1975

Result: Cowboys, 17; Minnesota Vikings, 14

What happened: This is the one that is called the "Hail Mary" game, on account of Roger Staubach's saying that he closed his eyes and threw a prayer of a pass that Drew Pearson caught for the winning touchdown in the playoffs against the heavily favored Vikings. A lot of Vikings fans say that Drew Pearson pushed off illegally, but I think they just feel bad because they lost.

Why I remember it: After Drew Pearson scored the touchdown, my father swept me up in his arms, put me on his shoulder, and paraded me around our living room, saying, "The Cowboys are going to the Super Bowl! The Cowboys are going to the Super Bowl!" It was just conjecture at that point—the Cowboys still had to win the NFC championship game—but he was right: The Cowboys went to the Super Bowl. I just wish they had been able to beat the Pittsburgh Steelers.

Game number 3: January 17, 1993

Result: Cowboys, 30; San Francisco 49ers, 20

What happened: After a Super Bowl drought of fifteen years, the Cowboys got back in the big game by beating the hated 49ers in the muck and mud in San Francisco.

The Cowboys sealed it with a long slant pass from Troy Aikman to Alvin Harper. After that, my father grabbed my shoulder and shook me and said, "That Jimmy Johnson has balls to make a call like that!" I think it was a compliment.

Why I remember it: It took my father a long time to forgive the Cowboys and owner Jerry Jones for firing Tom Landry in 1989. But when the Cowboys got back to the Super Bowl—and especially after they won it—my father buried his grudge. "You can't stay mad forever, Edward," he said. I thought that was very nice of him. Also, for at least a year afterward, my father would sometimes look at me and go, "Hey, Edward, you know what? How 'bout them Cowboys!" My father could be pretty funny sometimes.

Game number 4: January 3, 1983
Result: Minnesota Vikings, 31; Cowboys, 27
What happened: Tony Dorsett ran for a ninety-nine-yard touchdown on *Monday Night Football*. A lot of football experts think it's one of the best runs in National Football League history.

Why I remember it: This is one of only two Dallas Cowboys losses on my top ten, but Tony Dorsett's run was worth it. My father and I were watching the game on television, and when Tony Dorsett got loose, my father said, "He's gonna go all the way, Teddy! He's gonna do it! He's gonna do it! Oh my God, he did it!" The next day, he and I played catch with the football in our front yard, even though it was a really cold day, and my father pretended that he was Tony Dorsett running for a ninety-nine-yard touchdown.

Game number 5: January 23, 1994

Result: Cowboys, 38; San Francisco 49ers, 21

What happened: For the second straight year, the Cowboys reached the Super Bowl by beating the 49ers. (They would go on to beat the Buffalo Bills in the Super Bowl for the second straight year, too.) This time, the game was at Texas Stadium. Also, Jimmy Johnson called a radio station earlier in the week and guaranteed that the Cowboys would win. "Brass balls, Edward," my father said. "The man has brass balls." This is also a compliment, I think.

Why I remember it: It was the last game Grandpa Sid and Grandma Mabel ever went to, and they called us in Billings afterward to tell us about it. When my father was hanging up with Grandpa Sid, he said, "I love you, Pop." And then he told me he loved me, too. I liked it when he would do that.

Game number 6: January 16, 1996

Result: Cowboys, 38; Green Bay Packers, 27

What happened: The Cowboys, after a one-year hiatus, returned to the Super Bowl, this time under Coach Barry Switzer. They haven't been back since. My father hated Barry Switzer. "That guy couldn't coach a dog to lick his balls," my father said. "How they got to the Super Bowl, I'll never know." My father talked about balls a lot.

Why I remember it: As my condition was worsening, my father and I were growing apart more and more and weren't talking as often or as nicely as we had before. When this game was over, my father said, "You're the best football buddy I ever had, Edward." That made me feel good.

Game number 7: January 4, 1981
Result: Cowboys, 30; Atlanta Falcons, 27
What happened: The Cowboys scored twenty points in the fourth quarter in Atlanta and rallied to beat the Falcons, which allowed them to go on and play the Philadelphia Eagles in the National Football Conference championship game. They lost that one, though, which is why it isn't on my list.

Why I remember it: My father was despondent when Roger Staubach retired. "That's the greatest Cowboy ever, Teddy," he said. (That's a subjective judgment, not a fact, but my father was never the stickler for facts that I am.) On this day, Roger Staubach's successor, Danny White, led a comeback every bit as good as any Roger Staubach ever led. That pleased my father very much.

Game number 8: October 27, 2002
Result: Seattle Seahawks, 17; Cowboys, 14
What happened: Emmitt Smith, the last of the Dallas Cowboys' so-called "Triplets"—the other two were Troy Aikman and Michael Irvin—set the all-time National Football League rushing record with an eleven-yard run against the Seattle Seahawks. It was really neat: They stopped the game and everything to recognize Emmitt Smith's achievement.

Why I remember it: Much like the other loss on my top-ten list, the result didn't matter. My father and I saw National Football League history together. "That guy's the greatest player in Cowboys history, bar none," my father pronounced, perhaps forgetting that he had already made that judgment for Roger Staubach. But that's the nice thing about subjective judgment, if there is a nice thing about it: you can change your mind.

Game number 9: September 5, 1983

Result: Cowboys, 31; Washington Redskins, 30

What happened: The Cowboys rallied from 23–3 down after the first half to beat the hated Washington Redskins in Washington, DC. The truth is, I could have picked ten times the Cowboys beat the Redskins as my favorite games, because I dislike the Redskins just that much. I would say hate, but I think it's a misapplication of the word.

Why I remember it: I didn't see it. It was a *Monday Night Football* game, and because the Cowboys were losing so badly, my mother suggested that I didn't need to stay up and see the rest of the game. The next morning, I sat down to have breakfast with my mother and father and asked how the game ended. "Oh, you know," my father said. "About how you'd expect…They won!" I couldn't believe it, but he said yes, the Dallas Cowboys had won, and he showed me the proof in the *Billings Herald-Gleaner*. It was really neat.

Game number 10: November 22, 2007

Result: Cowboys, 34; New York Jets, 3

What happened: The Cowboys beat the stuffing out of the New York Jets on Thanksgiving. It really wasn't that great a game.

Why I remember it: Because I realize now that it's the last game I ever saw with my father.

Today's Dallas Cowboys–New York Giants game definitely would not make my top-ten list, even if my father were here to see it with me. For a moment, I think it's better that he's not here, but that makes me feel bad. I think Dr. Buckley would say that it's only football and that I ought to have more perspective about things. Dr. Buckley is a very logical woman.

But even someone with perspective would say that the Cowboys are terrible today. I wish Tony Romo would hurry up and get better from his broken pinkie, because the guy who is playing in his place, Brad Johnson, cannot play very well. The New York Giants are a very good team, and I don't know if the Dallas Cowboys could beat them even if Tony Romo was healthy—how could anyone know such a thing? But maybe if Tony Romo were playing, the Dallas Cowboys wouldn't be trailing 21–7 at halftime, with the seven points coming only because the Giants did something uncharacteristically sloppy.

The way the Cowboys have been playing lately, it is not much fun to pull on my blue or white Tony Romo jersey and root for them.

— • —

The knock on the front door comes while I am rummaging around in the freezer for that Häagen-Dazs chocolate sorbet, only to remember that I tossed it out after my father died, a decision I am now regretting. I head across the living room to the front door and peek through the spy hole.

It is Donna Middleton. Holy shit!

I consider backing slowly and softly away from the door and pretending that I am not here, but now Donna Middleton is saying, "I heeeeaaaar you, Edward."

Holy shit!

I open the door.

Donna Middleton is not wearing her nurse's scrubs, even though Sunday is a day she works. She is wearing a jacket and gloves. Behind her, Kyle is sitting on the Blue Blaster.

"Hi, Edward," Donna says. "I'm off today. We thought you might want to come outside for a while."

"I—"

"No way!" Kyle says, standing up and pointing at my chest. I look down at my white Tony Romo jersey.

"The Cowboys suck. Denver rules."

"Kyle!" Donna Middleton snaps, looking over her shoulder at him. She then turns back to me. "I hate it when he says 'sucks.'"

"You don't know, Kyle!" I say. "Dallas doesn't suck. Dallas has won five Super Bowls and gone to eight. Denver hasn't done that."

"Edward! You're fighting with a little boy," Donna says.

"He started it by saying Dallas sucks," I say, and then I shout again at Kyle, "Dallas doesn't suck!"

"He started it? Edward, he's nine."

"So what? What are you doing here, anyway?"

"We thought you might want to come out and watch the Blue Blaster, but that was obviously a bad idea."

"Yes, it was. I'm busy, and you shouldn't be here."

Donna looks shocked, and then she looks mad. "Don't worry about it, we'll leave."

"Good."

"Let's go, Kyle." They leave, hand in hand.

The Blue Blaster stays.

— • —

I sit down for the second half of the Dallas Cowboys' game against the New York Giants, but I don't really watch. What difference does it make? The Dallas Cowboys are stupid. Donna Middleton is stupid, and her stupid kid says stupid things. The whole world is stupid.

— • —

By 10:00, I'm still frustrated, but I decide that I'm calm enough to at least try to watch tonight's episode of *Dragnet*. It's called "The Big Bookie," and it's one of my favorites.

This episode, which originally aired on April 13, 1967, is one of the few in which Officer Bill Gannon isn't Sergeant Joe Friday's partner. This is because the case that's being worked is in North Hollywood, where Officer Bill Gannon apparently worked for many years, and so there is concern that he will be identified if he is working undercover.

For this episode, Sergeant Joe Friday is paired up with Sergeant William Riddle, who is also the department's chaplain.

Sergeants Joe Friday and William Riddle are investigating a bookmaking operation, and they're posing as surveyors who frequent a bar, where they try to win the confidence of the bartender, who sets up the bets. Meanwhile, Officer Bill Gannon stakes out the home office, where the bets come in.

Eventually, the gambling ring is busted, and Sergeants Joe Friday and William Riddle take the bartender, Richard Clinger (played by Bobby Troup), to jail.

It turns out that Richard Clinger has a little girl with a bad heart, and she dies while he is in jail. He calls Sergeants Joe Friday and William Riddle and asks if they can help him make the funeral arrangements, since he is in jail.

He says he wants a nice service for his little girl and asks if they know anyone who can do that for him.

Sergeant Joe Friday tells him, "We have someone," then gives him a nice pat on the arm.

And so it is that I am sitting here, in the living room, crying. And I cannot stop.

— • —

Donna:

I wish I could tell you why I cannot speak to you. I suppose I could, but somehow, I think you would think less of me if you knew that I had signed an agreement not to. Perhaps it's better that you just think I am mean.

I wish I had not yelled at Kyle. You were right: That was childish, and when I tell Dr. Buckley about it, I bet she will tell me the same thing. I am not feeling very secure about the Dallas Cowboys these days, and I overreacted.

It would be easier for me if you would just quit coming around here. Then I would not have to be mean and I would not have to see the disappointment in your face. And perhaps I would not be so disappointed in myself.

Maybe you could think about this the next time you're tempted to come over and knock on the door.

Regards,
Edward Stanton

Just before midnight, I slip outside and see the Blue Blaster still sitting in my front yard. I quietly roll it up the driveway and put it inside the garage.

MONDAY, NOVEMBER 3

Donna Middleton and Kyle have just told me the funniest story, and we are all laughing hard. I don't think I have ever laughed so much.

I glance out onto Clark Avenue from the front porch, and I see my father's Cadillac going by. My father rolls down the window as he passes and looks at us there, and he shakes his head disapprovingly.

I stop laughing.

"What's wrong?" Donna Middleton asks.

I don't say anything, but I reach into the mailbox and fish out today's letters. There is only one.

It says Lambert, Slaughter & Lamb, Attorneys at Law, on the envelope.

I open the letter.

> *Mr. Edward M. Stanton Jr.:*
>
> *You have broken the agreement set forth with your father regarding fraternization with Donna Middleton. This will have serious consequences.*
>
> *Regards,*
> *Jay L. Lamb*

A wrecking ball crashes into the house my father bought for me to live in, destroying it with a single swing.

— • —

It's 7:38 a.m.

I am awake.

I am out of breath.

I have been awake at 7:38 a.m. 226 times out of 308 days this year (because it is a leap year).

I am not looking forward to day number 308, the fourth full day without my father.

I reach for my notebook and pen to record my data. The pen does not work. I reach for backup pen number one. It does not work. I reach for backup pen number two. It does not work.

I do not believe in omens, as what people call omens usually can be explained as coincidences, and although coincidences are facts, the belief in omens is not a belief in science. People who put stock in omens believe that some mysterious, mystical force is guiding what happens in our lives. I believe in science. I believe in facts.

But if I did believe in omens, I would not be enthused about the fact that none of the three pens on my nightstand works. Until I get up and find an operational pen, my data will not be complete.

— • —

The same perfectly put-together, impossibly pretty secretary is the gatekeeper to Jay L. Lamb's office. Today, however, I am not waiting alone in an uncomfortable chair to find out my father's displeasure with me. I am sitting next to my mother, who is also in an uncomfortable chair, waiting to find out what my father has intended for us.

"Can we go in yet?" my mother asks the impossibly pretty secretary. It is 9:11 a.m. We have been waiting eleven minutes longer than we should have to see Jay L. Lamb.

"It should only be a few more minutes," the impossibly pretty secretary says apologetically. "He's had a conference call that ran a little long."

"Thank you," my mother says, an edge in her voice.

"Oh, and Mrs. Stanton," the impossibly pretty secretary says, "I am so sorry about your husband. He was the sweetest man."

"Thank you," my mother says, and now her lips are pursed. I think about *Dragnet* actor G. D. Spradlin and his mouth tighter than a chicken's asshole. That's what my mother looks like right now. I stifle a giggle.

At 9:16, the impossibly pretty secretary tells us we can go in.

— • —

"Maureen, I am so sorry about the wait," Jay L. Lamb says, getting up from behind his desk to meet my mother. He takes her hand and guides her to a chair. He has never done that with me, and I've been here many, many times, although it occurs to me that I never bothered to count them. No matter. I wouldn't want Jay L. Lamb to touch me.

"Edward," he says, nodding at me and gesturing for me to take a seat. As I sit down, he goes back behind his desk and sits in his big office chair, which looks far more comfortable than the chairs my mother and I are occupying.

"So," he says, clapping his hands together, "we're here to go over Ted's estate and how it will be apportioned. Maureen, of course, you know all of this, being Ted's wife. Edward, I'll go over it with you, and please ask any questions if you're unable to understand."

"I'm developmentally disabled, Mr. Lamb. I'm not stupid."

Jay L. Lamb looks momentarily dumbfounded, and then he smiles thinly. "Yes, of course. Let's get on with it, shall we?"

— • —

My father is rich—really, really rich. You would be shocked if I told you just how rich, and that's why I am going to tell you:

My father has an estimated $27.85 million in assets—that's stock holdings, savings, pensions, and the like, as Jay L. Lamb tells it—and that doesn't even include the house and cars and boat and cabin on Holter Lake. As Jay L. Lamb tells it, my father had a remarkable penchant for getting into and out of investments at just the right time. He left the oil business before it tanked in the early 1980s. He invested heavily in tech throughout the 1990s, and then he shifted his holdings before the bubble burst in 2001. He bought a lot of Google stock in the initial public offering and has seen that investment grow. My father, it seems, was as good a businessman as he was a politician.

Jay L. Lamb explains that, because my mother is my father's direct survivor, the bulk of the holdings will go to her. "The money, the stocks, the house, the cars," he says.

"I have my Mercedes," my mother says. "I don't need that Cadillac, too."

"You own it, free and clear," Jay says.

"But I don't need it. Edward, would you like to have your father's Cadillac?"

"Well, my Toyota Camry did get hit by a careless driver outside Rimrock Mall."

"It's settled, then. The Cadillac is yours."

"If that's how you want to do it," Jay L. Lamb says.

"That's how I want to do it," my mother replies.

"OK, let's talk about Edward," Jay L. Lamb says. "When Ted bought the house on Clark Avenue, it was in his name and yours, Maureen. The house passes along to you. Ted's will makes it clear that we're now to have you and Edward sign a quit-claim deed listing Edward as a co-owner."

"What's a quit-claim deed?" I ask.

"It essentially says that when your mother dies, the house goes solely to you."

"So it's my house now?"

"Yours and your mother's, yes."

"It means, Edward," my mother says, "that you can stay in that house for as long as you like."

Jay L. Lamb also explains that my father has set up an annuity for me, with enough money behind it to ensure that my living expenses are taken care of for the rest of my life. My bills will continue to go to Jay L. Lamb's office, and he will administer my annuity and pay my expenses.

"You'll need to budget, of course," Jay L. Lamb says. "But you have plenty in reserve should you occasionally go over."

"How much in reserve?" I ask.

"Five million dollars."

Jay L. Lamb then explains what happens to the money after my mother dies—that some will go to me, some will go to taxes, and that some should probably go to charity while my mother is still alive so that the tax burden is reduced, but I'm not listening all that closely. Five million dollars is more money than I would ever need, I think.

— • —

After Jay L. Lamb has finished going over money matters, he asks if I have any questions.

"Yes," I say. "My mother says I can stay in the house on Clark Avenue for as long as I want. Does that mean that the memorandum of understanding is over?"

"What's this?" my mother asks.

"I...I think..." Jay L. Lamb is stuttering, and I've never seen him do that before.

"Last week, the day before Father died, he made me sign a promise that I would not spend time with Donna Middleton ever again, or I would have to move out of the house on Clark Avenue and find a way to pay my own bills," I say.

"Who is Donna Middleton?" My mother is sitting forward in her chair.

"She's my friend. She lives on my block."

"You made a friend on your block, Edward? That's wonderful."

"Yes. If I can stay in the house as long as I want, no matter what, I want to keep being friends with Donna Middleton. That's why I'm wondering about the memorandum of understanding."

"Jay," my mother says, "what is this memo?"

Jay L. Lamb reaches into one of his desk drawers and pulls out a green office folder, just like the ones I use to store my letters of complaint. He thumbs through it, picks out a sheet of paper, and hands it across the desk to my mother.

My mother reads the piece of paper. A couple of times, her mouth drops open. Finally, she turns to me.

"Your father made you sign this?"

"Yes."

"Jay," she says, turning away from me and toward Jay L. Lamb, "what is this all about? Why would Ted make Edward sign a document like this? Even if Ted had a problem with Edward's knowing this woman—and for the life of me, I can't imagine why—what business is it of yours?"

"Jay sends me lots of letters," I say.

"This isn't the only one?"

"No."

"Jay," she says, "you better let me see those letters, right now."

— • —

By the time my mother works her way through the file with my name on it, she is quaking with anger. She reads letters informing me that I have spent too much money, letters summoning me to meetings at Jay L. Lamb's office, letters correcting me for mistakes made in taking care of the house. I count eighteen of them as she reads them and dismissively tosses them back on Jay L. Lamb's desk, one at a time.

"I just can't believe this," she says. "How dare you? How dare you, Jay?"

"Maureen, please, I was acting on behalf of my client."

"It's absurd. It's positively ridiculous. Did you never think to tell Ted that he was being an idiot for doing this?"

"Maureen, he was trying to protect everybody—you, him, and of course, Edward. I don't know. A lot of it seemed to make sense at the time. Ted wanted to separate his duties as a father from his duties as a legal benefactor."

"It makes no sense to me. This is his son. If he wanted to talk to his son, he should have just talked to his son."

I have never seen my mother so worked up about anything.

"Point taken, Maureen."

"I can't believe this," she says, shaking her head. "I can't believe this was going on and I had no idea about it."

— • —

Eventually, my mother cools off, and she even apologizes to Jay L. Lamb, telling him, "Ted did a lot of dumb things he shouldn't have done, and I guess I failed in not knowing what some of them were. I understand that you were just doing your job, Jay. But listen to me: Never again. You do what you've been hired by this family to do. I will do the talking to Edward. Do you understand me?"

"Yes, Maureen, I do."

"OK, then. Edward, let's go."

We're heading to the door when Jay L. Lamb says, "Oh, one more thing. I nearly forgot. Edward, this is for you."

Jay L. Lamb hands me an envelope with my name written in across the front: "Edward."

"What's this?"

"It's from your father. Read it when you get home."

— • —

Because I don't like Jay L. Lamb telling me what to do—in fact, my mother just instructed him not to do that anymore—I wait until I'm in the parking lot to open the envelope from my father. I turn the ignition far enough to get the stereo playing, and it's one of my favorite R.E.M. songs playing on the CD I have in the player.

I fish out the contents of the envelope, and it's a two-page handwritten letter from my father, in his precise block letters that, when I was a child, I would try to emulate in my own penmanship. I could never do it.

Dear Edward,

As I write this letter to you, I do so with the hope that you never have to read it. For one thing, if you're reading it, it means that I have died. More than that, it means that I did not get a chance to do in life what I'll do now.

You have been a challenging man and a challenging son, Edward, and I have not always performed admirably in my role as your father. I never quite figured out how to deal with your mental illness. For a long time, I tried to convince myself that I had tried my best. But I know the truth: I never tried hard enough. When I sent you away from the house in 2000, I did so out of anger and exasperation—I felt like your illness was overwhelming me and that episodes like the Garth Brooks incident were exposing the family to ridicule. I was selfish, Edward. I put myself before you.

But then something wonderful happened: You thrived in your little house there on Clark, and Dr. Buckley made great progress with you. I was so happy about that, but I was also so sad, because I knew that I had thrown you out of the house and you weren't coming back. You wouldn't have wanted to, and I wouldn't have known how to ask you.

So even though you got better, you and I got worse. And I need you to know this, Edward: It's not your fault.

It's mine. I can write this letter and say that, knowing that you aren't going to be reading it any time soon, but I cannot bring myself to say these words to you in real life. I've tried. I am weak. I will keep trying. It will break my heart if you have to read this.

Edward, I love you. I am proud of you. I know that life can be challenging for you and that it's sometimes easier to retreat to a place where no one can intrude on you. I understand that. But you have been a great gift to your mother and me. You are a beautiful, gentle, sweet man, and I am proud to be your father.

You're the sunshine of my life, Edward, as the song goes. If I never got to tell you when I was alive, I am telling you now.

I love you, son.

Ted Stanton
June 7, 2006

R.E.M. is telling me that everybody hurts. I can't leave the parking lot. I can't see.

— • —

I'm home at 1:08—I stayed in the law firm's parking lot for nearly a half hour, crying and listening to R.E.M. and reading and rereading my father's letter. I dig around in the refrigerator, but there's little to eat, since I threw out all my food, a decision that I continue to regret. I retreat to the kitchen table and sort through the surprisingly voluminous (I love the word "voluminous") amount of mail that I brought in after I returned home.

It's mostly advertisements—and a box from Amazon.com, which flummoxes me, until I remember ordering that book *He's Just Not That Into You*, which is of little use to me now. One other letter catches my eye. It has the *Billings Herald-Gleaner*'s logo on the return address.

I tear it open.

Dear Edward,

I was very sorry to read of your father's passing. He was a good man, and I know how much he cared about you. He'll be missed by a lot of people.

I've been meaning to drop you a line for a while now, but things have been so busy. When I saw the unfortunate news about your father, I decided that I shouldn't leave this undone any longer.

I'd like you to give me a call here at the Billings Herald-Gleaner *so we can set up a time to chat. You can reach me at 657-1315. I retired from West last year and took a job here as the operations director. It's a lot different than teaching high school shop, but I like it so far.*

Anyway, we can talk about my big move and what's going on with you after you call. Please do, Edward. I'm looking forward to hearing from you.

Best wishes,
Nathan Withers

Apprehensively, I dial the number in Mr. Withers's note.
"*Herald-Gleaner*, Withers."
"Mr. Withers, it's Edward Stanton."

"Edward, my boy. How are you?"

"Fine."

"Glad to hear it, glad to hear it. Edward, I was stunned to hear about your dad. How are you holding up?"

"OK, I guess."

"It's hard. You live long enough, it happens. Both of my parents are gone."

"I'm sorry."

"Ah, it's OK. Happened a long time ago. That's the nice thing, Edward. It doesn't hurt forever. Eventually, you just remember the good things. That's comforting."

"That sounds nice."

"So you got my letter, then. I want you to come see me, Edward."

"When?"

"When is good for you?"

"I'm busy tomorrow, and I'm helping my mother Wednesday."

"How about Thursday, then? Ten a.m.? Will that work?"

"Yes."

"Good, Edward, good. I'm looking forward to seeing you."

"Yes. Why do you want to see me?"

"Let's talk about that when you get here. I'll see you at ten a.m. Thursday, OK?"

"Yes."

"Good, good. Take care, my boy."

— • —

Tonight's episode of *Dragnet*, the fourteenth of the first season of color episodes, is called "The Subscription Racket," and it's one of my favorites.

In this one, which originally aired on April 20, 1967, Sergeant Joe Friday and Officer Bill Gannon are investigating a ring of young people who pose as students and fraudulently sell magazine subscriptions door-to-door by telling potential customers that the money will go for good causes rather than telling them the truth: the money will go into their pockets.

Sergeant Joe Friday and Officer Bill Gannon eventually arrest a young couple who are engaging in fraud—the young woman by changing the dollar amount on a check and the young man by using the Medal of Honor his father posthumously won and passing it off as his own. Sergeant Joe Friday takes a dim view of this.

The young man declares that his father gave his life for the medal. And Sergeant Joe Friday says that the young man will have to give up a little of his own life for using it. Sergeant Joe Friday seems to think that the young man's father would not be proud. I'm glad my father was proud of me.

— • —

Enough of my letters are turning out to not be complaints that I ought to rethink my description of them. I now have a large collection of complaint letters and a smaller collection of letters of regret, letters of pleading, and now, tonight, a letter of awe and thanks. I prepare a new green office folder for this one.

Michael Stipe:

One of your songs made me cry today. I don't like to cry, but I seem to be doing a lot of it lately, and to be honest, I think I would feel worse if I didn't cry. Also, to be fair, it wasn't just your song that made me cry. My father's letter made me cry, too.

I don't know how it is that you write songs that seem to sum up how I'm feeling. It's not because you know me; you don't. But you have a talent for it, and I want you to know that I've noticed.

"Everybody Hurts" is the perfect song to describe how I am feeling these days. I do feel like I am alone sometimes. But as you rightly point out, I am not alone. I have my mother. And I have a memory of my father that is a happy one.

Thank you, Michael Stipe, for writing such perfect songs.

I am, as ever, your fan,
Edward Stanton

TUESDAY, NOVEMBER 4

This morning, I sit calmly in Dr. Buckley's waiting room, the soft sounds of string music washing over me. I have rearranged Dr. Buckley's magazines; it wasn't so hard. I have hope—that word again—that perhaps Dr. Buckley's other patients are starting to care a bit more about maintaining order around here.

I awoke again at 7:38 a.m., the 227th time this year (because it's a leap year). For one of the few times in recent weeks, I slept soundly and dreamlessly. Well, that's not true: Nobody sleeps dreamlessly. But I don't remember any dreams, and that's nearly the same thing.

Today is the fifth full day without my father, and I don't feel quite so badly about that as I did yesterday or the day before. I wish he were here, of course, especially now that I know he isn't ashamed of me. But I also feel like it's all going to be OK. I can't explain this feeling. It is not based in fact, but rather in emotion. I prefer facts, but I don't mind this emotion. Perhaps Dr. Buckley will have some ideas about all of this. I find emotions difficult to explain.

Perhaps Dr. Buckley will have some ideas about Donna Middleton, too, because I have none. I wish I did.

I'll know soon enough. Dr. Buckley just ushered a man out of her office—the one I barreled into last week—and is signaling me to come in.

The man scowls at me as we cross paths.

"I'm sorry," I say.

— • —

"Edward," Dr. Buckley says, taking her seat. "How are you doing today?"

"I'm doing well."

"That's good. Again, I'm so sorry about your father. How is your mother?"

"I think she's going to be OK."

"And you?"

"I think I'm going to be OK, too. I feel…Well, it's hard to explain."

"Give it a try."

"My father wrote me a letter. His lawyer gave it to me yesterday."

"Oh?"

"But it's not like the other letters I've gotten from the lawyer. My father told me in this letter that he's proud of me and that he loves me. He apologized to me. I…Dr. Buckley, would you like to read the letter?"

"If you feel comfortable with that, Edward, I would love to."

I lean forward in my chair and pull the folded letter out of my back pocket, then hand it to her.

Dr. Buckley gingerly unfolds the letter and starts reading, and I can't be sure, but it looks like her eyes are getting teary.

After she stops reading, she looks for a while at the folded-up letter she still holds.

"Edward," she finally says, "this is an extraordinary letter."

"Yes."

"I have patients who have waited all their lives to hear something like this from a parent, or a spouse, or a child."

"Yes."

"You should put this somewhere special. Don't keep it folded up in your pocket."

"Yes."

She hands the letter back to me, and I hold it carefully.

"If I may, I think I can help you understand this feeling of peace you describe, Edward."

"OK."

"In the time we've been doing these sessions, what have been the constants in your life?"

"What do you mean?"

"The years change, the seasons change, the fashions change. What has remained the same?"

"I watch *Dragnet* every night."

"Yes, you do, and strangely enough, I think that figures in. But what else?"

"I take my fluoxetine."

"Yes. What else?"

"I complain about my father."

"Yes. But it's not just complaint. You've yearned for your father's approval. You've wanted a better relationship with him."

"Yes. But he's dead now. I can't have a better relationship with him now."

"I disagree. Your father has given you a great gift with this letter. It allows you to have the relationship with him in death that you didn't have when he was still alive."

"How do you have a relationship in death?"

"It's not a relationship in the way you're thinking of. You don't get to have coffee or share a conversation. But it's in the way you feel about him—that you can have happy memories instead of sad ones. When someone asks you about your father, you can talk about what a warm, good man he was, not how he made you feel at times. That's what he has given you. Do you understand what I'm saying?"

"I think so."

"Think of it this way: When I ask what you're thinking about your father, what do you say?"

"I miss him."

"Why do you miss him?"

"Because I love him, and because I know he cared about me."

"How do you know?"

"Because he told me."

"Exactly. That's the gift."

Dr. Buckley is a very logical woman. She knows how to look at things in just the right way.

"I get it," I say. "Now, tell me about how *Dragnet* figures in."

— • —

Dr. Buckley is right: *Dragnet* does figure in.

She asks me when I started watching *Dragnet*. It was 1994. I was changing channels and came across it on the TV Land network. I was immediately struck by Sergeant Joe Friday. Even though he is fictitious, he is the only person I've ever known who cares about facts as much as I do. Sergeant Joe Friday isn't interested in anything except the facts. That's the way I am.

But Dr. Buckley explains that it's more than that. As my relationship with my father deteriorated, culminating with the "Garth Brooks incident," my relationship with the fictitious Sergeant Joe Friday intensified. I began to see in him something virtuous, a quality I no longer saw in my father. That's what Dr. Buckley says.

"Sergeant Friday perhaps became your father figure," Dr. Buckley says.

That seems strange to me.

"But Sergeant Joe Friday never married," I say. "He didn't have any children."

"He's also not real," Dr. Buckley says. "That's why he's a symbol. He's not the real thing. Your father was."

"Are you saying I spend too much time with *Dragnet*?" It seems impossible to me that anyone could, but if Dr. Buckley says so, I might have to consider it. Dr. Buckley is a very logical woman.

"No, not at all," she says. "Believe me, there are far worse ways you could spend a half hour a day. Watch *Dragnet* all you like. But you have a father. Maybe you could just let Sergeant Joe Friday catch the bad guys. That's his job."

Dr. Buckley is a very logical woman.

— • —

Finally, we talk about Donna Middleton. I tell Dr. Buckley about the memorandum of understanding that my father made me sign, about how I pushed Donna away when she tried to talk to me about my father's death, about the episode out on my front lawn Sunday when I yelled at Donna and Kyle.

"You've not told her about the document you signed?" Dr. Buckley asks.

"No."

"Can you understand, then, how she might be confused about your actions toward her?"

"Yes."

I then tell Dr. Buckley that my mother fixed it with Jay L. Lamb where the memorandum of understanding is no longer in force and that my mother is proud of me for having a friend.

"But I don't know what to think," I say. "I saw Donna getting into her car this morning, and I'm pretty sure she saw me, too. I waved at her, but she just stood there for a few seconds, then got in the car and drove away."

"You're not sending her a very clear signal, Edward. First, you're her friend and you go to court with her. Then you're not her friend and you push her away. Then you yell at her little boy. Then you wave at her. What do you expect her to think?"

"I don't know."

"I want you to consider something. Your friend's feelings are probably hurt, and given what she has been through in her life, she may be asking herself whether she can trust you."

"She can."

"Yes, but you can't be the one who convinces her of that now, not after all of this. I think you need to give her some space. I think you need to prepare yourself for the possibility that she won't be your friend. Do you think you can do that?"

"Yes," I say. I am sad. "I don't want to, but if Donna Middleton doesn't want to be my friend, I will accept that."

"Good. We'll talk about this more."

— • —

"It's been quite a week for you, Edward," Dr. Buckley says. "What are you going to do now?"

"I don't know. Go back to the things I've always done. Find a new project."

"Anything else?"

"No, I don't think so."

"I'm going to be frank with you here."

Dr. Buckley has said this a few times in the years that I have been talking with her. What she has to say usually stings, but later, I find out she was right.

"OK."

"I don't know what you're waiting on."

"What do you mean?"

"Edward, do you know how long life lasts?"

"It depends."

"Yes, but let's just say you live a nice long life by conventional standards. Do you know how long that lasts?"

"I don't know. I read somewhere once that men live about seventy-two years."

"That's about right. Put another way, a full, long life is about 650,000 hours. What do you think when you hear that number?"

"Can I borrow a calculator?"

Dr. Buckley stands up and goes to her desk, and then she brings a pocket calculator back to me.

I check her math: 24 hours a day x 365 days a year x 72 years = 630,270.

"It's 630,270 hours," I say.

"So even fewer than 650,000."

I punch up the numbers again, just to double-check my math. Of course, there will be some leap years in there, so it's not exactly 630,270 hours, but it's close enough. It's hard to know how many leap years there are unless you know the first year, and I don't. This is a hypothetical situation.

"How long did your father live?" she asks.

I punch up the rough numbers: 24 x 365 x 64 = 560,640.

I tell her the answer.

"And how long have you lived already?"

That's easy. I know that, as of today, I am thirty-nine years and 300 days old.

I punch up the numbers: 24 x 365 x 39 = 341,640 + (24 x 300) = 348,840.

Holy shit!

I tell Dr. Buckley the answer.

"So I ask you again: What are you waiting for?"

— • —

Tonight's episode of *Dragnet*, which I start at just after seven— 7:04—is the fifteenth episode of the first season, and it's called "The Big Gun." It's one of my favorites.

In this episode, which originally aired on April 27, 1967, Sergeant Joe Friday and Officer Bill Gannon investigate the senseless shooting of a beautiful young Japanese woman. They find out that her husband had been killed in Vietnam several months earlier and that she has a young daughter, Miko, who apparently is somewhere in Japanese Town with her grandmother.

The shooting gets to Sergeant Joe Friday in a personal way, something that doesn't happen often. Maybe he's angry at all of the gun violence in Los Angeles. Maybe he's shocked that anyone could murder such a pretty, petite woman. Sergeant Joe Friday just wants the facts, but he's also human.

Eventually, Sergeant Joe Friday and Officer Bill Gannon zero in on a creepy man named Ben Roy Yoder, who lives with his highly religious aunt. When the police come to serve a search warrant at her house, the aunt castigates them, saying that they would go rooting around in a holy temple.

And Sergeant Joe Friday says that he would if he thought he would find a murder gun there. That's very logical.

I'm watching *Dragnet* almost three hours early and might even watch another episode, if I feel like it. I'm also munching on thin-crust pepperoni pizza from Pizza Hut. I didn't go to the grocery store today. I decided I didn't have to. Maybe I'll go tomorrow. Or maybe not.

I'll do whatever I feel like doing. You live only once.

— • —

Tonight's letter continues a recent theme. It's not a complaint.

I have written letters of complaint to Dr. Buckley before, especially early in our working together, when what she said to me didn't make much sense and before my dosage of fluoxetine balanced out and calmed me down a little bit. There were times that I wrote very angry letters to Dr. Buckley—seventeen such times, it turns out, as I retrieve the file with her name.

I am glad she never saw them. I wouldn't want Dr. Buckley's feelings to be hurt.

Dr. Buckley:

I want to thank you for my session today. I think it is one of the best ones we have ever had. You helped me to see things much more clearly where my father and Donna

Middleton are concerned. You are a very wise and logical woman.

I understand what you said about Donna, and I will give her the space she needs. I do hope you're wrong, though. I would be very sad if Donna Middleton were no longer my friend.

I am looking forward to talking again next week. Thank you for all you have done to help me.

I am, your patient,
Edward Stanton

WEDNESDAY, NOVEMBER 5

I have been thinking that perhaps I do have some rituals that aren't worth the time I invest in them. I don't think I could give up my tracking of the weather—you can learn a lot about the tendencies of a place by its weather patterns, and I take some enjoyment in seeing how often the forecasts are wrong. But perhaps I could stop counting the number of days that I have been without my father, especially considering that it's a recent addition to my data sheets. Plus, if I look at it the way Dr. Buckley suggested, I am not really without him. He is with me, in my thoughts and my memories. This is outside the boundaries of the strictly factual world I prefer to live in, but I think I would like to see if I can make it work.

I am thinking of these things at 8:17 a.m., thirty-nine minutes after I awoke. If you're challenged by math, that would be at 7:38 a.m., the 228th time out of 310 days this year (because it's a leap year) that I have gotten up at that time. It is also the third consecutive day that I have emerged from sleep at this most common of waking times, and I take that to mean that I am getting back to my normal patterns. I am relieved by this. I have been discombobulated for too long. (I love the word "discombobulated.")

A few minutes ago, I peeked through the front-window curtains and watched Donna Middleton load Kyle and his backpack into the car—for the ride to school, I presume. It was hard to stifle the urge to go outside and see if I could get Donna's attention in the hope that she would talk to me, but I remembered what Dr. Buckley said. Donna Middleton needs time and space. And though I have only 280,000 or so hours of life remaining—assuming that I live a life of average length, and I don't like assumptions—I am willing to spend some of them letting Donna Middleton decide what to do.

Now I am sitting at the dining room table for another of my nonnegotiable rituals: I am eating my corn flakes and reading this morning's edition of the *Billings Herald-Gleaner*. I see by the big headline on the front page of the newspaper that Barack Obama won. The headline says, in all capital letters, "OBAMA'S TIME." I am not impressed by that headline; it sounds like a beer commercial. I have half a mind to write a letter of complaint to the newspaper editor, but then I think again and realize that another of my rituals has run its course. I think I am going to see if I can get out of the unsent-letter-of-complaint business and try just dealing with the frustrations as they come. If they require complaint, I'll complain. If I can let them go, I will try to let them go, even though I know that will be difficult. A bad headline in the *Billings Herald-Gleaner*, while irritating, is the sort of thing I need to try to let go.

The newspaper also has a story about my father's now-empty seat on the county commission. He died so close to the election that there wasn't time to line up candidates for the job and put them on the ballot, so the county leaders have decided to have a special election in January to fill the spot. The Billings mayor, Kevin Hammel, says he is going to run for the position. As he has just been roundly beaten for the position of state schools superintendent—another story in this morning's *Herald-Gleaner*—he should have the time. I don't like his chances of winning, although that is merely an informed opinion and not a fact. I prefer facts.

I also see that my old boss in the court of clerk's office lost her race. I bet that Lloyd Graeve and the rest of the people who work there are celebrating this morning.

I glance at all the news I want to read and check out other parts of the *Billings Herald-Gleaner*—especially Dear Abby, who answers a letter from a fifty-nine-year-old man whose eyes are so bad that he can't see his girlfriend when they're having intimate relations. A good headline for that Dear Abby column would be "Love Is Blind," but of course the *Billings Herald-Gleaner* didn't do that. They have terrible headline writers at that newspaper. But I will let it go.

By the time I'm done reading, it's 9:05 and I have to hustle or I'll be late to my parents'—my mother's—house.

— • —

The living room of my mother's house is uncharacteristically cluttered today. She has been bringing down armfuls of my father's clothing and sorting it into piles.

"What's this, Mother?" I ask after she lets me in the front door.

"I'm giving your father's clothes to charity. Go through them and take anything you want."

"I don't want anything."

"Are you sure?"

"Yes. I don't like golf shirts."

A glance around the room tells me that he has hundreds of golf shirts, and slacks, and golf sweater vests, and fleece pullovers. These clothes, destined for the Salvation Army and the Montana Rescue Mission thrift stores, will be fine items for someone. I would not be surprised to see a homeless man in a St. Andrew's sweater this winter. That would be funny.

"Why are you doing this now, Mother?"

"Why not? No time like the present. And, frankly, it's too much. Your father is no longer here to wear it, and it's not right that we should have so much when others have so little."

That makes a lot of sense to me. And my mother seems invigorated with this project.

"There's another benefit to doing this, Edward."

"What's that?"

"Come here and smell this." She's holding out one of my father's shirts, an aqua-blue long-sleeved shirt with the Augusta National logo on the left breast.

"Smell a shirt?"

"Yes, it's not something bad. Give it a whiff."

I lean over but don't let my nose touch the shirt. Even so, I can smell the faint essence of my father's cologne, Canoe, on it.

"You spend forty years of your life in the same house with a man, and you come to know his scent," my mother says. "It's like he's here in the room with me. And that gives me comfort."

She smiles at me, and I back at her.

"Maybe I'll take one of them, Mother." She hands me the aqua-blue long-sleeved shirt, which I place away from the stacks of clothing, and then I come back and help her fold and sort the piles of unprocessed clothes still to go.

— • —

"I've made a decision, Edward."

My mother and I are eating tuna sandwiches and carrot sticks in the kitchen.

"What?"

"I'm selling the house."

I am surprised.

"Why?"

"It's too much for just me. I wouldn't feel right living here alone. It's too big and...Well, it's something your father and I shared. Now that he's gone, I think it might be time for me to find a place that's just mine."

"What sort of place?"

"There are some lovely new condos just downtown. They are small enough for just me, and they're near the places I like to go. As nice as the view is from here, I've never much cared for how far we are from town and for driving down that hill in the nastiest days of winter. I think I would like downtown living."

"Yes."

"Also, I won't be spending as much time here anymore."

"Oh?"

"Yes," she says. "It's like this, Edward: I've decided that I would like to split my time between here and Dallas. Your Aunt Corinne still lives down there, and I haven't seen nearly as much of her as I would like."

"Didn't Uncle Andy die last year?"

"Yes. We can be the two crazy widow sisters, on the loose in Texas."

"That's funny, Mother."

"Would that be OK with you, if I spent more time in Texas from now on?"

"Yes. Why would you ask?"

"I don't know. You're a grown man, Edward, and I know you can take care of yourself. But if you thought I was abandoning you, I wouldn't want to leave."

"I know you're not abandoning me, Mother."

"Good."

"I might even come see you sometimes."

"Edward, I would love that."

"I think I would, too."

She reaches out and clutches my right hand in hers. I squeeze back.

— • —

"Are you angry with me over some of the things your father did?"

My mother and I are in his office going through photo albums. She thinks that I should take some and keep them in my house on Clark Avenue, and I think it is a very good idea.

"No."

"I feel horrible about all the things I didn't know. When I saw those letters in Jay's file, I…I felt so betrayed. Betrayed by your father, and even Jay. Then later, I felt so stupid. I wondered, 'How could I have not known? How could I have become so detached from your life? How could I have let him make me so detached from your life?'"

"Dr. Buckley says that I should try to remember the good in Father and give him the benefit of the doubt that he was doing what he thought was best, even if it was off base."

"What do you think?"

"I think that is easier to say than to do. But I also think Dr. Buckley is very wise and that it's worth the effort."

"I guess so."

We keep looking at photographs.

"Edward, what was that letter that Jay gave you Monday?"

"Father wrote it a couple of years ago to tell me that he was proud of me and loved me, and that he hoped he would say it before he died so he didn't have to say it in that letter."

My mother's eyes fill with tears. "I wish he would have told you," she says softly.

"So do I, but Dr. Buckley says he gave me a great gift. She says that she has clients who have waited all their lives to hear those things from their fathers. I only had to wait until I was thirty-nine years and two hundred and ninety-nine days old."

My mother laughs as a tear runs down her face. "I love you, too, Edward."

"I know, Mother. And I love you."

— • —

Before I leave, my mother tells me that there's one last order of business between us.

"Leave your Toyota here and take the Cadillac."

My father's Cadillac DTS is sitting in the driveway, gleaming in the early afternoon sunlight.

"What will happen to the Toyota?"

"I'll have Jay dig up the title, and we'll include it in all the things we're sending to the Rescue Mission. Between your father's clothes, the car, and the check we're going to write, there ought to be enough to ensure some happy holidays for people who deserve some happiness, don't you think?"

"Yes. That sounds very nice."

"The keys are in the ignition. Enjoy your new car. Your father certainly did."

I kiss my mother on the cheek and then walk over to the car, which is a deep, beautiful cherry red. I open the door and climb in.

I turn the key in the ignition to get a look at the instrument panel, which is a lot different from the one in my Camry. As I'm slipping into the seat belt, my mother raps her knuckles against the window on my side of the car.

The DTS doesn't have manual-crank windows like the Camry. Finally, I find the automatic window button.

"Edward, it will take a while to sell this house, and I'm not planning to head to Texas until spring. Can I count on seeing you from time to time?"

"Yes, Mother. Of course."

"Because we're going to do better from now on, you and me, right?"

"Yes."

"Good. Take care, son. I'll call you in a few days, or you call me, OK?"

"Yes."

She puts her hand on my cheek and smiles, and then she steps away from the car and waves good-bye. I push the window button to roll it up, put the car in drive, and head down the driveway.

A few minutes later, at 4:26 p.m., I'm riding along Highway 3, back toward downtown.

The Cadillac DTS is a superior car in every way except one: I liked where the cup holders were on the Camry. It is yet another thing I will have to let go.

— • —

At home, I park the Cadillac DTS in the driveway, and then I get out and admire it.

It's a beautiful car.

The STANTON vanity plates will have to go. My father was more flamboyant than I. (I love the word "flamboyant.")

The Dallas Cowboys license plate frames will stay.

— • —

I spend the next few hours ostensibly sorting through the pictures my mother has sent home with me. I say ostensibly—a word I love—because every ten minutes on the dot, I get up and peek through the curtains on the front window to see if I can spot Donna Middleton and/or Kyle. Each time, I see no one, though I can see by the car that they are home.

The pictures I've selected span much of my life, but most of them are from the days when I was a young child and my father and I got along famously. As I thumb through the albums, I remove some of the ones I like best: my father and me on the Ferris wheel at the Montana State Fair, my mother and me standing outside a cave at Carlsbad Caverns in New Mexico, my mother and father splashing around in a lake in Minnesota. I decide that these pictures and several others should not be closed up in an album but instead should be framed on a wall. As my walls are empty, I have plenty of room for such things.

In considering where the photos I've picked out would look best, I find myself wishing that I had taken pictures of that snowy day in front my house when Kyle was riding his Blue Blaster and Donna and I were throwing snowballs. Photographs, it seems to me, are both moments in time and bits of memory. I have the memory of that day with Donna and Kyle, but I also know that memory is imprecise. If I'd had a camera, instead of just a memory, I could have caught the moments so that they would never escape me. If Donna has decided that she no longer wants to be my friend, I'll have to desperately hold on to those memories so that they never get away, because I won't have the chance to replace them.

As the second hand hits 12:00 and another ten minutes have passed, I go back to the front window and look out. They are still nowhere to be seen.

Though I want nothing more than to leave this house and find my friends, I decide instead to quit looking. Staring out the window doesn't violate the letter of what Dr. Buckley asked me to do in leaving Donna alone, but it does violate the spirit of it.

— • —

At 10:00, I start watching tonight's episode of *Dragnet*. Though I broke with protocol yesterday and watched *Dragnet* earlier, at 7:04 p.m., I did it only to make the point that I wasn't slavish (I love the word "slavish") to the clock. I also watched a second episode, the sixteenth of the first season of color episodes, called "The Big Kids," and that also was to prove a point. I wanted to show that I can watch my favorite show whenever I want and for however long I want.

But the truth is, I like watching *Dragnet* at 10:00 p.m. and only one episode. It works for me. Doing what you want and what feels right strikes me as being more important than doing something just to prove a point. I think Dr. Buckley would agree.

Tonight's episode, the seventeenth and final installment of the first season of color episodes, is called "The Big Bullet," and it's one of my favorites.

In this episode, which originally aired on May 11, 1967, Sergeant Joe Friday and Officer Bill Gannon investigate a reported suicide at a woman's house. She tells the officers that her estranged husband came by to visit, locked himself in a room, and killed himself with a gun.

But the clues don't add up that way. It turns out that the slug pulled from the man's body doesn't match the gun he was holding. Sergeant Joe Friday and Officer Bill Gannon return to the woman's house and go through her vacuum cleaner filter, as she has already cleaned the room where her estranged husband died. In it, they find the shell casing for the bullet that killed him. They talk with the woman's mother, who answered the door when the husband came by, and they come to find out that she shot him—because he shot her Bible.

The lesson, I think, is that we tend to be protective of the people and things we care about. It's easy to understand why.

— • —

In lieu of writing a letter of complaint, which I've decided to swear off, I break down my filing cabinet and box up my green office folders full of letters. I am tempted to count the number of letters I have written, but I resist the urge. If I'm not going to write them anymore, the number doesn't matter. I will box up the letter files and stack them up in the garage tomorrow. They can wait there for a while, until I decide what do with them. Perhaps I will eventually move them back into the house, unable to swear off writing the letters, after all. I hope that's not the case, but I just don't know. Anything along those lines is just conjecture, and I prefer facts. Facts are the most reliable things in the world. On that, Sergeant Joe Friday and I agree.

THURSDAY, NOVEMBER 6

I am not sure where we are. It's a flat, treeless, straight stretch of highway surrounded by fallow fields. We are in the Cadillac—I in the driver's seat, my father riding shotgun.

"Rides nice, doesn't she?" my father says, grinning at me from behind sunglasses.

"Real nice."

"You know why, right?"

"Why?"

"Because you're driving a goddamned Cadillac, that's why!" He lets out a belly laugh.

"But where are we going?" I ask.

"Anywhere you want, Edward. But first, don't you think you ought to go to..."

— • —

The grocery store. That's what I'm thinking when my eyes flutter open at 7:38 a.m.

A man needs a good breakfast on a day like today, and I am a man, but I have no breakfast. Skipping the grocery store on Tuesday showed that I can be bold and impulsive, but it doesn't help me today, when I am out of food. If not for the tuna sandwich my mother made me for lunch and my leftover pizza for dinner, I might have remembered to go yesterday. But I did not. That failure is my fault.

I pull on clothes in the dark of my bedroom and then hustle out the door. I can remember 7:38 a.m. After all, I have awoken at that time 229 times in 311 days this year (because it's a leap year). If I couldn't remember that, I would have to have my head examined, which I don't want to do.

I can ensure that my data is complete when I get back home.

— • —

It is dark and cold this early in the morning. The late-fall sky is a deep gray, like a gun barrel, and I would guess that it won't get much above freezing today. I would guess, but I don't like to. Guesses are conjecture. I prefer facts.

Inside the Albertsons on Thirteenth Street W. and Grand Avenue, though, it's light and airy, and I enjoy walking the aisles, picking up the groceries I need.

I have decided to try again with different kinds of food. I realize that changing my grocery list didn't have anything to do with what happened to my father; it was a coincidence. I still would like to see if I can learn how to cook a steak, and so I buy a package of two New York strip steaks, in case my first attempt goes poorly.

I also get corn flakes, as per usual (I love the phrase "as per usual"), and the makings of spaghetti, which remains my favorite food even though I said I felt like I was in a rut. A lot has changed since I said that.

I do try some of the Lean Cuisine meals, but I think it's OK to get a few Banquet dinners as well, because I like Banquet dinners.

I make similar decisions on ice cream and pizza. I get the Dreyer's vanilla and the DiGiorno pepperoni because I like them. It's OK to get the things you like. It doesn't mean that you're slavish to convention.

I think Dr. Buckley would agree with me on that.

— • —

"Don't think I've ever seen you in here this early." The woman at the checkout stand is talking to me.

"What?"

"You're early. Don't you usually come in later in the day?"

"Yes. On Tuesdays. I didn't this week, though."

"Forgot?"

"No. I chose not to."

"Yeah, going to the store can be a real pain sometimes." She continues sweeping my items across the electronic price reader.

"My father died. It sort of jumbled up my schedule."

She looks crestfallen. "Oh, I'm so sorry."

"It's OK."

"Well," she says, holding up the Dreyer's, "ice cream makes excellent comfort food."

"Yes."

She finishes ringing up my items.

"OK, that will be fifty-four dollars and seventy-eight cents," she says.

I swipe my card through the electronic reader, hit the credit option, and wait for the receipt to come up. When it does, I sign my name.

"Thanks so much. It was good to see you," the woman at the checkout stand says. "Take care."

I tell her good-bye.

As I'm walking back to the Cadillac, I think it's interesting that I've never before had a conversation at the grocery store. That was fun.

— • —

For what it's worth—and that's not much, until I get the actual facts tomorrow—the weather forecast in the *Billings Herald-Gleaner* agrees with me: It's going to be a cold one today, with a high of thirty-six and a low of twenty-two. It's all just conjecture at this point, and I prefer the facts. Here are two: Yesterday's high temperature was forty-eight, and the low was thirty-four. I record these things in my notebook, and my data is complete. I then finish off the last few bites of my corn flakes and chase my fluoxetine with orange juice, and my breakfast is complete, too.

Mr. Withers didn't say how I should dress for our meeting today, so I am going to err on the side of formality and wear my George Foreman suit and shirt with blue stripes. I wore the same thing on my date with Joy-Annette, which momentarily gives me pause. But I have known Mr. Withers for a long time, and I have no anxiety that he will wig out on me like Joy-Annette did. I think it will be OK. That I'm wearing the same outfit is just coincidence. It doesn't mean anything.

I head for the shower. I must keep moving so I am clean and dressed and at the *Billings Herald-Gleaner* by 10:00 a.m. sharp.

— • —

The woman at the front desk has a kind, cheerful face. "Can I help you?"

"Mr. Withers, please."

"Is he expecting you?"

"Yes."

"Your name?"

"Edward Stanton."

She picks up the phone and punches in a number. "There's an Edward Stanton here to see you. Yes, OK." She hangs up.

"He'll be right down."

I glance around the foyer of the *Herald-Gleaner*. The woman I've been talking to is behind a big glass wall, and through it, I can see dozens of cubicles, with people in them typing away on computers or looking down at paperwork. Along the wall to the left, on the north side of the building, are glass offices. In the middle of the big room beyond the glass wall is a small table in a small pit surrounded by what appear to be trees. I can't tell if the trees are real, though. They look real; some of the leaves are withering. But I also know that manufacturers have gotten very good at making fake things look real. I will have to ask Mr. Withers about this.

Beyond the trees is a room with glass windows on three sides, a big table, and lots of chairs. Important meetings probably go on in there. To the right are more cubicles and more glass offices along the south wall. The *Herald-Gleaner* is a very active, important-looking place.

"Edward, my boy!" The booming voice of Mr. Withers comes at me from behind the glass. I would recognize it anywhere. He pushes open a door and tells me to come in.

"How are you, Edward?" he asks, offering a handshake, which I accept.

"I'm doing well."

"Excellent, excellent."

I have seen Mr. Withers only a few times since I graduated from Billings West High School twenty-one years ago. Back then, he was probably younger than I am now, perhaps around thirty-five or thirty-six years old. Now he's in his mid-fifties, the reddish-brown hair that I remember gone fully gray. He's a little heavier and a little more crinkly around the eyes, but the voice and the manner are the same.

"Edward, again, I was so sorry to hear about your dad. He was a good man."

"Yes."

He claps me on the shoulder. "Well, my boy, come on upstairs with me. We have a lot to talk about."

— • —

On the walk up the stairs, Mr. Withers is telling me about his job at the *Herald-Gleaner.*

"I'm the operations director," he says. "That means, essentially, that I keep things running around here. That has to do with mechanical things, like the press, and the maintenance of the offices and the grounds. It's a lot of responsibility. It's a big place. I'll show you more of it in a bit."

"Why did you leave Billings West?"

"I'd been there thirty-three years. It was time. I had my full pension, and the principals and regulations were getting harder and harder to deal with. I felt like it was time for a change. You know that feeling, Edward?"

"Yes." I have been experiencing it a lot lately.

"Anyway, here's my office," he says, ushering me into a small room that overlooks Fourth Avenue N., one of the busier streets in Billings. "Have a seat."

I sit down, and Mr. Withers settles in behind his desk.

"The reason I wrote to you, Edward, is that I want you to come work for me."

I had not expected this, and so I can come up with only one word.

"Why?"

"I need someone like you. You're good with your hands, and you can figure out anything mechanical. This place is forty years old. It needs a lot of maintenance. I figure you're the guy who can help me."

"When?" I am simultaneously excited and scared. It has been a long time since I worked anywhere.

"I'm thinking I'll have you work what's called the swing shift. It's from the late afternoon until around midnight," Mr. Withers says. Then, his voice gets a little lower and more serious. "Edward, I know about how you need to be left alone to do work. I know why. This job, you'll be allowed to do that. You'll report to me, but when you're here, you'll be working on tasks that I assign and that you'll be able to do yourself. Do you understand what I'm saying?"

"Yes."

"Good," he says, reverting to his usual cheer. "What do you say we take a look around?"

— • —

Mr. Withers takes me all over the *Herald-Gleaner* and explains to me what each part of the building does.

The north side of the building, he says, is where the advertising and marketing staffs work, selling ads for the newspaper and its website and working on promotions and such. He introduces me to a lot of people, and I can't remember all of their names.

On the south side of the building is the editorial staff—the reporters and editors and photographers who cover the news and make a newspaper every night. I expect a frenzy of activity, like you see in movies about newspapers, but it's a quiet place at this time of day. A lot of people are on phones.

It turns out that the indoor tree is real. Mr. Withers smiles when I ask about it and points up to the ceiling, where there is a massive sunroof. "It's a real pain to keep the leaves swept up," he says.

He also shows me the press and the new packaging center, where the newspaper is merged with ads from department stores and other inserted items, like *Parade* magazine in the Sunday newspaper. Mr. Withers explains that the press is running much of the time—not just with each day's newspaper, but also with specialty magazines and jobs for other publications around the region. The packaging center is vast, an addition to the building that went up just in the past year or so.

"It's an exciting time around here," Mr. Withers says.

It looks like a nice place to work.

On the way up the stairs, Mr. Withers tells me that he can give me about $12 an hour to start, and that sounds good to me. It's more than I have ever made, except for when my father gave me $5 million.

— • —

Back behind his desk, Mr. Withers says, "So, my boy, will you come to work for me?"

I don't hesitate. "Yes."

"Excellent, excellent."

"When do I start?"

"Come on in Monday morning at nine, Edward. We'll get your paperwork filled out, show you what you'll be doing, and hit the ground running. How does that sound?"

"Good."

"All right," he says, standing up and clapping me on the shoulder again. "I'll walk you down."

A few minutes later, I'm back behind the wheel of the Cadillac. My father told me in my dream that it would take me anywhere I wanted to go. I never would have expected that it would be here.

— • —

I drive the Cadillac the short distance home, and my mind is swimming. I never thought I would be going back to work, but I trust Mr. Withers to take care of me. The hours he has in mind may lead to some changes in my routine. My 10:00 p.m. viewings of *Dragnet* will have to be moved. Maybe I can watch it after I get home at night. That means I won't be going to bed at midnight sharp anymore. My common wake-up time of 7:38 a.m. will probably change, too. Between getting home after work and watching *Dragnet*, it will be close to 1:00 a.m., at the earliest, before I get to sleep.

My 10:00 a.m. Tuesday appointments with Dr. Buckley are safe. We will have much to talk about in just a few days.

And the grocery store can be visited whenever I need to. My new job won't affect that.

I saw in the *Billings Herald-Gleaner* yesterday that Barack Obama, the new president, says "change is coming." I wonder how he knew.

— • —

At home, I'm retrieving the mail—all advertisements—when I spot the envelope taped to my door. It says "Edward," but it's not the precise block writing of my father. Instead, it's a pretty cursive. Whoever wrote this probably got good penmanship marks in school.

I set the mail on the stoop and tear open the envelope. Lined notebook paper, the kind I had to write on in school, is inside.

Dear Edward,

This is a letter of complaint. The difference between your letters of complaint and mine is that mine get delivered.

You have not been a good friend to me lately, and I want you to know that. You walked away from me when I was telling you how sorry I was about your father, and you yelled at me and Kyle when all we wanted was for you to come outside and be our friend.

Friends don't do that, Edward. Friends talk to each other, and friends try not to be rude, even if they don't want to come outside. If you're going to be my friend, you can tell me that you don't want to do something, and I will understand. That's what friends do. If I'm going to be your friend, I will tell you if I don't want to do something.

I have wrestled with myself over whether to write this letter. Our life has been hard lately, and I don't need to waste time with someone who isn't going to be a good friend to me. Your track record as my friend is unclear. I'm trying to figure out if you're the Edward who argues with a little boy or if you're the Edward who stood by me in court that day and brought me back here and made me feel good about myself again. Sometimes, I think you could be a really good friend for us. Sometimes, I don't.

You might be interested to know that Mike won't have a trial. After that scene in the courtroom, his lawyer advised him to accept a deal from the prosecutor. He will be going to prison for a while. Not forever, but hopefully long enough that he'll leave us alone when he gets out. I think he will. The prosecutor told me that Mike gets just how much trouble he is in.

Edward, I want you to think about a few things:

If you're going to be our friend, you have to be our friend all the time. That doesn't mean we can't disagree or want some time apart or even get mad at each other. But you can't shut us out. I don't have time for friends like that, and I can't let Kyle rely on a friend who will ultimately let him down. He's just a little boy, and he's had enough disappointment.

Also, friends share. You have never been to our house, though we have asked you over. You have never even come to our side of the street. Your house is fine, and we will hang out there sometimes, but you have to come over to our house, too. It's only fair.

What I'm saying is that our hearts and our door are open to your friendship. But you have to come over here and knock to get in.

We hope you do.

Donna and Kyle

Kyle appears to have signed the letter. Like his mother, he has excellent penmanship.

I fold the letter and put it back in the envelope, and then I turn around and look across the street to Donna's house.

Her car is there.

The curtains are pulled back.

She is home.

Nothing is moving on Clark Avenue except for the tree branches in the breeze and the leaves pushed down the street by the wind.

All I have to do is look both ways and cross.

THE END

ACKNOWLEDGMENTS

So many people helped shape this book, but a few deserve special mention: my wife, Angela, for her encouragement and her guidance on plotting out Edward's interactions with Dr. Buckley; Greg Tuttle, my colleague, for expertly guiding me through the workings of the Yellowstone County court system; Janelle Eklund, my high school English teacher, for igniting my love of literature and cheerleading this book; and Matt Hagengruber, Craig Hashbarger, and Stephen Benoit for being good sports and lending their names to the cause.

Edward would never have been on this ride if not for the original endorsement and hard work of Chris Cauble, Linda Cauble, and Janet Spencer at Riverbend Publishing, who believed in his story and were good shepherds, indeed. Alex Carr and the amazing crew at Amazon Publishing have been a joy to work with, and I look forward to seeing where Edward's story goes from here.

Finally, I'll just say this: With the exceptions of those who are (or were) obviously real—Jack Webb and the *Dragnet* ensemble, Matthew Sweet, the members of R.E.M., Garth Brooks, and the like—the characters in this work of fiction are just that, fictional. That said, some passages of the book were based on real events. Barack Obama was really elected president. Veteran character actor Clark Howat (may he rest in peace) really did answer a letter from a fan (me) and describe how *Dragnet* was filmed, and he could not have been more of a gentleman. I don't know if Garth Brooks's lawyer ever wrote anybody a cease-and-desist letter, but in this case, it's immaterial. He/she certainly didn't write one to Edward Stanton, who is fictional.

Oh, and the 2008 Dallas Cowboys? Sadly, they were all too real.

Edward's story will continue in:

Edward Adrift by Craig Lancaster, coming soon from Amazon
Publishing

What follows is the first chapter in Edward's new life.

WEDNESDAY, DECEMBER 7, 2011

I look at my watch at 3:37 p.m.—3:37 and 17 seconds, because
I have the kind of watch with an LED digital display for preci-
sion—and stop in the kitchen. I have another fifty-three seconds
and could easily make it to the couch, but I stand still and watch
the seconds tick off. The seven morphs (I love the word "morphs")
into an eight and then a nine and then the one becomes a two and
the nine becomes a zero, and I keep watching. Finally, at 3:38 and
10 seconds, I draw in my breath and hold it. Time keeps going,
and I exhale. I look down again and notice that I am standing
on top of dried marinara sauce that sloshed out of the saucepan
yesterday. And just like yesterday, I don't have the energy to clean
it up, even though it bothers me.

At 3:38 p.m. and 10 seconds, twenty-one days ago, on
Wednesday, November 16, 2011, Mr. Withers fired me from my
job at the *Billings Herald-Gleaner*. I know it happened at that
time because as Mr. Withers said, "I hate like hell to have to
tell you this, Edward," I looked directly at my Timex watch on
my left wrist, where I always keep it. Its display read 3:38:10,
and I made a mental note to write it down as soon as possible,

which I did exactly 56 minutes and 14 seconds later, as I sat in my car. A phrase like "I hate like hell to have to tell you this" is a precursor to bad news, and I think the fact that I recognized this is what caused me to look at my watch. I was right about the news. Mr. Withers finished by saying, "but we're going to have to let you go." He said a lot of other things, too, but none of them are as important. I couldn't listen very closely, because I needed to concentrate on remembering the time. The time is now logged, but that's purely academic. I don't think I'll ever forget it, although I hesitate to say that definitively. I can think whatever I want. It doesn't mean things will happen that way. It's easier to stick to incontrovertible (I love the word "incontrovertible") facts.

That I needed 56 minutes and 14 seconds to get to the car can be attributed to the fact that getting fired is no simple thing. In the movies and on TV, getting fired never seems complicated. Some boss, generally played by someone like Ed Asner, comes out of an office and says, "You're fired," and the fired person leaves. But Mr. Withers doesn't look like or sound like Ed Asner, and he made me sign a lot of papers—things like the extension of my health care benefits through something called COBRA and the receipt of my final paycheck, which included the hours I had worked in that pay period and what Mr. Withers called "a severance," which was two weeks' pay, or 80 hours at $15 an hour, minus taxes. The severance check came to $951.01. When I asked Mr. Withers why I was being fired, he said that I wasn't being fired per se (I love the Latin phrase "per se," which means "in itself") but rather that it was what the company liked to call "an involuntary separation." He said that often happens when a company needs to cut its costs. Labor, which is to say people, is the biggest cost any company has.

Mr. Withers said it was an unfortunate reality of business that people sometimes have to endure involuntary separations.

"So, Edward, don't think of it as a firing," he told me as he shook my hand, after he took my key and my parking pass. "You didn't do anything wrong. If we could keep you on board, we would. It really is an involuntary separation."

I think Mr. Withers wanted to believe what he said, or maybe he wanted me to believe that he believed it. I don't know. I veer into dangerous territory when I try to make sense of subtext, which is a word that means an underlying, unspoken meaning. I would rather people just come out and said what they mean, in words that cannot be mistaken, but I haven't met many people who are willing to do that. I will tell you this, though: Another word I love is the word "euphemism," which is basically a nice way of saying something bad. The incontrovertible fact is that "involuntary separation" sounds a lot like a euphemism to me.

— • —

Getting fired, or involuntarily separated, from the *Billings Herald-Gleaner* has made it a real shitburger of a year. Scott Shamwell, one of the pressmen at The Herald-Gleaner, taught me the word "shitburger." Scott Shamwell was always coming up with odd and interesting word combinations, and most of them were profane, which delighted me. One time, the press had a web break—that's when the big roll of paper snaps when the press is running, which means they have to shut everything down and re-thread the paper—and Scott Shamwell called the press a "miserable bag of fuck." I still laugh about that one, because the press is almost entirely steel. There's not a bag anywhere on it that I've ever seen, and now that I don't work at the newspaper anymore, I'll probably never see the press again. I don't know. Again, it's hard to be definitive about something like that. If I ever get a chance to see the press again, I'll take one last look and see if there's a bag somewhere. I don't think there is.

— • —

One of the things I learned from Dr. Buckley before she retired—and that is another thing that makes this a shitburger year—is that when times are difficult, I need to work hard at finding stability and things that bring me pleasure. Dr. Buckley is a very logical woman, and in the 11 years, two months, and 10 days that I worked with her, I came to learn that I should act on her suggestions. On that note, I guess I should focus on the brighter news that I continue to maintain my daily logs of the high and low temperatures and precipitation readings for Billings, Montana, where I live. I started keeping these logs on January 1, 2001, when it occurred to me that Billings, in addition to having wildly variable weather, has poor excuses for weathermen. Their forecasts are notoriously off base, so I've come to distrust what they say. I prefer facts. Every morning, my copy of the *Billings Herald-Gleaner* provides me with the facts about the previous day's weather. I then write it down, and my data is complete.

For example, yesterday, December 6, 2011, the 340th day of the year, saw a high temperature of thirty-four and a low temperature of sixteen in Billings. There was no precipitation, meaning we held steady at 19.34 inches for the year. It's been a bad year for precipitation in Montana, and a lot of places have had floods, although not Billings. Scott Shamwell lives in Roundup, which is

49.82 miles north of Billings, and his town flooded badly. He said one time that he was going to start driving "a cocksucking rowboat" to work, but I don't think he ever did. I wasn't there every day that he was, as our schedules didn't fully align, so while it's conceivable that he would have driven a cocksucking rowboat to work, I have to believe that he or someone else would have told me about it. Belief can be dangerous, of course. I prefer facts.

We did have an oil spill in the Yellowstone River, which mucked things up, and last year a tornado blew down our sports stadium, so it's not like Billings is getting off light as far as catastrophes go. I guess everybody is having trouble these days.

Anyway, tracking the weather data is how I maintain stability, as Dr. Buckley suggests. She also suggested that I find something that gives me pleasure. That has been more difficult, especially since I was involuntarily separated from the *Billings Herald-Gleaner*. I should just try harder, I guess. But how?

ABOUT THE AUTHOR

Craig Lancaster is a journalist who has worked at newspapers all over the country, including the *San Jose Mercury News*, where he served as lead editor for the paper's coverage of the BALCO steroids scandal. He wrote *600 Hours of Edward*—winner of a Montana Book Award honorable mention and a High Plains Book Award—in less than 600 hours during National Novel Writing Month in 2008. His other books include the novel *The Summer Son* and the short story collection *Quantum Physics and the Art of Departure*. Lancaster lives in Billings, Montana, with his wife.